Brunch
and Other
Obligations

Brunch
and Other
Obligations

A Novel

Suzanne Nugent

SHE WRITES PRESS

Published 2020
Printed in the United States of America
ISBN: 978-1-63152-854-5
ISBN: 978-1-63152-855-2
Library of Congress Control Number: 2019912668

For information, address:
She Writes Press
1569 Solano Ave #546
Berkeley, CA 94707

She Writes Press is a division of SparkPoint Studio, LLC.

For all my best friends and their other best friends.
And for Bill, who's the best of all.
With love and gratitude.

1

When Molly Granger included "Dancing Queen" on her funeral playlist, she couldn't have anticipated that it would go over this badly. This is the worst funeral ever. No one is dancing.

Christina, Leanne, and Nora have done their best to respect Molly's final wishes—wearing bright colors, playing joyful music, and generally making sure that her funeral is "not too lame." But many people are already violating the no-tears clause from the funeral contract Molly drew up in colored pencil and had notarized.

"Should we skip to the next track? Do we know where the rainbow pinwheels are? Have you seen Nora?" Leanne says, buzzing past the bathroom door that hides Nora. Leanne has honored Molly's colorful wardrobe mandate with a splash of fuchsia nail polish and a perky pink-and-teal scarf. She felt that wearing just a pop of color with a traditional black cardigan and black skirt struck a balance that would make all the guests feel welcome—even ones who may have missed the note in the obituary requesting cheerful attire. Still, she regretted wearing black at all when Christina showed up in an impeccably tailored lavender Chanel pantsuit—possibly winning the best-friend-of-Molly competition that started when they were nine. With the perfect poise of a seasoned hostess, Leanne breezes through Molly's death party and lingers briefly near Christina to make a command sound like a polite suggestion. "Maybe we should dance and that will show everyone that it's normal?"

It's actually not normal to enjoy the dance hits of a Swedish pop sensation when mourning the loss of a best friend. And, for that matter, it's not normal for a woman's life to end at thirty-four. Molly would have been quick to point out that abnormality is the thing that got them there in the first place. That's how the story of cancer begins.

Christina looks at her watch. It's only been seven minutes. She's never spent this much time with Leanne and Nora without Molly buoying the conversation. In her daily life, Christina bargains with time—minute to minute—cramming massive responsibilities into a teeny day. There never seems to be enough time, yet today—at the funeral of her best friend, in the company of childhood frenemies—time has expanded. They just have to get through the next three hours, three minutes, and three seconds together.

"Make everything three," Molly told each of them separately. Separate was their preferred configuration. "I love threes."

Molly's nomadic lifestyle made it easy for them to avoid each other for the last decade or so, but when Molly came back to their suburban hometown in Massachusetts to be sick and then die, they were forced to spend much more time together in the last season of her life than they ever wanted to—which is to say, they've seen each other twice this summer. Today will be the third time, and mercifully, the last.

"I'll give out water," Christina tells Leanne, who is swaying in a feckless effort to groove to ABBA near a casket containing the body of their mutual best friend.

"Yes, Nora was in charge of bringing water," Leanne says. "Where's Nora?"

"I don't know," Christina says, looking at her watch again. Now six minutes have passed instead. For Christina, being with Leanne has somehow slowed time into reverse.

"Dancing Queen" fades out as Nora steps out of the ladies' room for the second time in seven minutes and twenty-two seconds. The first time was to get a tissue. The second was to wash her hands. Both times were to avoid conversation with Christina and Leanne.

If Nora were doing a countdown of her top three most dreaded activities, they would rank as follows:

3. Small talk with anyone anywhere, particularly at the funeral party of her best friend.

2. A full day of errands that includes getting a root canal, going to the DMV, and attending a black-box-theater production of a one-woman show written and performed by that lady from HR who hands out "comp" tickets with a great deal of pressure, but writes "no pressure" on the back of the ticket.

1. Being in the presence of Christina and Leanne.

Today, there's an abundance of small-talkers to fill the room while Nora hides in plain sight. She conceded to dress colorfully at Molly's funeral but only if the color was beige. Large groups at parties can really save Nora. She often positions herself near a few average-sized adults so she can enjoy the shade of a human eclipse. But here, those average-to-tall people might engage with her about sad things, and that is absolutely not what she wants. None of the responsibility of conversation will fall on her as long as she can avoid social stagnancy by staying in motion. Trips to the bathroom will help. It can be embarrassing to go to the bathroom as often as Nora plans to go today, but she has prepared several excuses. She's already used two. Next, she'll say she's going in to fix her contacts. (Nora doesn't wear contacts.)

While looking for Nora, Leanne experiences that magical instant where grief grants a reprieve of forgetfulness, and she surrenders to her instinct to search the crowd for Molly instead. Parties are where Molly belonged. Leanne recalls Molly's habit of slipping out of parties when no one was looking. By avoiding goodbyes, it could seem as if she had been around the entire time. It wasn't until the next day that people wondered, "Hey, what ever happened to Molly last night?" She loved creating the mystery. Leanne had always hoped Molly would grow out of this, but it seems Molly thought her funeral could be the same way. Just a good ol' time at a cozy nonreligious venue that has more windows than the typical musty old funeral homes her family preferred. Perhaps no one would notice that Molly had slipped casually out of the celebration forever.

For now, Leanne must actively pretend that Molly is just off somewhere being impolite. Telling herself this lie will help her follow the rules, comfort Molly's parents, and make guests feel welcome. Most importantly, she'll keep conversations with Christina brief and she'll smile at Nora—if she can find her. She plans to grieve later in the shower. That's the most appropriate thing to do, she decides.

In the name of similar propriety, Christina has muted her typical bombastic conversation style for this event. For these three hours, she's sworn off swearing. When she wants to exclaim about the politics of Molly's less liberal relatives, she keeps it to herself. She's tried to volley some light banter in the direction of Molly's musician friends, but it was a fail, and she let it go. No one ever knows what to say when there's a box of human remains in the room anyway.

Christina stews in the quiet awkwardness, wondering why Molly seemed to only collect one of each type of person for her menagerie of friends. By the time she sees Sam, her unexpressed thoughts escape by way of exasperated exhalation.

"Totally," Sam says, in full agreement.

Christina and Molly agreed that the word *tragic* is overused, especially on the internet. Still, even Christina had to admit that Molly meeting Sam so close to her death could be considered a tragic love story. She wants to exclaim about this, as she exclaims about all grave injustices (and even minor infractions like when her name is misspelled on her Starbucks order), but she has gotten through half of this party without side-eye from Leanne—or clergy. Sam has heard

Christina's intended sentiment from enough people already today, so he responds by rote to what she isn't saying.

"Molly and I had crappy timing," Sam says finally, as he rallies against tears. The no-tears clause included the words *especially Sam*, as he can easily be felled by the sight of a Hallmark commercial.

Christina ponders timing, punctuality, and Molly's acceptance of Christina's overscheduled lifestyle. She wonders if she deserved such unconditional friendship. More than that, she wishes she had less time today to wonder about this. She wishes she could just go back to her office. She turns on her phone for a minute and it buzzes right away, firing up the deprived dopamine centers of her brain. She wishes the alerts were Molly sending her a vulgar GIF to make this awful day into a dark joke. But it's just Christina's assistant reassuring her to take all the time she needs. Time is the last thing Christina wants.

Just back from her fourth trip to the bathroom, Nora finds herself standing between Christina and Leanne when Mrs. Granger's pastor calls for a prayer. Molly compromised on the pastor for her mother's sake, though she called him "the Religion Guy," even at the end, when she felt comforted by his final blessings over her.

"Ladies and gentlemen," the Religion Guy says. "If we could all join hands in prayer . . ."

Molly's three best friends reluctantly join hands in their own personal hell. They spend the next few minutes sweating through the awkward intimacy of hand-holding and God talk. Christina exclaims (in her head) that Molly wouldn't have wanted any sort of religious reference at her funeral. Leanne closes her eyes and nods with exaggerated reverence. Nora feels a competitive grip on each of her limp hands from Christina and Leanne and searches for the quickest path to her bathroom sanctuary because, eventually, this prayer will end.

At last, the prayer does end, and Molly's girls nearly escape each other, until Leanne brings up a bit of business:

"Mrs. Granger wants us to come over in a few weeks. In three weeks, actually. You know Molly and that 'three' thing."

"Fine." Nora is quick to end this exchange, even though agreeing to the invitation will mean three weeks of dread and then more small talk at the Grangers' house. It's not fine, though. Nothing is fine.

"I can't," Christina says. She can assume this without looking at her calendar. Booking Christina takes at least six weeks' advance notice.

"We have to," Leanne insists. "This was Molly's request."

"I'll make it work," Christina says.

"Good then," Leanne says. "Mrs. Granger said there are some things Molly wanted us to have."

Nora feels herself choking as she excuses herself. She doesn't want Molly's stuff. She just wants Molly, and that's impossible. Nora fears any inhalation could flutter into a sob before she makes it to the bathroom, so she doesn't breathe at all. It would be better to suffocate than to break down in front of all these strangers. Worse, she might cry in front of Leanne and Christina—two strangers she's known all her life.

Molly's Funeral Party Playlist shuffles to the next track: "The 59th Street Bridge Song (Feelin' Groovy)" by Simon and Garfunkel. Enough time has passed, and it's easier to ignore the buzzkill casket in the room and pay attention to the music. The party guests desperately need to shift away from the somber present and back toward happy memories of this woman whose spirit was free until she became sick—and now, in death, is free again. They hear the message Molly wanted them to hear:

Life, I love you. All is groovy.

"Classic Molly," Christina whispers to herself. But Leanne hears her. Leanne smiles. "That's so Molly."

Nora hears them both but pretends she doesn't. She agrees though. It *is* so Molly.

But now, Molly is gone.

2

Nora's coworkers at Content Monkey sent condolence flowers to her apartment, and she kept them for as long as it took the deliveryman to walk away from her front door. She removed the card expressing lukewarm sympathies and felt a pain behind her eye. Before she even got a good look at the bouquet, inflamed sinuses told her there were lilies involved. Why should Nora have to tolerate allergies on the day after her best friend's funeral?

It's a no-brainer—these flowers must go to live with someone else right away. The fastest solution is to deposit the arrangement on the stoop next door. Her overly sunny neighbor, Francine, will assume a secret admirer left them. Pretty Francine does have a lot of admirers, but most have been merely assumptions on her part. Today, Nora is fine with adding to Francine's disturbingly healthy self-esteem.

Later, Nora will write in her composition notebook:

Francine is just the type who loves the stink of lilies and will probably rub their fragrance on her neck and later will make them into some kind of Pinterest potpourri sachet.

Nora doesn't know how she feels about things unless they're written down. Often, she writes things like: *Do I need new sneakers?* and then writes the answer next to it: *Yes, Go to Marshalls.* It's as if Nora's notebook and pen come together as a council of elders for all the sounding-board questions other people ask family members, friends, or spouses.

Some pages of her notebook are designated for grocery store lists. Then there are lists of why she can't sleep and lists of remedies for her insomnia. It's a lot of lists. Old-school composition notebooks that cost two dollars each work just fine for her. Twenty years of this kind of note-taking has filled closets of her home with composition notebooks—and not because she's sentimental or would ever reference any of them. No, she just can't guarantee their discreet destruction. What if her thoughts got into the wrong hands? In high school, Nora feared that the horrendous varsity queen-of-everything, Amy McCormick, would somehow find her notebook in the trash and circulate it to everyone at school. Times change, but Nora's fears stay the same. She continues to hoard her journals, convinced that if they were ever discovered in the recycling bin, she would become a viral comic oddity on a Twitter account started by dumpster divers.

"If I don't make it, burn my notebooks," she said to Molly one time when Molly forced Nora onto one of those bungee fling swings in Orlando. "You can read them if you want, but then burn them."

And then Nora and Molly were launched into the steamy Florida air, and for once, Nora screamed as loud as Molly did, but each for different reasons. Molly's scream reflected the same blissful abandon she brought to everything she did. Nora's scream was just plain old terror. Nora survived that bungee fling swing, and Molly never had to burn any composition notebooks.

Today, Nora considers a notebook bonfire. The death of a friend makes people wonder how their own death will play out. Nora doesn't worry about the manner of death—only who will find her stuff afterward.

Nora almost makes it back into her apartment when Francine chirps a greeting from next door, then interrupts herself to gasp over the floral arrangement.

"Who are these from?" Francine sings.

It was more of a reflection than a question, but Nora steps back down from her front doorstep to answer her. It's too late though—the assumptions have begun.

"Hmmm. There's no card!" Francine relishes the delicious rom-com plot forming in her imagination.

It has already gone too far for Nora to tell Francine the truth. At this point, telling Francine that these are hand-me-down sympathy flowers would be awkward at best and cruel at worst. Lying isn't kind either, so Nora shrugs. Saying nothing is the loophole of lies.

Francine has lived next door to Nora for three years, and despite Francine's exuberance about neighboring, they haven't become friends.

The last time Nora made a true friend, it went like this:

Molly: "Hi, I'm Molly. Wanna be friends?"

Nora: "Okay."

It really doesn't work like this in adulthood. Adults have schedules instead of playfulness, opinions instead of curiosity, and personas instead of personalities. Brick by brick, their ideas about who they should be cover up who they really are. And often, as was the case with Nora, the only people left inside the fortress are the people who got in when the wall was still low enough to hopscotch over.

And now, Francine has bopped into Nora's newly empty fortress a day after the windows had been blown out and the foundation had been cracked.

"Are you home today?" Francine asks, her eyes growing huge. Francine's shiny strawberry blonde hair swirls around her peaches-and-honey complexion.

Francine is a fruit salad, Nora will write in her notebook later today.

Nora considers another lie loophole, but she's already reached the one-shrug-per-conversation limit Molly set for her a few years back. Now, she has to speak.

"Yes, home today. All day. Maybe bookstore," Nora says, and immediately wonders why she sounds like Tarzan.

Those aren't even sentences! Why do I talk? is what she would write if it were socially acceptable to take notes during a conversation. She has considered this many times. She might get away with it if she switches to note-taking on her iPhone. She could pass it off as an important incoming work-related text. People do this all the time.

"Bookstore! Perfect! I'm in!" Fruit Salad Francine accepts the invitation that Nora has not extended. Francine has assumed, as Francine does.

Nora can only muster shrugs and Tarzan talk, so there's no getting out of this.

"Okay," she says.

Typically Nora relishes a day stuck at home in her eclectic and cozy apartment. At home, she's comforted by the familiar structure of her inherited furniture that has become fully expressed with new quirky upholstery. She's inspired by her gallery wall that displays fine art alongside kitsch. She usually loves her stuff. But today, the pieces of her home radiate reminders and her stuff just makes her sad. Today, her gallery wall's focal piece—Gramp Shea's antique gilded frame surrounding a "Hang in There" kitty cat poster from Molly— makes her ache. Nora does not want to hang in there or anywhere.

She might even wish for the distraction of office life today, even though she's been pleading with her boss for months about establishing a telecommute situation. She's never understood why a content provider needed a brick-and-mortar headquarters anyway. Unfortunately, she has been banned from the office so she can grieve at home. Along with protocol flowers and standard sentiment, her coworkers have flooded her with a thread of texts urging her to take the "full bereavement leave" offered by their company. They fear if she doesn't, then HR will reevaluate the necessity for this time. It's likely some of them believe they are being kind by starting their texts with "Thinking of you" or "You are in my thoughts" before they push their self-serving agendas.

All of these texts show up as nameless phone numbers because none of Nora's coworkers have ever spoken to her before. And thanks to these ten-digit well-wishers and their burdensome sympathy, Nora faces a day of too much nothing.

$$\mathcal{C}$$

Getting into Francine's car was better than nothing. Nora didn't have enough words to express her preference for the local bookstore, the Well-Lighted Lit Shop, so Francine assumed they'd go to the massive book superstore at the mall. This time, Nora is fine with Francine's assumption. The multilevel mall bookstore will be a good place for them to part ways for a bit. Going forward, the Well-Lighted could still be Nora's private safe haven from run-ins with small-talkers. Nora typically goes to bookstores for public solitude. There, she can indulge her reclusive ways but still appear to participate in a community.

It would seem obvious to peruse the grief section, but Nora already brushed up on how to grieve about a month ago because she thought it might get Molly's hospice nurse off her back. Of course, hospice nurses are trained to stay off people's backs. That is pretty much their whole deal, actually. But they were saying things Nora wasn't prepared to hear yet, and even though the nurse's tone wasn't nagging, Nora's thoughts were.

Nora enters the massive bookstore with Francine twittering away about something she saw on HGTV. Francine works from home as a marketing consultant and has HGTV on as background sound the way most people play music while they work. Nora beholds the giant stacks of books and breathes in the peaceful access to knowledge in this place. Her shoulders soften and lower about five inches from where they've been hunched for the last week.

She's home.

What will she learn about this time? The idea of it is exhilarating. She might flip through a light ghostwritten memoir of a D-list celebrity or peruse a historical literary analysis of Keats poems. Maybe she'll look at some travel essays or a Crock-Pot cookbook? It could be anything.

There is, however, one section she will not browse today: Home & Garden. That's where Francine is headed.

"Let's go see if there's anything cute we can do with my container garden!" Francine says.

"Okay," Nora mumbles, but she's already paging through a spy novel. Francine assumes Nora is following her.

Nora explores the store and selects seven books to flip through. When she finds her spot on the floor in front of the map section, she takes out her notebook and pen so she can think better. No one ever shops for maps, so she'll be alone.

"Oh! There you are! Sorry I got lost. I found some good stuff," Francine says.

"That's okay, there's plenty to keep me busy around here," Nora says. A whole articulate sentence! She did it. Bravo.

"Girl, you got a lot of books going here," Francine remarks, grabbing from the top of Nora's stack.

"Good variety," Nora says, knowing she can never pull off calling another woman "girl" in that buddy way. Truth be told, Francine can't either. She just thinks she can.

"Here ya go! This helped my friend when she was in your situation," Francine says, presenting Nora with a self-help book called *Girl, You Got Dumped: How to Get Over Him and Under Someone Else.* "I totally understand what you're going through today."

Nora scribbles in her notebook, etiquette be damned:

No one understands.

It will be a while, if ever, before Nora accepts an invitation to spend time with another person.

Francine shouldn't have assumed.

3

When Christina screeches her Audi into the office parking garage, the valets prepare to hustle. They know she's in a hurry, as usual, and they don't mind indulging her polite yet demanding ways. She tips well and knows all their names.

"Louie!" she says. "Did you see the game?" Christina, a habitually barefoot driver, slips on her *YSL* shoes while Louie opens her door.

"Yes, ma'am," Louie agrees, his voice much quieter than his cologne.

"What a shitty call! Bunch of bullshit, right?" Christina towers over him, even without treacherously high heels.

Louie doesn't watch baseball, but there's never enough time to say much of anything during this morning greeting. So he just "yes ma'ams" her. Meanwhile, Christina doesn't enjoy baseball but accepts that knowing about it is her responsibility as a Bostonian.

"Welcome back, Ms. Ford," Louie says, but Christina is already in the elevator.

She texts "Arrived" to her assistant Julie, and when the doors open on the twelfth floor, Julie greets Christina with coffee.

"Thanks, Jules," Christina says, still in motion.

"Welcome back," Julie says.

"Thank you."

"How was your time off?" Julie dares to ask.

Julie, and everyone else at the Medeski, Pololuo & Ford law firm, would love to know why Christina was absent last week. It couldn't be illness, they've decided. Machines don't get sick. A vacation is even less likely because vacationing is just about the only thing Christina doesn't know how to do.

"Just fine," Christina says. "Thank you."

And that is that.

"I rescheduled your meetings, no problem, and canceled the deposition for this morning so you can regroup and—"

"Perfect, thanks. Can you make sure my salad gets here at one o'clock, and will you make my shake at ten, please? I'm just going to lock down and catch up."

"Sure, no problem. And your three-thirty chai latte?"

"Perfect. Thanks. You're the best!" Christina calls out as she closes her office door. Julie really is the best. She will never ask where Christina has been.

Christina lands in her overpriced ergonomic chair and slips off the torturous shoes that created the need for this special back-friendly office furniture in the first place. She hates wearing these unkind high heels, but she sticks it out. It's not enough for Christina to be taller than most women—she prefers to be taller than most men too.

A day ago, Leanne rolled her eyes when Christina was poking around on an iPhone at the funeral home, but setting a calendar alert is the only way Christina remembers anything. As soon as her desktop stirs awake, that reminder pops up.

Schedule awkward get-together at Molly's parents' house.

"Julie!" Christina calls. It's become Christina's habit to yell her assistant's name when faced with the task she wants to do the least. She immediately retracts. "Forget it!"

There's no way Julie can, or should, contact Christina's former frenemies to coordinate a meeting with their dead mutual best friend's mom. Though it would be so nice to outsource grief, even Christina hasn't figured out how to do that yet.

A torrent of pop-up reminders fills Christina's screen, but she gets the worst to-do over with first. She drafts an email to Leanne and Nora.

Subject: Molly's mom in three weeks
Hi—Just following up on funeral. Can we set a time for meeting with Molly's mom? Leanne, you said we're looking at three weeks out? Let me know so I can arrange.
—C

Christina has tended to exactly one of her other emails when a reply comes in from Leanne:

Hi, Christina & Nora:
Hope you're both doing well and recovering from yesterday. I was going to give Mrs. Granger some time to breathe, but she actually reached out to me this morning already. She seems to be doing okay, all things considered. She suggested we meet at her house on Wednesday night, three weeks from today, at 7:00 p.m.
    I hope you don't mind, I told her that would work, as I'm sure we'll all make it a priority. I'll see you there!
Yours,
Leanne

"Yours," Christina says out loud, mocking Leanne's formal closing. "*Up* yours."

While Christina is typing back, Nora replies to Leanne:

OK.

Nora can pull this off, but such pithy phrasing from Christina would come off as glib. She forces herself to write more than Nora did.

Thanks for setting it up. I will be there. Let me know if I should bring anything.
—C

She deletes the last sentence right away. What if Leanne asks her to bake something? She's said enough for now. In three weeks, she can come up with more to say. Until then, she has to get back on track. Two days off from work has been too much.

℮

At the stroke of 6:00 p.m., Louie gets the signal from upstairs— Christina is on the move. He bolts to her car, which he keeps parked in the first space next to the elevator.

When the elevator doors open, Christina strides to her waiting car and takes off her shoes for the drive to her Back Bay condo.

By 6:17, Christina arrives home and opens the door, two minutes off schedule.

Maeve has just plated dinner for two.

"Sorry, I'm late."

"Oh! You're not. You're okay," Maeve says, in a fading African accent. She scoots Christina out of the galley kitchen. Maeve's powerful stature takes up the entire narrow kitchen, and anyway, Christina has no place in a kitchen—even her own. "Dinner's ready. Let me finish up in here and then I'll let you be."

"Thank you. Is she awake?"

"Sure is. She hasn't slept at all today. She's been watching her TV shows."

Christina follows Maeve into the living room.

"Lilly!" Maeve says. "Look at who's here!"

Lilly looks up from *Wheel of Fortune*, which she doesn't really enjoy, but it comes on before the news. Watching the same channel all day helps her gauge what time it is. A moment before Christina arrived home, Lilly had started to worry. After all, it was almost half past *Wheel of Fortune*.

"Hi, Mum!" Christina says.

"Hi, sweetheart."

Lilly is a gentle-looking lady whose hair is still dyed the auburn color she chose in her late thirties. At the time, she reasoned that the only honest thing to do with one's hair was to go bold before going gray. Then, no one would wonder when the gray had appeared. It would be a more seamless transition, she'd decided. It was good thinking.

Now, at sixty-seven, she has the same decisively auburn hair, though she is no longer the one who makes the decision to dye it every month.

Christina flops onto the couch beside Lilly, so close their bodies touch. It doesn't matter how much space or available seating there is in a room, Christina has always sat this way with her mother. Christina repositions bed pillows around Lilly and finds an extra one to make herself comfortable. Back when Christina's interior designer chose this sleek modern couch, Christina had no intention of spending so much time sitting on it. Just like her shoes, Christina's home decor was designed for looks over comfort.

"How was your day?"

"Wonderful, sweetheart." Lilly smiles.

They watch a commercial for a pharmaceutical that, by the looks of it, provides the opportunity to ride a tandem bike, walk on the beach, and ballroom dance with a handsome silver-haired gentleman. It appears one must endure rheumatoid arthritis before living this well though. Or is it herpes? Yes, it's herpes. And man oh man, does this ad make herpes look like a good time. It's been so long since Christina had the opportunity to contract herpes that this commercial is making her rethink her lifestyle. The friendly voiceover speed-reads through the many side effects of this magic pill that makes holding hands at the farmers market with a good-looking fella look so delightful. Christina's successful career and role as caretaker for her aging mother has its own side effect: celibacy. She reflects on the time when she was more sexually prolific and wonders, *Should I have at least gotten herpes? It looks like I missed out.*

On the TV, young women with herpes are dancing up a storm at an outdoor concert when Lilly says, "Oh! Molly called, dear."

Christina puts her head on her mother's shoulder.

"No, Mum."

"She said she wants you to call her back at her parents' house," Lilly continues. "She's home for the weekend."

Maeve eyes Christina from the kitchen. In recent months, Maeve has been on Christina's case to set Lilly straight when she gets confused.

"It's good for her," Maeve always says. "It keeps her in the here and now."

Christina assesses the here and now. She decides that she, too, would like to live in a moment where she could call Molly back at her parents' house, and where Lilly could answer the phone on her own. She curls her knees up and stuffs her bare feet under her mother's thigh to keep them warm. Lilly kisses the top of Christina's head.

Christina hears Maeve close the front door on her way out. Maeve was merciful today. Mother and daughter are alone at last.

"I'll call Molly back later, Mumma," she says. "Let's have dinner, okay?"

4

Leanne revels in her space-saving packing techniques—one small suitcase will do for her and James to make the trip to Bermuda.

In her streamlined suitcase, efficient pods make it easy to find what she needs if she's in a hurry, and painstakingly double-bagged toiletries prevent spills or cross contamination. She would easily survive and probably conquer any sci-fi dystopian world plagued with space rationing, time scarcity, and spontaneous air-pressure changes. Future anthropologists might study her for this kind of thing. (Or current-day psychologists.)

Leanne lets James believe they're saving money by avoiding the airline checked-luggage fee, but in fact, the whole sensible packing ordeal is quite expensive. This kind of organization requires many hours and many dollars at The Container Store, where she talks aloud to herself as if she's alone in her own home.

"Will this fit in the—"

"Do I need two of these? Better get four."

Yup. It's like that.

In her bedroom packing zone, Leanne talks aloud to her clothing, her shoes, and her toiletries until James interrupts her trance. "Where's my—"

"Hold on!"

Leanne finishes counting pairs of socks.

". . . five, six." She turns to him. "Okay, what?"

"Where's my razor?"

"I packed it."

James rummages around the packing pods for his razor.

"Wait, wait, wait. I'll get it," she says.

"Nah, I can get it," James offers.

"NO! PLEASE!"

James snaps to attention.

"Sorry. I just know exactly where it is," Leanne says. "I'm in the middle of something. Do you need it *right* now?"

"Just have to shave for work, so . . ." James says, waiting for Leanne to acquiesce.

It will be a long wait this time.

"Uh, yeah, I do need it now," he says. James has always relied on his classic handsomeness to win hearts, score jobs, and get his own way. Leanne has always been his hardest conquest.

Leanne exhales as if this is the worst news she's ever received. It takes a moment, but she collects herself and complies with this extreme request. She retrieves a dark-blue pod from inside a larger light-blue pod. There, she finds a clear plastic case labeled "shaving items." She knows it's redundant to label clear cases, but label makers are really fun. Ask anyone.

She pops the case open and hands over the razor.

"Will you bring it back when you're done?"

"Hmmm. How about no?" James says with a playfulness Leanne doesn't see often enough. "I'll grow a vacation beard!"

Leanne suppresses a smile. The rare flirtation from James always breaks her out of the hypnosis of deep organization and serious planning. She resists letting him know he has this power even though she wishes he would use it more often.

"Operation Offspring commences in t-minus twenty hours!" James punches his fist in the air victoriously and walks into the bathroom. "Your mission, should you choose to accept it, is to get your wife good and pregnant on the pink sandy beaches of Bermuda! Do not fail!"

Leanne feels free to laugh now that James has closed the door and can't see her lighten up. This carefully planned conception trip is serious business.

"We're not having sex on the beach!" she calls.

"The future of the Stubin bloodline depends on Leanne Stubin getting laid properly! Do it for Leanne and do it for all of Stubinkind!"

Now she can't help it. Leanne laughs loud enough for James to hear. Satisfied, he starts singing the *Mission Impossible* theme song while he shaves.

Leanne shakes her head and puts her thermometer in the "last-minute items" pod along with a few other things she'll need in the morning. The app on her phone tells her she'll ovulate on her third day in Bermuda, but she doesn't want any surprises. Tomorrow morning, she's getting up extra early to take her temperature, just to be safe. If it turns out they have to have sex, she doesn't want to miss their flight.

Without thinking, Leanne reaches for her phone to text Molly her flight schedule. Her flurry of activity lurches to a stop. It occurs to her to send the text anyway. It might feel good to pretend again for a minute. Instead, Leanne curls into a ball amid the pods of partially packed resort wear spread across the bed.

"Can you come here?" Leanne calls to James, who has just turned off the faucets and begun whistling a stupid radio commercial.

"Hon?" Leanne squeaks one feeble syllable, but it's too late. James has already projected himself ahead into his workday, along with the mindless chatter of news, sports, and politics.

"See ya, babe," James says as he strides out their bedroom door.

Leanne remembers when James used to kiss her goodbye in the mornings. She remembers when he would spoon her to safety every time she curled into this helpless human heap. But now there's no more spooning from James. And it forking sucks.

5

Christina is the first to arrive at the Grangers' house. She knows that Nora will lag behind on purpose. It's awkward to be the first one to arrive at a social event, but it's especially terrible when the social event takes place at the home of your deceased best friend's parents. Nora always wants a human shield, but Christina has to admit that almost everyone would want one with this particular crowd. Nora, Christina, and Leanne have never had a conversation together without a buffer. And that buffer was buried three weeks ago.

"Hi, Mrs. Granger," Christina says when Molly's mother answers the door.

"Oh, Christina, call me Paula," Mrs. Granger says. "You're an adult."

"All right. Thanks . . . uh, thanks, Paula," Christina says, though it feels weird to call Molly's mom a totally different name after almost thirty years.

Leanne walks up the front walkway just in time to let some air out of the long pause between Christina's greeting and whatever conversation might have happened next. For the first time ever, Christina and Leanne are mildly relieved to see each other.

Christina attempts to break the ice for everyone. "Hey guess what? We're calling Mrs. Granger 'Paula' now. This is happening."

"Oh, we are? Lovely! Paula! Good to see you," Leanne lilts.

Mrs. Granger forces a smile. It seems she already dislikes the sound of her own name when said in these two women's voices. It's a reminder that Christina and Leanne aren't little girls anymore and therefore neither is Molly.

They make their way inside and Molly's big shaggy labradoodle, Fred, greets them with enough gleeful commotion to break most of their ice. Leanne changes the pitch of her voice and speaks in a language that she believes is dog.

"Herro! Suchagoodboy! Who's a good boy? You are you are you are."

It's embarrassing.

Leanne crouches on the floor and stays there, snuggling Fred into a loving smoosh. Christina loves that dog too, but she's not going to get on the floor. Don't be absurd. She's wearing Armani.

They catch a glimpse of Mr. Granger's shoulder as he closes the door to the basement stairs without so much as a hello. For weeks, Molly's dad has spent time in his basement office, finding ways to occupy his mind. He lets himself believe that Molly is just on another one of her "sabbaticals." It will be impossible for him to keep believing this comforting lie in the presence of her three oldest friends.

The doorbell rings and Fred gets very excited about it, but he wants to see how this tight hug with Leanne plays out first. There's no reason for him to leave a good snuggle until he's sure there's more than just a UPS guy at the door. Fred has been burned by the empty promises of a doorbell before.

"That'll be Nora," Mrs. Granger says, hurrying to the door.

"Hi, Mrs. Granger," Nora says with a casual wave to fend off any extra affection.

Mrs. Granger doesn't try to hug Nora. When Molly and Nora had sleepovers as kids, Mrs. Granger always asked, "Nora, can I have a little hug goodnight?" as if the hug were for her own benefit rather than for Nora's.

Nora's mother had always been very friendly to Mrs. Granger at Lamaze class when they were both pregnant, and Mrs. Granger often wondered whether they would have been friends if Nora's mom had lived through Nora's birth. When Mrs. Granger hugged Nora good-night at sleepovers, she always missed the woman she'd never gotten to know. And she sensed Nora did, too.

Now Nora looks exactly like that nice lady from Lamaze class, and it takes a few seconds for Mrs. Granger to pull herself out of the confusing layers of time and space. She often forgets how old she is until she accidentally catches her reflection in a shop window. Today, Nora is the window. She's a grown woman. They all are. Regardless, Mrs. Granger still refers to Molly's friends as girls. And she won't tell Nora to call her Paula.

"Girls, I made you some lemon squares," she says, brightening as she leads them to the "parlor."

"Wow, we get to call you Paula *and* we get to sit in the parlor?" Christina jokes. "Big day."

"Oh, you," Mrs. Granger says, relieved that her face remembers how to laugh.

Nora doesn't want to go into the parlor. It's as fancy a room as a middle-class suburban home ever gets, and she and Molly were abso-lutely not allowed to play in there.

Since Molly died, Mrs. Granger has fully occupied the parlor. It's the only room where there are no memories except for that one time she hosted the Neighborhood Watch meeting. Molly was a first grader when Mrs. Granger hosted angsty neighborhood ladies who raged about some local kids who'd been playing "mailbox baseball" on the street. A Neighborhood Watch gathering seemed like a lemon square occasion.

"I think it's what you're supposed to do, right?" Mrs. Granger asked her husband that day. She shuffled through the drawer where she kept her recipes on scraps of paper. She was looking for the easy no-bake lemon squares recipe she had gotten from a passive-aggressive PTA lady after Mrs. Granger had the audacity to bring store-bought cookies to a potluck.

Mrs. Granger had the further audacity to dislike hosting get-togethers even though she had a "parlor"—a room from a bygone era when people popped by for tea and whatnot.

"I think it's what you're supposed to do, right?" she asked her husband when they bought furniture for that room.

The Grangers always did what they were supposed to do. That's why Molly knew she could trust her parents to carry out her post-death requests. Mrs. Granger was grateful for the tasks, because for the first time, she couldn't even hazard a guess.

"What am I supposed to do?" Mrs. Granger asked her husband after Molly died. This time, the question wasn't about how other people might expect her to behave, but rather, how could she be expected to survive? What is a childless mother supposed to do, lost in a stormy wilderness full of monsters who feast on human heartbreak?

"What am I supposed to do?" she repeated.

Her husband handed her the folder Molly had stashed right where Mr. Granger would find it—on his desk in the basement. Inside the folder was a letter.

Hi Dad!

Greetings from the great beyond!

. . . Too soon?

Thank you for everything. I love you forever.

Take good care of Mom, like always. I have some savings that will come to you (all the account numbers are in this file along with a few other requests). I know you're both very frugal, but please use this money to do something fun with Mom—like go on that Alaskan cruise she wants to go on. You won't hate it, I promise. Just in case you do slightly dislike the cruise, take my iPad and learn how to use it before the trip so

you can play solitaire onboard. There are iPad classes for <u>free</u>
at the Apple store in the mall.

Some other quick stuff:

There are three things I've left for Christina, Nora, and
Leanne. They'll know what to do with them.

See you soon! But not too soon I hope. (wink) Just kidding,
Dad. Seriously though, do lay off the fatty foods. You'll just
feel better.

Love love love,

Molly Molly BoBolly Banana Fanna FoFolly Me My Mo Molly

The rest of the file had instructions for Mrs. Granger. Directions to grief support groups, a few drawings, a list of some books she should read—all of them already on Molly's bookshelf. Molly should have left a longer list because in the last three weeks Mrs. Granger has read all the books on Molly's list—day and night. That's all she's done, as if she's cramming for the biggest test of her life. Now Mrs. Granger has moved on to the other books in Molly's bookcase, even though they weren't on the list. This is her way of being close to her daughter. She wonders why they never read the same books together before. They could have talked about them.

What did we ever talk about anyway? she wonders. She already can't remember exactly. It seems they talked about nothing, but that was everything.

The nothing talks are what she misses most. Molly's books are her comfort. But Mrs. Granger would be wise to pace herself. Eventually, she will run out of the books on Molly's shelf, and it's going to be very awkward when she finds the erotica.

Molly's books are stacked up all over the parlor, along with a few empty tea cups. Christina sits on the couch and crunches some reading glasses that have slipped between the cushions. She bounces back up and blurts out an apology.

"No problem. I have them everywhere," Mrs. Granger reassures Christina, who's trying to straighten the busted-up readers.

Molly always advised her mother to keep only one pair of glasses because a person with one pair of glasses is more careful to never lose or break them. Mrs. Granger has at least twenty (in her house, purse, and car) and none of them has value.

"No, Molly. The reason I have twenty is *because* I lose them and have to keep buying more. And then the lost ones turn up," Mrs. Granger told Molly.

"But Mom, if you didn't just go get more, you'd look harder for the ones you have," Molly said.

This is the kind of thing Mrs. Granger plays over and over in her mind now. She tries to find meaning in everything Molly ever said.

Last week, Mrs. Granger cried to her husband in the middle of the night, "Frank, I should have looked harder for the one I had."

Mrs. Granger spent a lot of time wondering whether Molly's being an only child was a detriment to her social growth, which is why she let Molly have friends over as much as possible. When PTA ladies asked how many children she had, Mrs. Granger would shrug with a weird apologetic smile and say, "Just one."

She regrets using the word *just* in that answer. But there's no succinct word—like *orphan* or *widow*—to describe a mother who has lost all her children because no one can name it. Mrs. Granger lives in a nameless space, poring over the words in Molly's books to find a phrase that will connect her back to the daughter she's lost.

When Leanne releases Fred from nearly ceaseless smothering, he darts to greet the newest guest. Nora recoils and gives him a little wave.

"Hi, dog."

Fred doesn't read Nora's boundaries the way Mrs. Granger does. He circles Nora as she makes her way to the couch.

"All right, dog. All right," Nora says, shrinking her limbs in toward herself.

"I got him, Nora," Leanne says, taking a seat on the floor of the parlor. She beckons Fred into more relentless snuggling.

"Sorry the place is a mess," Mrs. Granger says.

"Are you kidding? I love it in here," Christina says, diving into the lemon squares. "I'd spend all my time in here if I were you."

Mrs. Granger feels validated. The girls look comfortable, so she summons the strength to bring out the folder Molly left.

"Girls, Molly left me some instructions," she begins. "It's kind of like a will, actually, when you get right down to it. Nothing too extravagant. She loved you girls."

Nora pretends she has to cough. Mrs. Granger pours Nora a glass of water. Christina takes another lemon square without even thinking about it. Leanne uses her flood of sorrow to drown Fred in affection.

"She has a few things she wanted you each to have," Mrs. Granger says. "She said you would all know what to do with them."

Nora anchors herself to the glass of water she hasn't sipped yet.

"So first, there's Fred," Mrs. Granger continues.

"Oh, but you'll want to keep Fred, won't you?" Leanne protests.

"He's a good dog, but we're not dog people," Mrs. Granger says. "Frank's allergic to almost everything. He's been staying in the basement all day to get away from Fred. Molly thought it would be best if one of you took him."

"Of course," Leanne says, as if offering to take Fred herself.

"So, Molly's instructions are that Fred should go live with Nora," Mrs. Granger says.

Nora looks up from her water glass for the first time since Mrs. Granger gave it to her.

"What?"

"She said you would know what to do with him and that you'd understand this note," Mrs. Granger says, handing Nora the note:

Go ahead and love him.

"I actually don't," Nora says, staring at the paper. "I don't understand this."

"I don't either," Christina says, laughing. "No offense, Nora, but I would have thought Leanne would be better suited for this."

Leanne thinks so too. She hasn't let go of Fred—in fact, at this point, her hug has escalated to a full-on cling.

Nora tries to find another way out of this.

"Well, what about Sam? Doesn't he want Fred?"

Mrs. Granger pets Fred with the type of long, soothing strokes that would probably do Nora some good right now if it were a normal, non-creepy thing to do to a human on the verge of panic.

"Sam offered to help with Fred whenever you need," Mrs. Granger says. "He's been coming over and walking him for us. He can't have a dog in his apartment, and besides, Molly's instructions are for you to—"

"Okay. I'll do it," Nora interrupts, staring at the note. The long strokes of her best friend's familiar handwriting soothe her. "Okay," she says again.

"I'll give Sam your number and you can coordinate if you need a break or anything," Mrs. Granger says.

Nora nods.

Mrs. Granger turns her attention back to the folder.

"Christina, she left you this note," Mrs. Granger says, handing over a slip of blue paper.

FLOAT

"And something else," Mrs. Granger says, getting up from the couch as if she's the Wizard of Oz looking for that plastic clock heart for the Tin Man.

Christina shows Leanne the note to decipher. Leanne shrugs.

Mrs. Granger returns, lugging a wicker, oval-shaped seat with a purple paisley cushion. She plops it on the floor and Fred plops himself on top of it.

Christina tries to make sense of it. "A dog bed?"

"No, she used this to, uh, meditate or something," Mrs. Granger says. "It's a meditation chair, I think. I Googled it. As the instructions say, you're supposed to know what it means."

Christina absolutely does not know what it means, and she squirms. Being confused comes so unnaturally to her.

"Thank you, Paula. I love it. I know exactly what to do," she says. It's not a total lie. Christina does know what to do. Research. She will research meditation chairs until this gift makes sense.

"So, now for Leanne," Mrs. Granger says, clasping her hands together. "Follow me."

Fred is the first one to follow her. Leanne is the last.

As they make their way out to the garage, Nora avoids eye contact with Leanne even more than usual. Leanne's anguish is palpable. Her thoughts are so loud, it's possible even the neighbors can hear her.

Doesn't Molly think I'll be a good mother? Why wouldn't she leave Fred to me? I told her James and I are starting a family—maybe she thought having a dog would be too much? Isn't a dog part of having a family? But I can handle it. Doesn't she know I can handle it? What does this mean? Nora hates dogs. This is a mistake. This is a mistake. This is a mistake. This is a—

"This is for you, Leanne," Mrs. Granger says, gesturing now as if she's Vanna White.

Leanne beholds the gift left for her in the Grangers' garage: Molly's bubblegum pink, pristine Vespa with its glittery matching helmet.

"What?" Leanne can't even pretend to be polite about this.

Nora's lips disappear as she bites away a smile. Christina releases an involuntary snort. They're relieved to absorb the comedy. It may have been exactly what Molly had planned—a moment of entertainment in case she was able to watch from somewhere in her afterlife.

When Molly bought the Vespa three years ago, Leanne was adamant that it was the biggest mistake ever.

"You *do* know that ER doctors have nicknamed those things 'donor cycles,'" Leanne said to Molly, who had just driven up to their brunch session in the Vespa. "You *know* that, right?"

"No, that's *motor* cycles. See? That's why that 'donor cycle' thing is so clever. It almost rhymes," Molly said, trying to change the subject. "Donor cycle. Motor cycle. No, that doesn't really even go. What else rhymes with motor? Voter, odor, boater—"

"What's the difference? This is the same thing as a motorcycle," Leanne scolded.

"No. It's a Vespa! It's Italian."

"Still dangerous."

"How can something so pink be dangerous, Leanne? There's glitter on the helmet. *Glitter!*"

"Well, I'm not going to tell you what to do but—"

"But?"

"Don't ride that thing," Leanne said. "It's going to kill you."

Leanne recalls her constant nagging about the Vespa and regret washes over her. She wonders if Molly was sticking it to her. It wasn't the Vespa that killed her after all.

"How am I going to get it home?" Leanne asks Mrs. Granger.

"Drive it?" Nora chimes in.

"Absolutely not!" Leanne says.

"It *is* a vehicle, Leanne," Christina reasons.

"It's a death trap!" Leanne says. "I told her that!"

"At least take this tonight," Mrs. Granger says, handing Leanne the sparkly helmet. "We'll figure out how to get the scooter to you later. Maybe Frank can drive it over in the morning."

Leanne moves closer to Mrs. Granger to take the helmet and

notices a tag hanging from the Vespa's handlebar. It's Molly's handwriting.

Allons-y, chérie!

"She said you'd understand what she meant," Mrs. Granger says, as Leanne stares at the note.

Leanne doesn't understand and looks to Christina for the answer. Christina subtly nods, indicating that Leanne should pretend—for a grieving mother's sake—that she does understand.

"Thanks," Leanne says, her eyes welling up with tears.

Mrs. Granger assumes the tears flooded in with the meaning of this note. But in reality, the tears came from guilt for thinking angry thoughts about a dead friend. Leanne is furious at Molly for mocking her concerns about the safety of a two-wheeled motorized vehicle, for giving Fred to Nora, for leaving her a cryptic note in French when Molly has never spoken a word of French to Leanne in her life, and for dying when she still has so many questions and so much of her life left to live without her best friend.

Now, Leanne's thoughts are loud enough to be heard in neighboring towns.

HOW COULD SHE DO THIS TO ME?

But she smiles.

"All right, girls. Just one last thing," Mrs. Granger says, opening the folder again. She takes out Molly's final message to her best girls. "Here, Nora. Can you read this? I left my glasses inside."

(All twenty pairs of them.)

Nora hesitates, but takes the note. Looking at Molly's handwriting, Nora can easily hear her friend's voice, and can barely summon her own voice to read aloud.

C, L, N—

Hello! Weather here is wonderful, wish you were here. (kidding!) Hope you liked my little gifts. I miss you already. I have one last request. Please have brunch together on the first Sunday of every month for the next year. If you don't, I will haunt you!

Also, I love you.

—Molly

Molly's last message to them hangs in the air.

"Every month?" Leanne finally says, not even trying to disguise her reluctance.

"That's what it says." Nora looks over the message again. Maybe she read it wrong?

"That's uh . . . weekends are tough but, uh," Christina says, starting to negotiate.

"We have to do it," Leanne snaps. "It's for Molly."

"Okay, okay," Christina says. "No one said we shouldn't, I'm just trying to work it out in my head."

Nora is already out of the garage, on her way to her car. "'Kay, bye, just email me where you want to meet," she calls over her shoulder, starving for solitude. This evening has already been way more conversation than she can handle and she's just been sentenced to monthly conversation with those same old strangers. She can't resist her urge to flee to the safe embrace of her Honda Civic and NPR.

Nora slams her car door. Sweet solitude. She starts her driving ritual checklist: check the back seat, fasten seat belt, plug in podcasts, lock the doors. She's alone at last, until there's a knock on the window. It's Mrs. Granger, holding Nora's new passenger:

Fred.

6

Nora stares at Fred.

"Are you hungry?" she asks.

Fred stares at Nora.

This is not the type of language barrier you'd hope for in a love affair. Maybe a beguiling Mediterranean guy or even a Scotsman with an absurd manner of speaking English would be fun. But instead, Nora got this silently expressive dog. At any moment, she suspects, Fred might stand on his hind legs, unzip his belly, and a bearded Muppeteer will climb out, stretch, and call it a day. Nora doesn't really want to talk to that guy either.

"How about I just give you some food and if you don't want it, then you won't eat it and that will be your way of saying you're not hungry," Nora says. "Sound good?"

She waits for an answer, defeating the purpose of the communication system she just laid out.

"Or just keep staring at me. That is equally effective," she adds.

Fred whimpers, but only coincidentally. Fred is probably not smart enough to understand sarcasm. Well, not yet anyway. A few more months with Nora and he'll at least be able to deadpan with more intention.

Nora assumes (correctly) that Fred means to imply she is being rude.

"Look, it's nothing personal, Fred. I know you've heard about me. I'm just not one for general togetherness," Nora says. "Please understand."

Fred doesn't understand. His cuteness is usually enough to break any human-to-dog barriers. He lies down next to the bowl of food to let Nora know he's not hungry. He's lost his appetite, having just found out that he can no longer rely on his good looks. It's a tough day for him.

"I'll figure it out, Dog. Just, uh, stand by," she says, as much to herself as to Fred. She jots down some dog care titles in her notebook for her trip to the library later.

The day Molly met Fred, it was pouring rain in that delicious July way. It was the kind of rain that comes urgently, as if every drop of moisture in the world has heard how much fun it is to pour down on summer. All the raindrops want in on this drippy, wonderful party.

Molly was on her way to nowhere in particular that Sunday, and an animal rescue organization had popped up some canopies on the sidewalk to lure farmers market types into dog adoption. The only commitment she had planned to make that day was to the inevitable heartburn that follows the hangover-friendly breakfast burrito she just couldn't live without. But the animal rescuers drove a hard bargain, as they always do. For one thing, their canopies provided the only shelter from the downpour. Molly figured she might as well play with the puppies until the rain let up. Once she was in their lair, she was under their spell. When Molly saw Fred, she knew her next stop would be the pet supply store. Organic dog food, of course. Nothing's too good for her Fred.

Molly crouched close to the doggie playpen where Fred had been humoring a Chihuahua into thinking she was the toughest dog in the area. Fred smiled at her, Molly would tell everyone afterward when she retold the story of their meet cute.

"Hi. I'm Molly. Wanna be friends?" Molly asked.

He didn't have to answer in so many words. He licked her face and she got the message—they belonged together.

Naturally, a gal wants her best friends to get along with the love of her life—especially when the best friends in question can't even get along with each other. Nora was going to be the toughest sell, so Molly told Nora the dog's name was Fred.

"I see what you're doing," Nora said.

"What?" Molly shrugged with feigned innocence.

"You're trying to endear this dog to me," Nora said.

When they were kids, Molly and Nora spoke in code about their mutual school crush. In sixth grade, it really didn't matter that they both had a crush on the same boy. He was older and their relationship potential was wholly imaginary, so they shared him happily. They called him "Fred" as Audrey Hepburn called George Peppard in *Breakfast at Tiffany's*. It was the perfect code because normal children had not seen this movie. Nora knew she wasn't a normal kid, based on her pop culture references. It seems that a lot of kids are desperate to be considered "normal," but Nora also knew the true gift of childhood is finding another kid who is abnormal in exactly the same way you are. With a friend like that, no kid would trade their weirdness for any amount of normal in the world. When Nora spoke in code with Molly, she felt understood and she embraced the weird.

Earlier that year, they had been eager to see *Dirty Dancing* for the first time and planned a big night of snacks, sleeping bags, and matching T-shirts. Nora's grandfather, Gramp Shea, offered to pick up the movie and swung by the library to get it. Gramp Shea had heard you were supposed to join the video rental stores, which required a credit card, but he didn't believe in credit cards. The video store also collected a great deal of personal info for membership, which was sure to bring about more telemarketers—the only thing in the world that made Gramp Shea furious. Ultimately, getting videos from the library was simply more efficient; he made weekly runs there anyway to check out books for Nora's insatiable reading appetite.

"Well, they didn't have that dancing movie you wanted, but you'll love this one," he said, handing them the video of *Breakfast at Tiffany's.*

The truth was the library *did* have *Dirty Dancing,* but Gramp Shea was concerned about the content. It was called *DIRTY Dancing* after all, and he just wasn't too keen on Nora and Molly seeing anything that was dirty. Never mind that *Breakfast at Tiffany's* is about a call girl and a gigolo. Audrey Hepburn is so adorable, she even made shoplifting look whimsical. To this end, Gramp Shea's efforts to shield them from a movie about debauched dancing backfired when Nora and Molly made a halfhearted attempt to emulate Audrey Hepburn's behavior by fleecing a twenty-five-cent piece of Bazooka Joe bubblegum from Cumberland Farms. Their guilt consumed them before they made it out the door with their loot.

Even delightful memories of shoplifting and sleepovers hadn't swayed Nora into loving Fred on that raining July day.

"I'm allergic to dogs, you know," she said.

"Oh, I know. That's why I got a poodle breed—so we can still all hang out together," Molly told Nora. "He's a labradoodle."

Nora recoiled when Fred sniffed her ankle.

"Aw, he ruvs you," Molly said.

"Are you gonna talk like that all the time now?" Nora asked.

"Rike what, Nowa?"

Wherever Molly is now, she is privy to all the truths in the universe from the profound to the mundane. The latter will reveal the truth about Nora's dog allergy, which Molly always suspected was fake. A person who dislikes dogs is even more unpopular than a person who dislikes people. Nora avoids most humans, but she knows better than to dig the hole deeper by having a dog issue as well. So, she invented an allergy.

"You'll have to go straight home from work every day and get up at the crack of dawn to walk the dog—you'll never sleep late again," Nora warned Molly when she first adopted Fred.

"Eh, I don't care about sleeping," Molly told her. "I'll sleep when I'm dead."

Is she sleeping now? Nora wrote in her journal the week after Molly was gone. She answered herself:

> *No way, she's probably haunting some girls at a slumber party who are playing with a Ouija board, just to freak them out. I'm sure she thinks being a ghost is hilarious. I wonder if she's watching people have sex. I bet she is. She so would.*

With Fred at her feet, Nora scribbles in her notebook, trying to work out her feelings as if they were a math problem. (And Nora sucks at math.)

> *This dog squeaks a lot. I don't know what he wants. I gave him food. Perhaps I should accept that this is his nature. Is this just what dogs do? I don't think this much whimpering is normal. Maybe he misses M? Is he crying?*

Her eyes sting for a second, but she catches herself.

Fred's forehead furrows in the twitchy inquisitive way that makes Nora "ruv" him for half of one second. Fred looks up at Nora in earnest. He squeaks again.

> *I'll ~~call~~ email Sam and see if he can ~~come over~~ meet me at the park. Maybe Dog will cheer up when he sees Sam? Dog is clearly not into me. I don't know what he wants from me. I gave him food. I took him out earlier. How many walks a day am I supposed to take him on? I'll Google that later. I don't*

even know how I'll be able to tell when he has to pee. There must be some sort of way dogs communicate.

Fred squeaks louder.

I'll ask Sam.

Fred shuffles at Nora's feet and wags his tail.

Or maybe it will be in that book.

Fred squeaks one more time before he gives up and pees on Nora's rug.

Nora regards this without emotion. She flips a few pages back to that list of dog books and supplies. She adds:

Rug cleaner.

7

Stretchy saliva froths from a panther's foamy mouth. Leanne can feel its hot breath as the gravelly sound and bitter darkness clamp down on her throat, and she can't scream. The panther rips her in half. She'll have to watch him devour her lower body unless she wakes up first.

Leanne gasps awake and pulls at her bedsheets. The panther is gone. Leanne is intact. And she has full license to use this nightmare to justify extra calories for the rest of the day.

Later, at Kauffee Café, she allows herself to order a pumpkin spice latte. She won't actually drink the fully caffeinated gooey goodness, but merely smelling it won't harm the Bermuda baby. It's not official yet, but Leanne feels that everything lined up perfectly on her baby-conceiving trip with James. She almost even enjoyed it.

She inhales a few quick whiffs of latte, but serenity is still farther away than the nightmare she can't shake. Cinnamon nutmeg can make a lot of things nicer, but it cannot erase the horror of a panther attack—not even a dreamed-up one.

Leanne is less terrified of a real-life panther than she is of her dark, unchecked mind. When she dreams like this, she's alarmed that such sleeping darkness exists, despite her waking sweetness. Leanne locked in her nice-girl persona right around the time her mother explained that making friends might not be that easy for a girl like her. It was the closest Leanne would ever get to hearing her mom call her pretty. The comment made Leanne wonder what kind of girl she was, but she deduced that she must be the kind of girl who wasn't naturally worthy of friendship. It was important for this kind of girl to make sure she was never too mopey, too happy, too loud, too quiet, too silly, too serious, too human. But the mopey, happy, loud, quiet, silly, serious, human stuff exists in Leanne even when she pushes it away. It has to go somewhere, so it gangs up on Leanne in her dreams. She has begged God for a peaceful dreamless sleep, but because prayers and dreams are so closely related, one can't cancel the other. Leanne dreads sleep.

Lots of people tell Leanne that once she becomes a mom, she'll love sleep. Leanne doubts this. She hopes she'll be so exhausted she won't have the energy to dream. She'll finally be at peace—maybe.

As she smells her pumpkin spice latte, Leanne considers the entire dream. The worst thing about the panther ripping her in half was that she was screaming for help and no one could hear her. No, maybe the worst part was being trapped, knowing the panther was about to rip her in half and she could do nothing but wait for it to happen. Or maybe the worst part was after she'd been sewn back up, no one believed her when she told them she'd been ripped in half. She remembers lifting her shirt to show a jagged, stitched wound across her midsection. No one was impressed. Faceless people in her dream shrugged and told her to stop complaining. But she'd been *ripped in half*!

Ultimately, Leanne concludes that the worst part was the mere existence of the dream itself.

Leanne mindlessly sips the latte, then panics and spits out every last drop.

How could I be so careless? She rages at herself in that panther mind of hers.

She spikes the coffee cup into a trashcan in a way that is almost athletic but mostly menacing. She snaps right back into her sweet demeanor, reminding herself that she's not in her dreams, but at Wellesley, where such lack of composure is historically unpopular among the staff.

"Whoops!" she chirps. She hopes this adorable "whoops" will convince passersby that her emotional outburst was merely a silly, clumsy slip. But because she is the only witness to her own darkness, it will require a lot more convincing.

There's one week left before the students return to campus, and Leanne relishes the slow pace as she walks toward her office. Her work in the Wellesley College Alumnae Office is year-round, but with fewer people looking over her shoulder during the summer, she has had more time for off-campus lunches, late mornings, and personal days. Somewhere in a place she wouldn't ever acknowledge, Leanne is relieved that Molly had the good manners to die during this less hectic time of the year. No one would ever say it, but dying during winter holidays is just plain rude.

Leanne soaks up the extra oxygen while she can. Soon, the new work-study student will be up in her grill, asking how to use the copy machine, how to mail merge the donor appeals, and, most annoyingly, what year Leanne graduated from Wellesley College. The intern will mean no offense—it's a fair assumption that a woman working the Alumnae Office is, in fact, an alumna herself. The poor work-study gal will be taken off guard, however, by how charged Leanne's response will be:

"Actually, I went to Framingham State and I *really* loved it and it was *really* perfect for me at the time and I *really* made the right choice. For me. At the time."

. . . Really?

Each year, some poor unsuspecting undergrad tumbles in Leanne's tidal wave of regret. And even though Leanne smiles when she describes her college choices, the message still knocks over anyone in its wake. It's not easy to piss Leanne off, but she holds Wellesley

College undergrads in a special place of contempt. It might even be why she gets so flustered by Christina, who at one point was one of those girls . . . *women*. Wellesley students hate to be called girls.

Katherine Riker bounds across the green pristine lawn (footpaths, be damned), waving both arms over her head as if she's trying to land a plane. Indeed, Leanne's focus is somewhere in the clouds, until she notices the very noticeable Katherine, draped in a billowy cotton kaftan, a head scarf, and layers of colorful beads. Somehow, it all works.

"Bonjour! BONJOUR, MON AMIE!" Katherine bellows.

Katherine's miniature collie pauses to greet a squirrel, an exchange Katherine can barely tolerate. Her little baby should exhibit as little canine behavior as is possible for a dog.

"Non! Non, Corbu. Allons-y, monsieur. Dites 'Bonjour' à Madame Leanne!"

Of course, Corbu can't say "bonjour" to Leanne. He's a dog, for crying out loud. He does seem to understand French, as does Leanne—fluently, in fact. And just like Corbu, Leanne refuses to speak it.

"Good to see you!" Leanne says, quickening her pace from a saunter to a full walk toward Katherine. Leanne is relieved that Katherine is the first faculty member she encounters this year.

"Thank God no one's here yet! I need the quiet! J'adore le silence! Le silence est glorieux!" Katherine yells.

Katherine removes her sunglasses and helps herself to Leanne's personal space. She takes a dramatic breath to say something upbeat and hilarious (*en français bien sûr*), but then Katherine becomes still. Something in Leanne's face makes Katherine forget all about that hilarious thing she was about to say.

"When did it happen?" Katherine says instead.

"Five weeks ago. She was ready. It was okay," Leanne says, still somehow presenting a smile.

"Oh, mon amie," Katherine says, never a sucker for fake grins or rehearsed pleasantries.

Katherine wraps Leanne up in a warm hug and rocks her gently. Katherine's stature matches her personality and dwarfs Leanne, who looks like a wounded child in Katherine's embrace. When Leanne is ready to pull away, it doesn't bother Katherine, who will always hug someone for an amount of time that is well past the normal threshold for friendly intimacy.

Leanne launches into her grief script again.

"I was lucky to be with her at the end," Leanne says. "I'm glad we got the chance to—"

"Yes. I know. I'm sorry," Katherine says.

"Oh, thank you. She was ready, she—"

"No. You. I'm sorry for you," Katherine says. "It's awful."

Leanne can't remember where in her death spiel she left off, dammit. What's the next line? Most people let her cycle through the death-of-a-loved-one speech while nodding and tilting their heads in sympathy. Some even say the lines for her to hurry the whole thing along. Katherine has no such script. She's all improv. "Grief is a beast," she says.

Leanne has nothing to say to this, because now she's thinking about the black panther from her psychotic dream.

Is that the beast?

"A beast, my friend. You can't fight it. It will win," Katherine says. "You just learn to make friends with the beast. *C'est la bête la plus féroce.*"

Leanne resists her urge to talk away the pain and concedes. "It is a beast."

"Allons-nous promener?" Katherine asks, linking her arm with Leanne's.

"Yes," Leanne says.

And so, they walk. Since there's nothing else to talk about, they don't talk at all. And the silence is glorious.

8

A narrator's lilting voice coaxes Nora awake. Nora believes that listening to audiobooks doesn't count as reading, but until she can learn to flip pages in her sleep, this will have to do.

The first Sunday of the month has come too quickly for Nora. Her normal Sunday ritual includes going to the Well-Lighted Lit Shop to flip through the new releases. A year ago, she stopped her Sunday newspaper delivery because she was feeling guilty about spending so much time at the bookstore without actually making a purchase. She feared the Well-Lighted would succumb to the same plague that killed her other two favorite bookstores, so she started buying the *New York Times* and the *Boston Globe* there. A bookstore's biggest hope for survival is a voracious reader like Nora, but she still has to hit up the library every week because, as she says, "I'm not a Rockefeller." It's one of many antiquated phrases in Nora's vernacular—a side effect of having been raised by a grandparent.

Nora's budget is so tight she would have to live in a house made of books if she actually purchased everything she reads. She would not particularly mind living in a house made of books, however. It should be a thing.

Today, Nora will have to skip the bookstore altogether. She writes in her composition notebook:

Take the dog outside.
Shower.

Eat oatmeal.

Leave by 9:45.

Get newspapers at Dunkin Donuts with coffee.

11 a.m.: Meet L & C at Sunnyside's.

I only have to stay for ~~an hour.~~ ~~45 min~~ 30 min.

Get to the library at noon when it opens.

Come back home and read, do laundry, reset for the week.

Bring books to return, Dunkins coupon, Fred.

Yesterday, Nora wrote down a few topics she might be able to talk to Christina and Leanne about.

Without M, we have nothing in common, she scribbled. *What can we talk about?*

The answer came out of her pen.

Ask them about work. Tell them about that book you read last week about Queen Liliuokalani. What was that called? I can't remember, never mind, tell them about that bouilla-baisse recipe you read in NYT. I think Leanne likes to cook. Do people ever cook bouillabaisse at home? I really doubt it. I should get some at Jimmy's this week for lunch.

It is inevitable they will talk about Molly, but Nora doesn't want to. She feels better now that she has a list of topics she can deflect onto them. That should take up a half hour. Then she's allowed to go.

When she was a kid and Gramp Shea dropped her off at birthday parties, he always gave Nora a dime and showed her where the nearest payphone was.

"Give it thirty minutes, love," he encouraged her, pressing the dime into her little hand. "You might have fun."

She felt the dime in her pocket like a totem and it made her brave. It never mattered that the payphone was going to cost more than a dime, because she usually ended up having fun. And anyway, Gramp Shea was always parked right next to that payphone, reading the newspaper until it was time to pick Nora up.

Nora attaches the leash to Fred and gathers her NPR tote, composition notebook, and car keys.

"I'll give it thirty minutes. I might have fun," she tells Fred.

℮

Nora arrives at Sunnyside Café with plenty of time to spare. She considered purposely arriving late so she wouldn't have to endure the painful one-on-one time with whomever arrived first. Ultimately, she decided she might as well get there on time and relax before Leanne and Christina arrived. That way, she could preview the menu and order quickly, moving this brunch thing right along from the start.

Nora doesn't realize that efficiency was also Christina's priority when she picked Sunnyside's as their meeting place. It ranked eighty-seventh on Yelp, and therefore would certainly not have a swarm of foodies willing to wait in a long line to get in.

Nora gets to the door of the café and feels the sudden tug on the leash she forgot she was holding. *Fred.* It's the first time Nora has taken him anywhere besides the park.

She doesn't have time to write the question in her journal to ponder what dog people do in these situations. She'll have to ask Fred.

"Ah, crap," she says. "What do we do now?"

Fred doesn't know either.

"Can you stay outside?"

Fred can stay outside.

"I'll get a table next to the window, okay?"

Fred is okay with it.

She ties his leash to the wrought iron window box full of geraniums. Nora gags because she hates the smell of geraniums. Fred makes a random dog noise that sounds a lot like gagging and Nora assumes it's because he too hates geraniums.

"Okay, okay, I'll put you over here instead," she says. She slips the leash loop under an easel holding the chalkboard brunch menu. It's not a very heavy item, so Fred could conceivably drag it away if he wandered off. Nora knows this.

"You won't wander off, will you?" she asks.

The question is, of course, rhetorical.

Fred lies down. This exchange has been too exhausting for both of them. Nora has already had enough of this brunch adventure and it hasn't even begun. She takes the table next to the window where she can see Fred. She waves to him. He acknowledges her in his way.

"Lemme get you a menu," the waitress yells across the café.

It's a lot more loud attention than Nora is really comfortable with. She regrets taking the table next to this conspicuous window where she's exposed to sunlight, street noise, and every pedestrian's gaze. She glowers at Fred. It's his fault she's not in the corner where she belongs. Nora swears she just saw Fred shrug.

Since Nora compulsively reads every word that comes into view, she notices the waitress's nametag: Diane. Nora will never use this information because that would constitute some sort of friendly banter, which is out of the question.

Diane passes Nora a menu.

"Can I get ya somethin' ta drink?" Diane bellows.

"Yes, thank you. May I have tea with the bag out, please?"

"What kind of tea?"

"Doesn't matter. Thank you," Nora says. "Oh, and I have two more people coming, so could I have two more menus?"

"No problem!" Diane says.

She's so loud, Nora writes in her notebook.

Diane comes back with two more menus, a cup of hot water, and a Lipton tea bag on the side. Diane clangs it all down on Nora's table and yells over to a guy who's been trying to get her attention. "Ya want some creamahz, hon? Oh buttah? Sure thing!"

And Diane dashes off to get butter for that guy in the corner.

Nora is relieved by Diane's distractible nature. It makes it easier for her to sneak a bag of Trader Joe's Decaf Irish Breakfast Tea from her tote and drop it into the cup of hot water.

Nora hears a muffled cooing coming from outside. She sees Leanne crouched in front of Fred, fussing over him in a babyish voice. She's speaking nonsense. Nora steals one serene sip of her tea before acknowledging Leanne and beginning the brunch she's been dreading for two weeks. Nora taps on the window and waves.

"Hi!" Leanne chirps. She nuzzles Fred one last time before she leaves him outside. "Is he okay out there, you think?" Leanne asks Nora as she walks into the café.

"He seems fine." Nora shrugs.

"Oh, sorry, he's your responsibility, so I shouldn't butt in," Leanne says, though it's too late.

Spoiler alert: Leanne will butt in again.

"So how have you been?"

It's already come to this. Small talk.

"Pretty good," Nora says. "How's uh . . ."

"James! James is good," Leanne gushes. "We just got back from Bermuda."

Nora braces herself for more gushing. Then, thankfully, Diane returns to the table to yell some more. "Hiya, you want somethin' ta drink?" she says, practically knocking Leanne over.

"Oh, some coffee—uh, decaf. Decaf! No! Orange juice, eh, better get water. Never mind. Just water. Water would be great, please. Thank you," Leanne says.

Diane instantly dislikes Leanne.

Now it's over. They've lost conversational momentum. A crushing impasse. Leanne asked how Nora was doing. Nora asked about Leanne's husband, What's-his-name. What else is there? Oh, yeah, the dead friend. In her discomfort, Nora looks down at the menu.

"Oh! So, what are you getting? What looks good?" Leanne asks.

"I'm not sure," Nora says, though she's considered an omelet.

"What am I in the mood for?" Leanne asks. "Lunch or breakfast?"

Nora's not sure if she's supposed to answer this question.

"I'm getting the omelet special," Nora says, punctuating this decision with a definitive sip of tea.

"What do I want, what do I want, what do I want?" Leanne thinks out loud. "Christina's coming, right?"

"I think so, I haven't heard from her," Nora says.

Just outside, Christina parks her Audi almost perpendicular to a parallel space. She turns off the radio as a priority—it's only acceptable to play '80s heavy metal at such a decibel when driving full speed. Everyone knows that. That's why she always turns down the volume at red lights. And you better believe she clicks the window controls to be sure no one can hear her singing along with Def Leppard. Christina's penchant for '80s metal clashes with the cultured image she has so carefully constructed. During the decade when she rebranded, Christina gave up metal and bought only albums of "indie" artists or classics like the Beatles. Currently, she's having an '80s Hair Band renaissance. When she can't quiet her mind, the next best thing is to drown out her thoughts.

She climbs out of the car in a fitful manner that startles Fred to his feet. When Fred sees that it's Christina, he resumes his lounging.

"Hey poochie," Christina says, greeting Fred with more enthusiasm than she gives most humans. "Where's Nora?"

Fred believes the answer is obvious, so he doesn't comment.

Christina thrashes the door open to get into the café. This time, Fred doesn't even flinch. He knows that's just how Christina is.

"Hi," Christina greets Nora and Leanne. "Sorry I'm late."

"No problem," Leanne says, as she stands to give a forced hug to Christina. Christina one-ups Leanne and gives her an air kiss.

Nora has none of the air kisses. Instead, she waves.

"How's it going?" Nora says.

"Pretty good, pretty good, and you?" Christina says. She catches a glimpse of Diane in the distance. "Coffee?"

Diane has met her match. Christina is louder and more in charge. Nora shrinks a little more and sips her tea, which is almost gone. She would like to order more, but she'll wait until Diane offers.

"How are things going at work?" Nora asks, already regretting that she used up her go-to conversation starter so quickly.

"Ugh. Hectic. Crazy. Awesome," Christina says. She can't remember what Nora does for a living. She'll figure it out later. "How about you? Your job going well?"

"Good, no big news," Nora replies, providing no career clues for Christina to decipher.

"Leanne, how was your trip to Bermuda?" Christina asks.

Nora is relieved that Christina's arrival means this topic can be recycled.

"Oh, just wonderful," Leanne chirps. "Have you been there?"

Nora shakes her head no, as if she's part of this exchange, but she's not, really.

"Yes, I went with my parents when I was really little. They loved it there." Christina knows how to chat. "Where did you stay?"

"The Ritz."

"Fabulous!"

"We splurged," Leanne says in a well-rehearsed modest tone used by people who are embarrassed by luxury.

Nora looks out the window to check on Fred. He checks on her right back.

"I love the Ritz. Have you been to the one in Vail?" Christina asks them both.

Nora doesn't bother to answer this one.

"No. Just in Bermuda. It was a special occasion," Leanne leads.

"What's the occasion?" Nora lands that question like a pro. She's proud of herself for interjecting in a natural manner. It bought her a few more minutes of polite silence.

"Ohhhhhh . . ." Leanne acts coy, forgetting for a moment that this is not the right crowd for talk of "babymoons." She adjusts her tone accordingly and states a fact. "Anniversary. It was our anniversary."

"Fabulous," Christina lies. She doesn't think anniversaries are fabulous. She's never had one.

Diane returns with Christina's coffee and a glass of water for Leanne.

"Ready to order, ladies?" she asks.

Nora is very ready to order. She's been staring at the menu as if she's trying to memorize it.

"I'll have the omelet," she declares.

"Am I in the mood for lunch or breakfast?" Leanne wonders aloud again. A sip of tepid unfiltered tap water, and she's rethinking her drink order already.

"You need another minute?" Diane offers.

"No. I'll have eggs Benedict," Christina says. She doesn't want this dragging on any more than Nora does.

"Cobb salad, no bacon," Leanne decides. "And I guess I *will* have a decaf coffee, please. Thank you. Decaf."

"Gotcha." Diane turns to walk away.

"Oh my GOD!" Leanne screams, startling Nora and getting Diane's attention. "No bleu cheese! No bleu cheese, please!"

"Got it," Diane says. "No bacon. No bleu cheese."

"Really. *No* bleu cheese," Leanne says again.

"Absolutely. No bleu cheese," Diane assures her, heading toward the kitchen. She has the decency to turn away before rolling her eyes.

"No bacon, no bleu cheese? Is it technically still a Cobb salad anymore?" Nora says, trying to make a joke.

"I can't have bleu cheese," Leanne says in defense. "It, uh, gives me migraines."

"I read it can do that to some people," Nora agrees. "I avoid it myself."

Christina doesn't buy this bleu cheese story. She's not going to play into the fuss. She correctly suspects Leanne is hanging bait and wants someone to ask her if she's pregnant. Christina is accustomed to these kinds of conversational manipulations in her circle of friends. Her crowd can spin any subject in the direction of an anecdote from when they "went to school in Cambridge," so they can casually mention that they went to Harvard. It's the modesty loophole that's taught in an Ivy League freshman orientation—it doesn't count as bragging if someone has asked about it. Christina will never take such conversational bait. She won't be played.

"I think what makes it a Cobb salad is the egg," Christina circles back to Nora. "I don't know why it's called *Cobb* salad, though."

"It's after the owner of the Brown Derby Restaurant, Robert Howard Cobb," Nora chimes in without thinking. "Robert Cobb. Bob Cobb? He went into the kitchen late one night and put all the leftovers he could find into a salad. Some people dispute that he, and not his chef Paul J. Posti, invented it. And, technically, the cheese in a Cobb salad should specifically be Roquefort, but everyone uses any old bleu cheese. I suspect Roquefort would be even more likely to give you a migraine because Roquefort is aged in caves whereas others have controlled humidity. Either way, the chemical tyramine is what causes the migraine, and that happens in the aging process. Commercial bleu cheeses aren't aged as long as a Roquefort, usually."

Leanne and Christina are silenced by this exposition.

"I guess," Nora adds, as if a shrug will erase it all. She mutters to herself, "Bob Cobb."

It's quiet again. Their thoughts all drift to Molly—how impossible it seems that they'll be able to stand coming together like this every month for a full year.

"So, did you figure out what you're supposed to do with that dog bed?" Leanne asks.

"It's a meditation seat," Christina says.

Dianne plunks down a mug of decaf coffee in front of Leanne and pours a caffeinated refill for Christina.

"Oh, that's right. That's what Paula said. I forgot. That night is kind of a blur," Leanne says. She takes her coffee mug and interrogates Diane. "Decaf? It's decaf, right?"

"Right!" Diane smiles and this time, she's not quite fully turned when her eyes roll.

Nora catches Diane's expression and smiles genuinely for the first time all day.

"Well, I guess I'm supposed to sit on it?" Christina surmises.

"No, but isn't there a meaning?" Leanne insists. "There must be some kind of riddle to it, don't you think? Or a message? Otherwise, why would Molly have given Fred to Nora?"

"What do you mean? I'm taking care of him. He's happy, right?" Nora says, looking out the window at Fred again.

"Yes, but you're not," Leanne says.

"So? She never is," Christina says.

"I've been happy," Nora says. "At most points in my life. More often than not."

"I didn't mean it like that," Christina says. "I'm not saying you're not happy. You're just not demonstrative about happiness. *She* means you don't seem happy about it. And *I'm* just saying you're not someone who's outwardly smiley."

"Because I don't feel like smiling," Nora says, simply. "I'm still content."

"Okay, never mind. I don't know how we got off track," Leanne says. "I just wanted to know if you've done anything with the meditation seat, Christina."

"I keep it in my bedroom. I had it in the living room at first, but my mom . . ." Christina starts, but snaps out of it. Brunch is the place to get real, but only if you're with your best friend, which she is not. She censors herself. "It was just better to keep the space clear."

"Your mom doesn't like it?" Leanne presses.

"Not really," Christina dodges. Christina has decided that it is none of Leanne's business that Lilly paces almost constantly these days. As her disease advances, new furniture throws off her wandering pattern, and she can't adjust her gait quickly enough to accommodate new obstacles.

Nora notices the strain in Christina's voice, because Nora notices everything.

Diane interrupts with perfect timing. She delivers their food. "Cobb salad no bacon, no bleu cheese, omelet special, eggs Bennie," she announces. "Anything else, ladies?"

"Thanks," Christina says. "I think we're . . ."

She notices Leanne inspecting her salad for traces of bleu cheese. It passes inspection.

"Yup, we're good," Christina concludes.

Now they can talk about the food. Talk of the food leads to talk of other food and other restaurants. It's enough to fill the rest of the time. Mercifully, Diane wants to move them along to make way for new customers, and she brings the check before they've finished eating.

Nora keeps the promise she made to herself, and she's back in the car with Fred by noon. As she drives away, she feels a euphoric and familiar Sunday morning sense of relief. It was that same feeling she had as a child when she was forced to go to church. The relief was not from a spiritual awakening or soul cleansing. Rather, the relief came from the mere completion of an activity she dreaded beforehand and barely tolerated during.

She's free now. And she's going to the bookstore—her chosen church.

Meanwhile, Leanne and Christina linger on the sidewalk.

"I'm sorry I was so brisk about the meditation seat. I honestly don't know what it means," Christina apologizes to Leanne.

"No, it's okay. I didn't take it in a weird way at all," Leanne says, though later she will try to deconstruct Christina's tone over dinner with James.

"I'm doing some research about meditation to see if I can figure out what she meant in her note," Christina says.

"Oh, that's great," Leanne says. "Meditation is supposed to be really good for you."

"I'm not meditating, I'm just researching," Christina clarifies.

"I see. Well, let me know if you find anything good. I've always been curious and I'm supposed to be reducing my stress now," Leanne leads again.

"Okay, I'll let you know," Christina says, still refusing to take the bait. "I better get going."

"Me too. James and I have to get some errands done," Leanne says.

"See you next time," Christina says.

"Yes. Good to see you." Leanne wonders if they're supposed to air-kiss goodbye. Neither of them knows for sure, so they don't.

9

"Okay, Mum. We're here," Christina says, pulling into a handicap parking spot. "VIP."

Lilly knows she's at the doctor today, but she remains quiet about it in case the next time is different. She clings to the idea that consistent silence may protect her daughter from witnessing a slow, painful loss of memories.

Christina used to spare her mother the long walk from the parking lot to Dr. Breyer's office—dropping Lilly off at the door and scurrying back to meet her after she'd parked. The whole thing took only about five minutes, but now that's plenty of time for things to go wrong. When Lilly wandered off that last time, Christina was outraged that there wasn't a valet at the hospital, and she took out her anger on Dr. Breyer. He responded by offering a handicap tag for Christina's dashboard. Dr. Breyer is always willing to bend rules for Christina, because he finds her wrath to be more than a little bit terrifying.

Dr. Breyer is the seventh doctor Lilly has had. He was also the second doctor. Christina has made the rounds with her rage and cycled through all the top specialists in the city. Dr. Breyer's degrees weren't from the fancy schools that typically impress Christina, but he did have one skill that the other doctors did not have—a forgiving spirit.

The word *burly* must have been coined on the very day that Dr. Breyer hit puberty and was able to grow facial hair. He's a Jewish

Santa Claus who wears a bolo tie and orthotic sandals with wool socks. From where Christina sits, he spent too much of his life in California to make sense in New England anymore. Indeed, he did spend a lot of his life in Marin County, but returned home to Brookline when his own mother was sick with Alzheimer's. It hasn't occurred to Christina that Dr. Breyer has experienced the same sorrow, even though he's always asking Christina about the headache at the base of her skull, the tightness in her right shoulder, the ringing in her ears from grinding her teeth at night. Christina remained oblivious to these clues that pointed toward his empathy. Instead, she surmised that he must have picked up some skills at a psychic convention he attended on the West Coast. Christina has always been full of ideas of what the West Coast is like. When she was in high school, she always wanted to move there and spoke hopefully about how different it must be. At that time, the "different" was spoken with a wistful romanticism. Now that her life is so irrevocably locked into northeastness, she mocks the West Coast, saying it's full of pod people and hippies.

"They don't have tradition there. They can't possibly! It's the newest part of America. I like it here. It's better. New England is steeped in culture and American history! It's just"—she pauses, searching for an important word to make her point, but fails and opts for emphatic repetition—"*steeped* in history!" she exclaims. Christina exclaims a lot.

Dr. Breyer adjusts his teeny, wire-rimmed glasses. He's massive and short at the same time and smiles at Lilly tenderly. Dr. Breyer and Lilly are about the same age, but he treats her as if she's his grandchild and Lilly doesn't seem to mind.

"Hiya, Lilly!"

His warm greeting to Lilly is why Christina gave Dr. Breyer a second chance. Dr. Breyer lets Christina believe that she is the one giving out second chances.

When he gets down to the medical stuff, he addresses Christina. He gives her the straight scoop, but with a tone that sounds as if Christina is his grandchild, too. At first, this foreign tenderness from an older male sent Christina reeling.

"It's so patronizing!" she exclaimed to Molly after the first meeting with Dr. Breyer.

Now she takes comfort where she can get it, even though she still thinks she doesn't need any comfort.

"It is what it is," she says, with no exclamation whatsoever.

Dr. Breyer waits for Lilly to reply to his greeting. When she doesn't, he pats her hand and moves on to the serious part of this exchange.

"So! She looks good, Christina," Dr. Breyer says.

"Yeah?" Christina says, shocked by this assessment. She does, however, understand the relative nature of the word *good*.

"Who knows? She could be like this for thirty years," he shrugs.

Christina brightens in her most fake way.

"Oh! That's good. So, we'll stick with what we're doing and . . ." Christina says, realizing there's nothing more to say to this terrible yet optimistic prognosis. "Okay, we'll see you next time."

℃

With Lilly settled at home with Maeve, Christina makes it to the pool for a rare second time in one day. Her morning swim was her usual routine, but this afternoon swim comes from primal need.

Christina explodes through her laps. She's often scoffed at casual swimmers for not having "lane etiquette," but now Christina is the one who looks like the novice—flapping and splashing with little to no form whatsoever. Today Christina swims as if a shark were chasing her. She is trying to survive.

"I would dive right into the shark's mouth. Headfirst," she declared when she and Molly first watched *Jaws* in seventh grade.

She brought it up again a few years ago, when they were too old (it would seem) for this kind of nonsensical thinking. It was Shark Week on the Discovery Channel and the whole discussion started again.

Molly couldn't let it go this time.

"You would *not*," Molly said.

"There is no way to outswim it!" Christina said, as if Molly were the irrational one.

"No, you would not," Molly said in a calm way that made Christina feel just the opposite.

Molly said "No, you would not" in as many variations of pace, intonation, and volume as one could say the phrase "no, you would not." She even sang "no, you would not" at one point, because there was no point raising counterpoints to such nonsense. It just delighted her to get Christina riled up like this—and repeating the same phrase without discourse or debate just made Christina even more fiery.

Christina continued to make her point. The absolute worst part of the shark attack would be the terror and pain. Christina said she had no intention of surviving a shark attack. She just wanted it to be as quick and painless as possible. Christina knew death wouldn't be all that bad, but getting your flesh ripped off? Eaten alive? Well, that would really suck.

"I mean . . . they have three thousand teeth! THREE THOUSAND teeth, Molly!"

"No, you would . . . NOT."

"They weigh over two thousand pounds! How am I gonna fight that off? It's better to just give up!"

"No . . . youwouldnot."

Today, Christina knows that she has no choice about diving into the shark's mouth. She is going to be eaten alive and there's nothing she can do about it. There's no painless way to lose a mother, and having the pain gnaw away at Christina for years is agony far worse than three thousand teeth gnawing away at her flesh while in the grip of a two-thousand-pound beast. This terrible disease simultaneously tears her mother away and dangles her just out of Christina's grasp, taunting Christina with the ferocious paradox: *your mother is still here and yet she is never, never coming back.*

Christina runs out of furious energy and stops splashing mid-lap. She musters one last frog kick and glides, facedown, with her arms in front of her. She bubbles out all the air in her lungs and floats, turning over gently onto her back when she needs more air. She inhales pure relief. She stares up at the red-and-blue lane flags and lets the water cover her ears. There is no sound, just a weightless calm that cradles her sinewy body.

FLOAT.

Without warning, the stillness becomes too foreign for Christina to bear and she startles, whips herself upright, and repossesses her body. She pulls at the water in a panic—this accomplished swimmer gasps and fights the foreign sensation of drowning. She holds on to the lane line and grapples toward the side of the pool. She reaches for the edge and lunges herself forward, draping as much of her upper body as will fit in the gutter around the edge. When she finally feels safe again, she surveys the pool to make sure no one has witnessed her meltdown. Though it seemed major to her, it went completely undetected by other swimmers, as is the way with all dramas in life.

Christina draws a steady breath and feels her weightless self below the surface of the water. She struggles to keep her head up. The parts of her that are unprotected by water feel impossibly heavy. Christina knows she cannot change her circumstances, but she has to find the same peace on dry land. If she doesn't find it soon, then she will surely drown.

10

When Nora and Fred arrive at the park, Nora beelines for an empty bench. Fred finds the idea of sitting down in the presence of all this open grass completely preposterous. But since Nora is new at this whole outdoor thing, he concedes.

Nora rummages around in her NPR tote bag. The impossible has happened—she's forgotten her notebook. She'd made a list of all the things she should remember to bring for this walk in the park with Fred and Sam. Perhaps it was presumptuous of her—she should have written *notebook* on the list, or even *list* on the list.

Disaster. Nora at the park on a Sunday without a notebook. She feels the sudden familiar ache of a migraine. But it's worse than a migraine. This pain has been brought on by being paperless in a world that's full of people. Her thoughts are trying to Shawshank their way out of her skull.

She grips her iPhone and types into the notes app.

Whyyyyyyyyyyyyyyyyyyy?

It doesn't feel as good as letting the words drip from the pen in her hand, but she's desperate. On the day she's seeing Sam for the first time since Molly's funeral, she can't scribble words into her notebook during her last few minutes of solitude. How will she mentally prepare for this excruciating experience?

Fred rests his chin on Nora's lap.

"Hello, dog," Nora says, her voice raspy as she speaks for the first time today. Talking to a dog in public (or at all) isn't usually her thing, but it's good to warm up.

Nora glances at her phone, which has lit up with eleven new text messages. She's never seen this many texts in a whole week. All were sent within last the hour—and all are from Sam.

> Running late.
>
> Sir sorry.
>
> Do sorry.
>
> So sorry.
>
> Not sir.
>
> Nor do. haha. for that matter.
>
> Almost they.
>
> Alms it. there.
>
> Almost there. haha. soryr.
>
> See ya in a min.
>
> I see you. Heading your way.

This many spelling errors could cause a wordsmith like Nora to go temporarily blind. By some miracle, she retains her vision and looks on the bright side—at least he didn't use LOL or emojis.

Fred breaks free of Nora's distracted grasp. He charges at Sam and they tumble on the ground together as if they are twin puppies— both sandy haired, playfully fit, and willing to make a mess of their grooming if there's fun to be had. At five years old, Fred has long outgrown his puppy stage. Sam never will.

Nora ponders the age ratio of one dog year to seven human years. "Are you thirty-five?" she asks.

"We both are," Sam says, continuing his dog bromance with Fred.

He presses his forehead against Fred's for deeper eye contact. "If Fred were a dude, I mean."

Fred bristles at the insinuation that he is not, in fact, human. Nora bristles at the idea that Sam knew what she had been thinking. She really prefers to have her thoughts all to herself. Based on his eleven misspelled texts, she expected Sam to be dumber. She'll have to be more careful.

"Should we walk?" Sam poses the question to both his companions, but neither of them speak. Fred answers by leaping. Nora answers wordlessly as well but with far less enthusiasm than Fred. She gets up off the bench and stashes her phone away in her bag.

Sam and Nora walk at a good pace, with Fred a couple of feet ahead of them. Nora scrolls through the files in her mind, trying to find a chatting topic that doesn't involve the elephant in the room. But the files are empty and she knows Molly wouldn't have wanted to be called an elephant.

"How are you?" Sam asks Nora in a way that seems like an actual question rather than a social nicety.

The sincerity of his voice startles Nora enough that she turns her head to see him—as if he'd just tapped her on the shoulder. She's even more startled when she sees his green eyes, looking straight at her, still wanting to know the answer. How is she?

"Um. I'm . . ." Nora can't bring herself to say she's fine.

"Fine" is the breezy lie she commits every time the question "How are you?" is served to her as a polite greeting. Polite greetings require reciprocal polite greetings. Sam has asked honestly, so Nora should answer honestly. And she will . . . later, in her notebook.

"Got it. Me too," Sam says, accepting her silence. "Sucks."

Nora regrets judging Sam for his inability to spell. He sure can read.

"We'll just keep going, right?" Sam asks in an attempt to rally both Nora and Fred, knowing that Nora won't answer him any more than Fred will.

They walk together and the early afternoon sky grows dark. The air smells like rain.

"I had a list of questions to ask you about Fred," Nora starts, "but I forgot my notebook."

"It's okay, just call me later."

Call him? A medium requiring Nora to talk as the exclusive method of communication? No. She will not be calling him.

Sam reads Nora again.

"Or text me, that's cool," Sam says. "Anytime. It's cool."

"Cool," Nora says, for perhaps the first time ever. Casual vernacular comes from Nora in a decidedly uncasual manner. She makes the word *cool* sound exactly opposite of its meaning.

"I can come get him on weekends if you want," Sam offers. "I'd love to help out with him anytime. I just can't have him overnight in my place because of the lame-ass condo board. I'll take him all day though. Whatever you need."

"Thank you," Nora says. "I think he would like that."

Fred would, indeed.

"Do you want to set up a regular schedule?" Sam offers.

"Yes."

Sam waits for Nora to give him the schedule.

"Text me the schedule?" Sam says.

"Yes."

Heavenly rain rescues Nora from this awkward stroll.

"Better get going," Nora says. It is no accident that they headed in the direction of her car from their first step. She clicks her key fob and her doors unlock. "This is me. Where are you parked?"

"Oh, I walked," Sam says.

Nora faces it. She has to offer Sam a ride. For crying out loud, it's raining.

"Get in," she says, defeated.

"Thanks!" Sam says, climbing into the back seat with Fred.

"You can sit in the front if you want."

"Oh, totally." Sam laughs and climbs through the two front seats, his limbs contorting and knocking Nora in the side of the head. It really would have been faster and more graceful to exit the car to get in the front seat, but that's not who Sam is. Sam is a man who still puts on his jacket by sticking his arms in both sleeves at once and flipping the whole jacket upside down over his head, the way they taught him to do in preschool.

With the grace of a cartoon cow on roller skates, Sam comes to rest in the front passenger seat with a final tumble. He lets out a whoop, as if he's just finished an exhausting feat of athleticism.

Nora takes him in. Her stare prompts him to smile and offer a high five. She declines, and instead presents a thumbs-up and a forced smirk. Very uncool, but it doesn't bother Sam at all.

"Right on," Sam says.

While Sam fumbles for his seat belt, Nora starts the car—along with the dulcet tones of Josh Groban on full blast. Nora grabs at the radio and turns it off, hoping she was quick enough that Sam didn't notice the music. Too late, though. Everyone in the whole city block noticed.

"A J-Gro power ballad! *Nice.*" Sam pushes his fist toward her to punch it out, but Nora doesn't punch things out . . . *ever.*

"He's got some good songs," Nora says, on the defense.

Sam stops buckling his seat belt to turn his whole body toward her.

"You're goddamn right he does," Sam says with sober gravitas. He leans back in his seat again and buckles his seat belt. "The guy is *legit.*"

Nora can't tell if he is mocking her or not, so she doesn't play along one way or another. She just drives.

Sam reaches over and turns the radio back on. Within seconds, he's singing along (badly) to the Josh Groban power ballad. Sam's spirit is incapable of participating in mockery. And based on the reckless use of his terrible singing voice, he is also incapable of feeling shame.

"When you say you love meeeeeeeee," Sam bellows along with Josh Groban. It's pretty awful. He has no idea.

"For a moment, there's no one else aaallllllliiiiiiiiiiiiive."

Okay, it's bad enough that maybe he does have an idea, but he certainly doesn't care.

Guess who else doesn't care?

Fred pokes his head between the two front seats and howls along with Sam and Josh.

Nora's grip on the steering wheel tightens every time Sam, Fred, and Josh hit a higher note. After driving three blocks, Sam still knows every word of this song, proving that he was sincere in his belief that Josh Groban is legit.

Nora turns up the volume to drown out Sam's singing, but Sam takes this volume cranking as a sign that they've bonded. It only makes him sing louder.

Sam smooshes his face against Fred's and they sing as terribly as a human-and-dog duo possibly can. Fred slobbers on Sam's face and Sam doesn't wipe it off.

Nora cannot make sense of this man or this dog, though she will try later. But no notebook in the world has enough pages, and no pen has enough ink.

11

On a crisp fall morning, Leanne walks along the damp paths that wind toward her office. The rising sun competes with flame-red leaves for brightness, and Leanne wonders if there could possibly be a better moment in time and space than autumn on a New England college campus. She takes a sip of her decaf pumpkin spice latte and she's sure of it—education is the secondary purpose of this place. This place was obviously built for strolling in sweaters and comfortable boots that go with everything while drinking hot beverages in take-away cups.

The shrill voice of this semester's work-study student snaps Leanne out of her bliss.

"LeANNE! LeANNE!"

It's Olivia.

Olivia is a freshman who hasn't taken Katherine's French history class yet. Aside from French history, Katherine is determined to impart important life lessons to the women in her class. Most notably, using their voices correctly. Sure, other mentors encourage these women to use their voices for causes, to be assertive, to stand up for themselves. But Katherine means it literally.

"I don't know why you all talk like babies," Katherine tells her students on the first day of class. There's no point for her to try to mince words because her powerful and rich voice already adds enough meaning to everything she says.

"Get your voices out of your heads and into your chests," Katherine says, her voice luscious and resonant. Most of the time, Katherine can't even hear what some students are saying at all because they've almost matched pitch with a dog whistle. "Nobody thinks you're cute here. Do you want to be taken seriously or do you want to be cute?"

Inevitably, there will be girls in Katherine's class who always choose cute. Olivia is one such girl. In Olivia's junior high, all the pretty girls were the sopranos in the school choir, and that was the same year Olivia decided she wanted to be pretty. She learned the vocal placement for a soprano voice and has been speaking in that place ever since.

"I can't help it!" she will tell Katherine in a year when she does take French history. She'll insist that her voice just naturally sounds like an anime baby doll, and there's nothing she can do about it. She'll switch right out of French history and take rhetoric instead. She will lose every debate. Why? Because Katherine is right. Cute never wins.

"Hi, Olivia, how are you?" Leanne says in a chesty tone. She's trying to set a good example for Olivia. The voice thing has begun to bother her too, now that Katherine has pointed out the "sexy-baby phenomenon" so many times.

"Doing *sooooo* good," Olivia says. "How are you doing?"

"I'm doing *well*," Leanne says. There's something about Olivia that makes Leanne want to correct everything she does. Olivia doesn't notice—she doesn't care about being correct because back in junior high she learned to be pretty instead.

"Oh my God, so crazy," Olivia explodes, unprovoked. "I'm sworn to secrecy, but I have to tell someone—"

"No," Leanne says.

"What?"

"If you're sworn to secrecy, you actually *shouldn't* tell someone. That's how it works," Leanne says, correcting Olivia again. Typically,

Leanne might relish dishy gossip, but Olivia's personality dulls the shine of this glittery bit of secret news, whatever it is. There's no way it can be that good, Leanne has decided. Olivia is too vacuous.

"Okay," Olivia says. "But I'm *literally* dying!"

"*Figuratively*," Leanne says, taking a slow sip of her latte to telegraph boredom. The message never lands; Olivia's short attention leaps to the next shiny thing: her roommate across the quad.

"Lizziiiiiie! Lizzziiiiiiie!" she chirps. Lizzie waves, and Olivia sprints to join her without excusing herself or saying goodbye.

"So rude," Leanne mutters.

Corbu scampers to join Leanne, with Katherine a few steps behind him.

"Ah, vous souvenez-vous du silence glorieux?" Katherine says with a wistful longing for quiet.

"Yes, I miss it too," Leanne agrees. "Remind me never to trust that girl with a secret."

"I don't think you'll ever need reminding," Katherine says. "What is she squawking about? Oh, nevermind, I don't really care. How are *you* doing?"

"Good," Leanne says, dismounting her grammatical high horse. "You?"

"Oh just great," Katherine says. "Ya see that girl with Olivia?"

"Lizzzzziiiee?"

"That's the one," Katherine says. "She puked in my class this morning."

"Lovely. Rookie drinkers."

"Not this time," Katherine says. "I am pretty sure it wasn't a hangover. That girl is knocked up."

Leanne smirks. She's been having trouble saying the word *pregnant* or *baby* out loud. She doesn't even say it to James. She just calls it their "situation." It's as if she's afraid saying it out loud may accidentally summon Beetlejuice or something.

This is Leanne's chance to share the news without saying the words. Leanne spits out two harmless syllables. "Me too."

Katherine flails her arms up in victory before wrapping them around Leanne.

"Mon amie!"

Katherine makes a scene. It's the kind of fuss Leanne would want from her mother, but unfortunately, Joan will misappropriate that joyful moment and make it all about her own journey to grand-motherhood instead. Leanne is relieved to share her news, but greedy grief invades even this happy moment. The insidious sadness has slithered back in, along with the impossible wish that she'd rather be telling the news to Molly.

"It's still early," Leanne says. "So I'm not saying anything to anyone around here."

"Bien sûr, bien sûr. My lips are sealed," Katherine says in as hushed a tone as she is physically capable. "Merci de me faire confiance."

"Of course!" Leanne replies, thinking how easy it is to trust Katherine.

Katherine hightails it to class and sends Leanne an air kiss and very conspicuous wink as they part ways. Across the path, Leanne sees Olivia and Lizzie who are rapt in a deep moment of crisis. She pretends not to see them. Leanne judges girls like Olivia and Lizzie and denies that she and Molly were ever that dramatic. She'd also like to believe that she never had an unplanned pregnancy scare of her own.

When they were sophomores in college, Leanne and Molly went to a music festival on the quad at Molly's cousin's liberal arts school. The afternoon faded into night with a series of relentless jam bands. By the end, everyone had stopped pretending to care about the music.

That day, Molly was particularly fixated on having the best time ever, and she noticed that Leanne was being even less fun than usual. Molly understood that Leanne was probably the worst choice to bring along to a place like this, but Leanne was already on campus because she was visiting James, whom she'd just met at her summer internship. Molly took Leanne to the concert to congratulate her for finally losing her virginity the previous month. It was possible that this rite of passage meant Leanne was growing up, or—more important to Molly—that Leanne was loosening up.

Unfortunately, the deed had only made Leanne more paranoid about her virtue, her relationship, and all the consequences she'd been warned about throughout her Catholic upbringing. According to the people who raised Leanne, the course of one's life after premarital sex was as follows: If the AIDS didn't kill you right away, then you would die of a torturous childbirth after an unplanned pregnancy, at which time, you'd go straight to hell to cleanse your filthy soul. Extra fun bonus: the illegitimate child you bore before death would be diseased, unlovable, and also hell-bound! Hooray!

So, Leanne wasn't in a very music-festival-y place that day. She was sure she was pregnant. And it was very bad news.

It's not as if Leanne typically added to the fun of an outdoor concert or party. But this time, Leanne was a full-on deterrent to Molly's fun. Molly was ready to get to the bottom of it.

The nearby gas station mart sold pregnancy tests, among other things like windshield wiper blades, snacks, and condoms. Molly bit the ends off of a Twizzler and stuffed this sugary straw into a can of Mountain Dew.

"Drink this," she said, presenting the drink to Leanne as if it were medicinal. "Then we'll pee and get some answers."

Based on their food choice and Leanne's paranoid energy, the store clerk assumed that Leanne was high, so he banished them both from the store before they could use the bathroom. Their only option was a Porta-Potty on the quad.

"I can't go in there," Leanne protested as they approached a green plastic portal to hell.

"I'll go with you," Molly said. "No big deal."

"I mean, I won't be able to *go* in there," Leanne said. "You shouldn't have made me drink all that Mountain Dew!"

Molly opened the flimsy door and pushed Leanne inside. They'd both barely cleared the doorframe when the rusty spring snapped the door closed against Molly's shoulder.

"Cozy!" Molly joked, as their bodies pressed together.

Leanne was afraid to touch anything in this poop booth, but Molly held on to the walls to balance. Even fearless Molly had a feeling that this thing was just a centimeter from tipping over at any given moment. They steadied themselves as if they were in the hull of a boat—a boat, that by the smell of it, was sailing through a sea of angry shit.

"I can't pee in these conditions!" Leanne said, as Molly unboxed the pregnancy test.

"Get it over with. Let's go," Molly said in a stuffy-nose tone. "And don't breathe through your dose, just breathe through your bouth. It's dot dat bad."

Leanne tried and quickly failed to squat over the filthy toilet. Her quads fired with fatigue, and she cursed the spinning class she had taken that morning.

"You can do it," Molly said. "Hold on to me."

Leanne put her arms around Molly's neck while Molly widened her stance to support them both. Outside, waiting drunks had formed a queue while still dancing to the music. At this point, the jam band onstage had been playing the same song for twelve minutes.

"I need to hear running water or something," Leanne said, clearly a rookie at Porta-Potties. There was no faucet in there.

"Okay, sssssssssssssssssssss," Molly hissed in Leanne's ear, hoping the sound effect would do the trick.

Up until that moment, Leanne had been sure that none of this was funny. Her legs buckled some more when she let out a snort of laughter.

"Oh my god!" Leanne screamed, losing her balance over the toilet. "Hold on to me! Hold on to me! I can't hold myself up and hold the pee stick at the same time. It's all too much."

"I got you, ssssssssss," Molly said, taking the pregnancy test from Leanne. "Don't worry, sssssssss."

Leanne laughed so hard, she forgot where she was and successfully used a Porta-Potty for the only time in her life.

"Sssssssssssssss, and let's never speak of this again, sssssssssssssss," Molly said, holding the pregnancy test in the line of fire. And three minutes later, Leanne was free to have fun.

Today, Leanne walks through the world with a very intentional pregnancy and still, the fear of the unknown grips her gut. There's no one left to whisper encouragement or help manage the gory goings-on of pregnancy and childbirth. The strength of Leanne's legs fail her again today and she wants to collapse. Her mind floods with memories of her lost friend and she prays:

Hold on to me.

12

For most people, the path to enlightenment might involve going where the universe takes them and believing in divine guidance. Christina doesn't have patience for such nonsense. When faced with her newly inherited meditation seat, she means business. She's made an Excel spreadsheet that includes the address of each meditation center, its approximate distance from her office, their schedule of classes, and their "suggested donation" rates. She's uploaded the document into her iPhone and has carried it around for three weeks, during which time she has not meditated even once. Planning to do a thing can sometimes feel like doing the thing. And that might be as good as it gets when it comes to meditation and Christina. The nirvana she experiences from a well-scheduled lifestyle surely outweighs anything she could get from any stinky meditation center anyway.

Molly's path to spirituality began in a way that's common for many in her generation—in a tattoo shop in New Hampshire. Molly had heard that New Hampshire was a great place to get tax-free alcohol and underage tattoos. It was the summer Christina got her driver's license and a car, while Molly got bored and a boyfriend. It was Molly's idea to drive north, cross the state line to Hampton Beach, and try to find trouble. Molly came back with a tattoo; Christina came back with a sunburn.

No one could stop Molly from doing a thing once she had the idea to do it—and that day, she was determined to get a tattoo. She was also determined to bring along a well-built doofus for the ride to New Hampshire. Molly almost never referred to guys by their real name—only by code names—and this one was no different. This one was called Oats.

Rumor had it he was hung like a horse, so Molly gave him the secret moniker Oats, after the diet of a workhorse. At least, that's what workhorses ate on *Little House on the Prairie*. This was the extent of Molly's understanding of farm life.

Christina, more accurately, called this guy "Oaf." The day of their road trip, Oaf helped himself to the shotgun position in Christina's car. He was a giant and very unwilling to cram his large limbs (and potentially large other appendage) into the back seat of any car.

In conversation, Oaf used the words *ironic* and *literally* with great frequency and staggering inaccuracy. His inability to speak his native language correctly, coupled with ignorant statements about people who don't speak the language at all, drove Christina to silence. Christina's deafening music and the loud wind from the sunroof made it impossible for Molly to hear any of the conversation. Christina had given up talking after the ninth time Molly yelled "What?" from the back seat. Later, Christina told her all about it.

"I wasn't going to debate that guy," she said. "I'd be bringing a gun to a knife fight."

As if Oaf had the dexterity to wield a knife! No, Oaf was actually more like those gorillas at the zoo who throw their own feces. While Christina could aim fierce weaponry with a marksman's precision, Oaf would be armed only with a handful of poo.

They arrived at the tattoo place, Molly still hoping inspiration would strike her. While Molly was deciding, Oaf got his tattoo right away. For Oaf, the decision was obvious; he would get a tattoo on his thigh of a chipmunk wearing Oaf's football jersey.

"Because girls think chipmunks are cute," he said, as a sweaty man with rudimentary art skills etched a permanent image of a chipmunk on Oaf's skin (it can't be emphasized enough) *forever.*

"I guess," Molly said, losing any vague long-term interest in him. She would later discover that the rumor about Oaf was false, and she'd missed the perfect opportunity to point out the correct use of the word *ironic.* The truth: Oaf was more of a chipmunk.

"Sure. Right. Rodents are adorable," Christina said, searching the walls for an image she wouldn't mind seeing on her best friend's arm for life.

"How about this one?" Molly said, pointing at a Chinese character. "The guy said it means 'forever.' It's like *us,* Christina! Friends *forever*! You can get one too!"

"A *tattoo* that says *forever*? That's really a hat on a hat, Molly," Christina said. She wasn't going to address the suggestion that she would get a tattoo herself.

"Good point," Molly agreed.

"And we don't even speak the language," Christina said. "We have no way of knowing it really says that. For all we know, it could say 'gullible.' Just get a flower or something."

"Nah, I want something meaningful," Molly said, still flipping through binders of tattoo photos as Oaf admired his freshly finished tattoo.

"How about a lotus?" the Sweaty Man offered. "The lotus flower floats above the muddy waters of attachment. It has meaning in many ancient religions. Ya know, like, it signifies purity and divine beauty. It has these, like, unfolding leaves that represent spiritual awakening and expansion of a soul. And, like, a *ton* of other stuff."

"*Totally,*" Molly said, offering her unmarked wrist to the Sweaty Man. The lotus spiel was frequently used by the Sweaty Man because he was simply much better at drawing a lotus than any other flower.

Getting a tattoo first and living up to its meaning later was much like putting the cart before the horse. (A real horse, not a rumored one.) For Molly though, it worked. Each time she met someone who admired the lotus on her wrist, they gave her more directions to what she needed to learn. It sparked conversations with people who would become mentors. And, when she got sick, she came to know that the tattoo was no more permanent than its body canvas.

"Ironic," Molly said in her final days, half dozing from medication. Christina stared at the lotus on Molly's wrist and held her hand.

"What is?" Christina asked.

"I just finally figured out how to use that word right," Molly said.

Always the efficient getting-her-ducks-in-a-row, synchronize-your-watches type, Christina had tried to get Molly to think of a code word they could use after Molly "crossed over" so she could know once and for all whether those TV psychic medium shows were real or not. This paranormal fascination had been Molly's only hope that Christina had even an ounce of mumbo jumbo in her. But Molly's hope fizzled when it occurred to her that Christina was plotting a scientific study of something that could have been her chance to just have faith for once.

Toward the end, most of Molly's friends wanted to say important things like "I love you" or "I'm sorry" or "thank you" or all those things people are always wishing they'd said before someone dies. But Christina?

"So, Molly. What's our code word?" Christina asked Molly right around the time the word *hospice* started entering the conversation.

"What?" Molly wanted to be awake, but needed to sleep.

"If I go to a psychic and you want to contact me," Christina said, "how will I know it's you?"

Unfortunately, Nora was in the room for this conversation. Nora squirmed when Christina brought up end-of-life topics.

"Seriously?" Nora whispered at Christina. It was the kind of whisper that weirdly sounds like a yell. Nora changed the subject along with her tone, hoping Christina's annoying question—and perhaps Christina herself—would disappear. "Mol, you want some water?"

Fear lives too far away from Christina's preferred neighborhood of emotion. She enjoys living next door to logic, even though logic hosts mortality as its unwelcome and ongoing houseguest. Christina was pissed off about Molly's young death, of course, but she'd accepted it and she wasn't afraid. Her way of dealing with it was to say, "See you later."

Even though Molly was barely awake, she could feel Nora about to explode. Molly tried to diffuse their squabble by coming up with an actual code word, preferably one that would embarrass Christina if it actually worked.

"The code word is cunnilingus," she said.

"Have some water," Nora said, stuffing a straw into Molly's mouth.

Molly sipped the water and played it out in her mind. Christina would go to a TV psychic like that sassy blonde lady from Long Island. The medium would get all deep and say to Christina, "Does cunnilingus mean anything to you?"

Christina would exclaim on national television, "YES! YES! Cunnilingus means so much to me!"

"Come on. Wouldn't that be funny?" Molly said to Nora, not realizing that she hadn't been thinking out loud.

"Okay, Molly," Christina said, solemnly. "Cunnilingus is a good idea."

And then they laughed together for the last time.

13

Sunday morning, Fred stares at Nora until she wakes up. Before Nora is conscious enough to remember that Fred is there, Nora knows she is not getting out of bed. Not today.

It's here.

Migraines have plagued Nora since her early twenties. No one's ever given her a clear answer as to what causes them. A few years ago, Molly's WebMD-fueled hysteria led Nora to schedule a precautionary brain scan. The doctors concluded that her migraines were just "one of those things." One of those things that wouldn't threaten her life but would sure make it really painful. Nora made her peace with doctors who had made their peace with medical mysteries.

The vise grip on Nora's head sends shooting pains into her eyeballs, and there is little reason to torture herself more by opening them. Still, she feels Fred staring at her.

"I can't," she says and the sound ricochets though all her sinuses, causing more pain.

Nora never wanted a dog in the first place, but here he is and he can't stay inside all day. Nora gropes at her nightstand, blind with pain. She feels her phone and clutches it with both hands, scrolling through her contacts. She squints, letting only enough light in to find the number she needs.

"Hiya!" Sam's voice blares from the phone and pierces Nora's skull. She turns down the volume desperately and holds the earpiece far from her face.

Even the sound of her own voice intensifies her pain. She whispers, "Hi, it's Nora, I—"

"Hey! How's it going?" Sam says without pausing. "I didn't expect to hear from you on a Sunday. I thought you had your—"

"Shhh. Shhhh," Nora shushes. It's involuntary.

Sam's boundless, friendly enthusiasm crushes Nora's brain. It's too much noise first thing in the morning, on Sunday, with a migraine. Fortunately, Sam complies with the shushing.

"Is everything okay?" he whispers.

"No," Nora says, whimpering as the sound of the syllable bounces off the bones in her face.

"Are you trapped?" Sam asks. "Should I call the police?"

Sam watches absolutely too much TV.

"What? Oh my God. No. No. I just need you to come get Fred. I have a migraine and I just can't," Nora says all at once. It is the longest sentence she's ever said with a migraine, and hopefully it's enough information that she won't have to speak again.

"Got it. I'll be right over," Sam says. "Okay if I just use my key so you don't have to get out of bed?"

For a minute, Nora gets lost in a lucid dream where she receives a genius medal for giving Sam a key so he can walk the dog while she is at work. Sam is still talking.

"When my sister gets migraines, she can't get out of bed," Sam says. "So, I know how it—"

"Shh! Yes. Use your key. Thanks."

"Okay, bye."

Enough is enough.

Nora hangs up.

Having heard the plan, Fred lies down in his dog bed to wait for Sam.

Nora rummages through her nightstand to find her migraine pills. They never work, but the hope of relief is better than no relief at all.

Nora imagines calling Christina to say she's not coming to brunch, and even an imaginary conversation with Christina's voice makes the pain worse. She opens her eyes just long enough to type a succinct message.

CAn't make it today im sick

Nora's phone rings right after the text swishes into the ether. The urgency to make the noise stop overrides her need to avoid talking to this cruel caller.

"Hello?" Nora whispers.

"What's happening?" Christina says, her words bursting through the phone.

"Shhhhhh."

"Oh my God. Are you being held hostage? I knew it!" Christina says, having assumed Nora's uncharacteristically misspelled text was a coded distress signal. Christina searches her mental files—have they ever discussed a code word for this scenario? "Stay on the phone! I have a plan!"

Christina also watches absolutely too much TV.

"Stopstopstop," Nora says. "It's a migraine."

"Oh," Christina says, seeming disappointed by the mundane. "You still get those?"

"Yes. I gotta go," Nora says.

"You should get Botox," Christina suggests.

"What is wrong with you?" Nora meant to say that in her head, but pain dissolved her filter and she said it out loud instead.

"No, I'm saying it's supposed to be a migraine treatment now—the wrinkle thing will be a nice side effect," Christina says. "Shit, you'll get your Botox covered by insurance, I bet. Jealous! You should get a hookup on that, I—"

Nora hangs up.

She is devastated to discover that there's no water beside her bed. Why? Why isn't there a bottle of water? A carafe? Why isn't there a faucet in her headboard? At the moment, it seems so reasonable.

Nora dozes off in a way that feels like a long blink. Her pain awakens her again, and this time she wills herself to sit up and put her feet near the floor. Through her squinting gaze, she makes out a shape on her bedside table. It's a glass of water.

And Fred is gone.

Sitting up consumed so much of her energy, Nora has barely enough left for something as extraneous as embarrassment. Still, she musters mortification because Sam definitely witnessed her deep, drooly, sickly sleep. And (oh God!) on the floor, in prominent view, is her underwear. The *comfortable* kind. But Nora is too grateful for the water to care about what he may have seen. She pops her pills, guzzles the water, and covers her head with blankets. She'll sleep for six more hours.

And later, when she finds the energy, she'll be embarrassed.

℮

Leanne shows up for brunch right on time at Sunnyside's. In case Christina is running late again, she doesn't want to torture Nora by arriving early. When she doesn't see Nora already sitting at the table, she wonders if she has the wrong day. Her mind has been all over the place for the past few weeks and she happily blames all mishaps on "baby brain."

"It's a real thing," she told James just before she left the house. She dashed around to find her car keys. "And where are my sunglasses?"

"I believe you," James said, eyeing the sunglasses on top of her head.

Running even later than she meant to, Leanne gives up the search for the keys and ultimately takes James's car instead. She will later find her keys in the dishwasher, which may also shed light as to why there's currently a fork in her purse.

Leanne consults her phone while she waits for Christina and Nora. Just in case "baby brain" is not, in fact, a thing, she types into Google:

Am I stu—?

Thanks to the search algorithm and other spiraling pregnant women before her, Google auto-completes her thought with a suggested search.

Am I stupid now that I'm pregnant?

Leanne checks the calendar on her phone. Their brunch is in fact this Sunday. But is today Sunday? Her phone says it is. If today is Sunday, then what did she do on Saturday? She can't remember. She is so stupid now. She scans a few blogs and finds some reassurance—baby brain is a real thing. It doesn't change a woman's IQ; it's just harder to think when blood flow has shifted to accommodate a new human. Leanne will definitely tell James all about this article later, if she can remember to do so.

Too late. She already can't even remember what she just read.

Christina arrives with her normal lack of subtlety and makes eye contact with the waitress, Diane. Before Christina gets a chance to yell her coffee order across the café, Diane nods to acknowledge Christina's telegraphed request. They've come to an understanding very quickly. Christina has that effect on people.

"Hi. Nora must be running late," Leanne says, standing for air-kiss shenanigans.

"No, I talked to her," Christina says. "She has a migraine, so—"

"So she's not coming?" Leanne says, with more panic in her voice than she intended to reveal.

"Not this time." Christina shrugs. "She's too sick."

"I knew this would start." Leanne sighs.

"What?" Christina responds without really wanting to know the answer. She checks her phone one last time before she stuffs it into her purse. She keeps her keys on the table though. She's already pre-pared for departure just minutes after arrival.

"We have to keep doing this brunch," Leanne insists.

Diane shows up just in time with Christina's coffee.

"So, Nora's sick," Christina says, distracting herself with the menu. "What can ya do?"

Christina cleverly looks for something on the menu that doesn't need to be cooked. If Christina's not careful, Nora won't be the only one with a headache today.

"I'll have the fruit cup," Christina says before Diane can get away.

"Decaf," Leanne says. "I'll just have an egg white omelet with spinach please. Thank you."

The brunch will now last as long as Leanne's egg white omelet.

"And an order of hash browns, thanks," Christina adds. She might as well go for something delicious, since she's going to be stuck there for longer than a fruit cup anyway.

Diane makes a mental note of the hash browns and takes their menus.

"Molly made good hash browns for hangovers," Leanne says.

"Yeah, she did," Christina agrees. "They were so gross."

"Gross" is about the highest compliment a person can give when talking about good and greasy hangover food.

"I never feel like I can talk about Molly in front of Nora," Leanne confesses.

"Me neither," Christina says. "But I don't know why we shouldn't. It's not like Nora never thinks about her."

"She probably never *stops* thinking about her," Leanne wonders out loud. "She spends so much time alone. Maybe that's why Molly left Fred with her."

"Are you still pissed about that?" Christina says, smirking.

"I was never pissed!"

"Okay."

"I wasn't! Whatever Molly wanted is fine with me."

"Fine."

"Seriously, Christina."

"All right."

"Can we not do this?"

"Do what?"

"You know what."

"I honestly don't."

"Okay, fine. Whatever," Leanne says. "I'm just saying I worry about Nora because I think she really misses Molly."

"Of course she does," Christina says. "I sure do."

Diane delivers a steaming mug of decaf for Leanne and tops off Christina's you-bet-your-ass-it's-caffienated coffee. Diane has become Chrsitina's favorite person in the world.

"Thank you so much," Christina says in a soft tone that even Diane notices.

"No problem," Diane says, raising an eyebrow. Diane doesn't dash away as she normally does. "You need anything else?"

"Not right now," Christina says. "Thank you."

Leanne shakes her head no. She can't say anything out loud because the next thing she should say out loud is that she misses Molly too, but she's been very meticulous about keeping this unsaid.

"Do you talk to James about it?" Christina asks.

"About Nora?" Leanne asks.

Leanne's denial silences Christina in disbelief for a moment.

"No. *Molly*," Christina says. "About Molly."

"Oh, no. He knows," Leanne says. "I'm sure he knows how I feel."

"Doesn't sound like you even know," Christina says, mostly to herself because Leanne has already found a way to deflect.

"Do you talk to your mom about it?"

This silences Christina again.

"No," Christina says. "Mom's not . . . Molly must have told you this, right?"

"Told me what?"

"My mom's not doing well," Christina says with such finality, it seems that no additional details will follow.

"I'm sorry, I had no idea," Leanne says.

"Memory stuff. Alzheimer's, actually," Christina says, sharing more than either of them expected her to.

"I just thought you lived together because . . . well, because you were close," Leanne says.

"We were. We are," Christina says. "It's just different now."

"Sorry," Leanne says.

"Don't be. It is what it is," Christina says, with real finality this time.

It now occurs to Christina that insisting that Leanne express her grief about Molly is just as invasive as all the people who insist that Christina should go to Alzheimer's support groups and therapy. Maybe it just is what it is. So she changes the subject.

"How are you liking the scooter?" Christina says, smiling.

In unison they correct the word *scooter* in a mocking tone.

"*Vespa.*"

Despite their irreverent eye rolling over a dead woman's sense of style, Molly would have stood by this: A Vespa is an altogether transcendent mode of transportation. Calling it a "scooter" takes away its magic powers. A Vespa (especially a pink one) can transport people not just from home to work but from real life to *la dolce vita*.

"Um, it's a *lifestyle*, Christina!" Leanne jokes, imitating Molly's emphatic rant about Vespas. "What did she say? It was like, 'If you want to get from point A to point B, you get a scooter. If you want to get from living to being alive, you get a Vespa.'"

"'Cachet!'" Christina adds. "'It's *so* other level.'"

Diane brings their food and stops cold to observe their hysterics. Nothing here is as funny as their howling laughter would imply, but clearly they need the release.

"You girls give me whiplash," she mutters to herself as she walks back toward the kitchen.

"So are you riding it at all?" Christina asks.

"No way, I *can't* really . . ." Leanne considers telling Christina her news in this rare moment of bonding, but decides not to. "I can't really imagine riding it. I feel like it's a death trap."

"But Leanne," Christina says, straightening her face to land a punch of sarcasm. "Only scooters are dangerous. Vespas are merely an accessory. Is a scarf a death trap?"

Leanne laughs and wiggles out of the subject. "Anyway, what's the latest on your research?"

"I'm going to a meditation place for a lesson tomorrow," Christina says. "We'll see how it goes."

"Oh! That's cool," Leanne says. "I have been meaning to sign up for something like that, to reduce stress. I've just been busy."

Christina feels it's only polite to invite her.

"Well, do you want to come along?" she asks.

"Oh sure!" Leanne replies, delighted by this gesture. "Where is it?"

"It's called like 'The Now' or 'The Present,'" Christina says. "I don't know. It's something New Agey."

"Yeah, that sounds about right," Leanne says. "Very Molly-ish."

Leanne already regrets accepting this invitation. She's kicking herself—she should have known Christina would be going to one of those hippie places. It's not likely that Molly would have led them to a meditation class at the kind of rigidly traditional church Leanne finds easier to understand.

"I kind of wish it were called 'The Never,'" Christina says, mostly to herself.

But it's too late. They've made a plan and now they'll have to see each other again in "The Very Soon."

14

When Leanne and Christina arrive at the Eternal Present Meditation Center, it's dead quiet and reeks of incense. There's a sign next to the door telling them to remove their shoes.

"They should tell you this on the website," Christina fumes, flicking off her shoes. "I would have gotten a pedi. Or brought socks."

Unfamiliar serenity sends Leanne's shoulders quite a bit north of her typical aligned posture. It feels inappropriate to speak in this place, so Leanne expresses her discomfort to Christina through wide eyes and a jutted jaw—the universal sign for "Let's get the hell out of here."

Christina pretends not to notice. With shoes in hand (she's not going to leave her fancy heels by the door next to someone's smelly Crocs!), she rummages around her Chloé bag to dig her swimming nose plugs out of her purse. There is no universal sign for "Don't even think about wearing nose plugs outside of a swimming pool, you weirdo," so Leanne is forced to speak in a loud whisper.

"*Seriously*, Christina?"

"What? I can't stand the odor! Molly always burned this incense shit and it made me gag, so I came prepared," Christina says. "It fuckin' *stinks* in here!"

"Don't say the f-word!" Leanne says. "We're in a house of worship! Or something. I don't know what this place is."

"Fuck it, the hippies don't care if you swear," Christina says.

"Stop it, Christina!"

Christina puts the strap of the nose plugs around her neck.

"When places are loud, people wear earplugs," Christina says. "What's the difference?"

"There is a big difference between earplugs and nose plugs. Please don't put those on—you look ridiculous!" Leanne says. "You won't be able to breathe. I looked up this meditation stuff on YouTube. It's all about inhaling and exhaling and, *seriously*, Christina!"

Leanne grows increasingly desperate, trying to be respectful in a place she doesn't understand. This was supposed to be a chance to bond with Christina. Bonding is an appropriate thing to do in the aftermath of a mutual friend's death. She didn't count on Christina's nose plugs ruining the whole thing.

Regardless of how the bonding goes, Leanne plans to lie to her mother during the inevitable interrogation about what she and Christina did tonight. If Joan finds out where Leanne has been, she will assume Leanne needs an immediate mental health intervention. After all, Joan still thinks Molly was part of a cult because she had tattoos and stopped going to church. From Joan's perspective, any sort of meditation or prayer that isn't led by a Catholic man ordained by another more Catholic man is a ticket to eternal hellfire.

Christina and Leanne's whispery banter is interrupted when Collin enters the room. They no longer notice the incense stink that started their fight. All they can smell is the fresh, delightful scent of guy soap and man spice. His face is kind with creases around his eyes from laughing. His gray T-shirt clings to his broad shoulders and chest but hangs loosely over what Leanne assumes are incredible abs.

"Hi, how are ya?" Collin smiles. "Are you here for meditation instruction?"

Leanne's left thumb reflexively fiddles with the wedding band on her ring finger. She can't help wanting to find out if his abs are as chiseled as she assumes they are.

"Yes, we are," Christina answers for both of them because it's clear that Collin's appearance has stolen away Leanne's ability to talk. (And breathe.) Having been bested by decorum and her will to remain cool in the presence of coolness, Christina tucks her nose plugs away. "I'm Christina, this is Leanne. We got shoes off, phones set to airplane mode, ready to meditate. Where to?"

Collin smiles, letting an unusually long pause hang between them before he responds. He meets a lot of these checklist meditators. They're his favorite because they're the ones who want to "get it right" so badly. And they're also the ones who will only get it right when they finally get it wrong.

"We'll head back to the studio in a minute. I just have to reset the room from the last session," Collin says, pausing again. "There's tea or water for you while you wait. Help yourselves."

Once Collin is gone, Leanne exhales.

"He seems so deep. He's like . . ." Leanne searches for a reference within her very limited knowledge of mystics and sages. "*Yoda* or something."

"Sure," Christina says, sipping the free tea. "Except he's not green or small or five hundred years old or *fictional* or—"

"Well, yeah," Leanne concedes, mindlessly popping a breath mint into her mouth.

"So not like Yoda at all," Christina says, wincing and rejecting the tea along with Leanne's observations. "Complimentary tea gets no compliments from me."

"Fair enough," Leanne concedes again. "But he seems wise and stuff."

"And stuff," Christina agrees.

Leanne later will ponder whether Collin was a fat kid or had headgear in high school. Molly always told her to look for a unique balance between a man's current success and his failings in high school. Humble beginnings are reassuring. And a man who lost his virginity after age eighteen is ideal.

Leanne didn't take Molly's advice when she met James. He filled out Leanne's husband requirements at the time. Unfortunately, she was working from a list she'd made when she was nine.

Collin is "wise and stuff" because he lost a best friend too. They were on a spring break rafting trip in college when Matt slipped into the river without a life jacket. A better swimmer, Collin went in after Matt, but the current was too strong and the panic was too intense. In Matt's struggle to survive, he couldn't see his rescuer. Soon, he was gone.

Later, Collin was gone too. Gone to bars. Gone to the pill stash from his knee surgery. Gone into everyone else's stash too. Numbing only made the pain deeper, so he went to rehab, he tried churches, he escaped to ashrams. He was desperate to hear something that would explain everything and make the pain go away. Then he went hiking in Yosemite. When he stopped moving through the snow for a moment, he heard something—silence. Any minor movement sounded loud in the snowy calm. Collin wanted to see what the silence sounded like, so he stayed as still as he could. In the silence, he heard everything. In stillness, he could hear the answers. In fact, stillness itself was the answer. He caught that moment of peace for a flash and immediately set out to find it again. Someday, maybe he will.

In the meantime, he meets people like Christina and Leanne every day—people who are looking for mooring in the tumult of grief that they think is unique to them alone. In the vortex of loss, it's nearly impossible to consider someone else's pain when you're just scrambling to find the surface and breathe. Panicked and blind to the sight of a rescuer. It never occurs to Christina and Leanne that many other people around them—including Collin—might be gasping for relief too.

"Are you ready to get started?" Collin says, poking his head into the waiting room from the studio in the back.

Leanne can't stop thinking about Collin's abs. She crushes her breath mint into a million tiny pieces in her teeth. She decides it's her hormones. She read about the prenatal horniness some pregnant women experience, but she is shocked that it kicked in so suddenly. She wasn't in the mood this morning when James was. How did this shift happen in a matter of hours?

On the way down the hallway, they pass display shelves of books by Pema Chodron, Dalai Lama, and Deepak Chopra. Christina's allergy to stillness makes it impossible for her to pass the merchandise without grabbing at it. Leanne folds her hands in reverence, as if she's going to communion at a Catholic Mass. She doesn't know what else to do here.

In the small room, Collin instructs Christina and Leanne to get comfortable on the meditation cushions on the floor. That's when it occurs to Christina that she's wearing a skirt. It further occurs to her at this point how out of place she is in general—Corporate Christina in her lady suit. Beyond the practical aspect of comfort, she's furious that her dry-clean-only lawyer costume is being infused with incense stink. When she gets home later, she's going to wash her hair and hang her suit outside overnight to air out.

Leanne sits cross-legged on the cushion. Christina scans the room for a normal chair, as well as a place to put her posh bag and the fancy shoes she's been carrying since they walked in the door.

"I can't . . . I'm wearing a . . . can I just . . ." Christina wishes she could finish a sentence. Finally, "I can't sit down on the floor."

"Well, then I guess you can . . . leave," Collin deadpans, then smiles. "Don't worry, I'll get you a chair. There's no wrong way to do this."

Christina does not smile back. If there's no wrong way to do this, then how will she know that she's doing it the best? Winning is her thing. There must be a wrong way to meditate. That's why she's taking lessons. This is the point where Collin begins to annoy her.

Christina gets settled in the chair and closes her eyes, trying to assume the position of a meditator. Collin instructs them in a casual, familiar manner as if talking about how to change a tire or how to play football rather than how to achieve inner peace. His voice sounds as if he's been gargling with gravel. Yeah. It's like that. A rough-and-tumble guy who happens to be talking about inner peace. But Leanne still thinks it's her pregnancy hormones that are making her sweaty.

Leanne, who has really no intention of meditating at all, listens to Collin as he looks her in the eye and explains. "Okay, so just pay attention to your breathing and"—he looks at Christina as she shifts in her seat and adjusts her jacket just so—"just try to get comfortable." Collin grins. "So you just can look down, gaze about eight or ten feet in front of you."

Christina's eyes snap open. She's furious that she's already doing this wrong.

"You don't close your eyes? I thought you're supposed to close your eyes!" Christina protests.

"Well, you can, or if you're more comfortable, you just lower your gaze," Collin says. "If you have a thought, just let it float away and pop like a bubble. And just really pay attention to your breathing."

It's hard for anyone to pay attention to their own breathing in this tiny room because of Christina's huffing and puffing. In this unfamiliar place, Leanne's sure of one thing—it's probably rude to laugh at people when they're trying to meditate. She's also sure that Christina's theatrics are unintentionally hilarious.

At the parochial school Leanne attended with Molly, Christina, and Nora, the faculty had the crazy idea to force young children to attend Mass together every Friday. That was where Molly always did her best schtick. She knew exactly how to break Leanne down—just a quick cross-eyed face and she'd lose it. When you're in a place—like church—where such sounds are forbidden, it makes it so much more satisfying to make those noises. A giggle could turn into a laugh and then a snort. Molly's snort was what always sent Leanne into a real tailspin, laughing until she almost peed her pants. It was bliss for these girls—laughing about laughter itself.

Leanne purses her lips, trying not to laugh. She wonders if Molly is watching and it occurs to her that Molly had a code word to signal from the beyond. *Cunnilingus.* It's just too much for Leanne. A loud raspberry sound bursts through her pursed lips, until she lets laughter just fly.

"Sorry! Sorry. *So* sorry." Leanne regains some composure. Though silent, she cannot keep her shoulders from bobbing as she shudders to suppress giggles. Her nostrils flutter.

Christina shoots Leanne the stink eye.

That's when Leanne's laughter is joined by more laughter. It's Collin's.

"It's okay, Christina." Collin laughs. "This is a good start."

An hour later, Christina gets ready to leave with a stack of books about meditation. She'll study them because studying is how Christina has become the best at other things.

Leanne makes a beeline for the bathroom, having sipped a lot of the terrible-tasting complimentary tea during awkward moments. There were so many awkward moments.

"I'll see you at brunch, Leanne," Christina calls to Leanne through the bathroom door. "I have to head home."

Leanne panics at the idea of having a moment alone with Collin. When she emerges from the bathroom, she hurries to put on her shoes and feels the urge to quell unfaithful thoughts by mentioning faithfulness.

"My husband is probably wondering where I am," Leanne says, gesturing with her left hand, her wedding ring flickering in the dim light. "I mean, I told my husband I was coming here, but I didn't tell my husband that it would be so long."

Collin lets her keep talking.

"Had to pee," Leanne confesses further. "I'm pregnant."

That last confession comes as a surprise to Leanne herself, but there is a part of her that wants to make it clear she is completely spoken for.

"Congratulations! My wife and I are expecting our third," Collin says. "It's all just . . ."

Collin's whole being seems to swell while he selects a word. The word ends up being redundant because of the way he says it.

"*Amazing.*"

"Amazing," Leanne repeats, though she's commenting on something else. Leanne has never seen James's eyes look like that when he talks to her. And she can't imagine him saying something is "amazing" and really understanding the meaning of genuine amazement.

"I really enjoyed the meditation, thank you," Leanne says, eager to escape into a space where amazement is shallow and she can more easily keep herself from drowning in something so real. "I'll be back!"

Like every person who has ever uttered the words "we should do this more often," Leanne has just lied. She'll never be back. This was all just too amazing.

15

Nora stands outside her front door to meet Sam in an effort to avoid inviting him in. It was weird enough that he'd been in her apartment last week when she had a migraine—and extra awkward because she wasn't even conscious when he was there.

Fred can't figure out why he's on a leash, outside, but not moving. What a waste. He could be indoors napping.

When Nora greets Sam, he's still shouting distance away, so Nora shouts.

"Hi, here's his stuff. He just ate," she says, keeping the exchange strictly to facts over pleasantries.

Sam gets close enough to speak at a normal volume, though Nora can't imagine he'll have more to discuss. She's already said everything she planned to say.

"How's it going?" Sam greets her warmly.

"Good, he's been pretty calm," Nora answers.

"Anything new with you?" Sam asks.

"Not really," Nora says. She wishes she could dive back into her apartment and slam the door while a puff of smoke obscures the whole maneuver. Poof! She'd be gone. She curses the lack of pyrotechnics in her welcome mat.

The right thing to do is reciprocate interest in Sam's life. She'll do it in one word:

"You?"

"I got a new job," Sam says. "I'm a programmer. Not sure if Molly ever told you?"

"That's good," Nora says, avoiding the question. She knows almost nothing about Sam. Molly and Nora rarely discussed Molly's love life and Nora doesn't have one to discuss.

"You like the work?" she asks.

"It's totally boss. It's a cool company too. I work from home, which I don't mind that much," Sam says. "You make puzzles, right?"

"Yes, I do. I write crossword puzzles. I like doing it," Nora says.

"You must work from home too?" Sam asks.

"You'd think. I work for a content provider and they are really into office culture," Nora says. The words *office culture* drip with disdain. "The husband and wife who started it—John and Susan Miller— they're really into this bonding thing among coworkers."

"Your favorite thing!" Sam jokes.

"Ha, yeah," Nora says. "Are my reclusive ways that obvious?"

Francine's door opens and Nora darts to hide behind Sam.

"Um. Yes," Sam says.

Francine puts one hand to her forehead to block the sun and her other hand through her tousled hair to block any notion that she's down-to-earth.

"Hi!" Francine squeals at Sam. "Are you the dog walker?"

Francine is on the move. Personal space be damned, she's going to get right up in Sam's face. Here she comes.

"Sort of," Sam says, trying to shield Nora. "We're co-parenting."

"Adorable!" Francine grins. It doesn't occur to Francine to pretend she doesn't see Nora. It would be a polite thing to do in this case.

"Your ex?" she asks Nora.

"No!" Nora says, a little too adamantly.

"I used to go out with her best friend," Sam clarifies.

"The one that died?" Francine asks right away.

"Yupper! That's the one!" Sam says in a way that makes a laugh escape

Nora's lips before she has a chance to catch it. Meanwhile, Francine continues her oblivious streak and misses his flippant tone entirely.

"Awwwwwww." Francine squeezes Sam's arm tenderly. She scans him with her glance and assumes he looks great shirtless. Francine has assumed correctly for once.

"My kingdom for a trapdoor," Nora mutters, still trying to will herself invisible.

Sam chuckles and leans on Nora. He masks his laugh with fake sobbing. He pretends that he's so overcome that he cannot look at Francine anymore.

"I'm sorry! Will you excuse us?" Sam says to Francine. He walks away, using Nora as his human Kleenex. "I just—can't—I can't!"

Francine is moved to put her hand over her shallow heart.

The drama.

Nora goes along with Sam's charade and walks away holding him up. These histrionics rip her away from the haven of her apartment. When they clear the corner, Sam straightens up.

"You're welcome," he says.

"Thanks," Nora says.

"Aha! But now you're stuck with me," Sam says. "Pick your poison: small talk with your insensitive neighbor or a brisk walk with this tall drink of water?"

Sam raises his hands in the air victoriously.

"Ladies and gentleman," Sam announces to the neighborhood. "Nora has chosen the tall drink of water! Well, it seems like an obvious choice, no?"

"I have a lot of work to catch up on," Nora says. "I can't really hang out for long."

"No problem. Let's just do a loop. Once around the block. Good?" Sam asks. "I won't even make you talk to me."

"Oh, come on," Nora says. "I'll talk."

They proceed to not talk.

After a full block, Sam laughs.

"My kingdom for a trapdoor," Sam says, remembering Nora's comment. "Good stuff. I'll watch my step around you, kiddo."

"Nothing personal. I pretty much always fantasize that there's a trapdoor," Nora confesses.

"A trapdoor under the person you're talking to?" Sam asks.

"No, under me," Nora says. "It's a great escape, and really, I'd be doing everyone else a favor because it's very easy to come up with conversation after a girl falls through a trapdoor and disappears. It'll be fodder for every party they ever go to after that, actually. So. You know. I'd be doing it for other people too."

"Dude," Sam says definitively. It's an odd word choice when talking to a woman who makes a living through her vocabulary. Somehow, Sam always communicates layered meaning with this word though. This time, "dude" means he's impressed.

"I know," Nora says, already wondering why she has never used this four-letter slang in a puzzle before. It might be handy.

"So where does the trapdoor go?" Sam asks. "Won't you just be locked in some boring person's boring-er basement?"

"No," Nora answers right away. She's thought this through. "There's a slide. A curvy one that shoots me out to the sidewalk."

"It would be awesome if it was a waterslide. Like in *Goonies*?" Sam says. "You can leave the conversation and plunge into a refreshing swim. That would be dope."

Nora considers this. They've looped the block and now they are approaching her front door. Mercifully, it's Francine-free.

"Would I get the pirate's treasure?" Nora asks. "Like in *Goonies*?"

"Hells yeah," Sam says.

"Then yes. That would probably be very . . ." Nora considers saying "dope" but knows she simply cannot. "I'd like that."

For the first time, Nora feels a little less like a weirdo. All she had to do was get to know someone who is even weirder.

16

Complainers get annoyed by July rain because it ruins their barbecues or cancels baseball games, but Molly loved it because it cozied people up during a time of year when no one wants to be cozy. She loved sitting in a parked car, waiting for the torrent to die down before making a run for it. She loved splashing into a movie theater. She loved playing cards with other lifeguards in high school when no one came to the pool on the rainy day. She loved teaching card tricks to the two scrappy latchkey kids who came to the pool on rainy days anyway. Molly treated rainy days in July as if they were holidays, and she always wanted to be with her favorite people in the rain. Despite the percussive tatter of the rain, there was a stillness throughout a rainy day in July. And everything was funnier. Even Christina could be silly on a rainy day.

The summer between freshman and sophomore year of high school, Christina made Molly promise to spend the Fourth of July with her because the previous year, Christina had stayed home and lied to her new friends at her fancy school about how great it was.

Nora and Molly's Fourth of July tradition included walking to the town parade, and their small hometown full of New Englanders never let a little thing like rain get in the way of a parade. Christina agreed to join them in this "lame" plan because she didn't have any better options and she couldn't lie again. Leanne did have a better option, but her cool-girl cheerleader barbecue got rained out.

Molly was always loyal to tradition and Nora was always loyal to Molly. They were going to that parade even if it started to hail golf balls (which it did). Nora and Molly sloshed to the parade, dragging along with them two sourpuss teenagers who vaguely resembled their childhood friends.

All four were insensibly dressed of course. Fifteen-year-olds believe that their coolness can repel all kinds of weather, so they didn't bother with umbrellas or rainwear of any kind. By the time they got to the parade, Leanne and Christina had valid points about how lame it was. Nora suggested that because they'd all reached their maximum saturation points anyway, they might as well just stay wet and watch the parade. Another valid point.

They didn't see much of the parade because all their focus was spent trying to control their shivering. Shivering looks even dorkier than carrying an umbrella, but at that age, they weren't about to concede the cool.

Later, even after they were dry, shivering persisted. Nora had seen a documentary about Mount Everest and recounted the morbid play-by-play of what it must feel like to die of hypothermia. This information not only made the girls colder, it made them paranoid as well. They were sure they were going to die. Christina wondered out loud about whether they would be the first people to die of hypothermia in July in the balmy Northeast. Leanne, Nora, Christina, and Molly piled onto Molly's bed and huddled under an electric blanket. While all snuggled up, Christina began describing a *Dateline* report she had seen about defective electric blankets.

Leanne covertly wiggled around in the blankets to conjure up static, while Christina detailed the body count in her lethal electric blanket story. Just when Christina escalated to report the most gruesome and terrifying statistic about accidental electrocution, Leanne zapped Christina's earlobe with static electricity. Christina screamed and fled while Nora and Molly roared with laughter.

It was the type of laughter that was so delicious they kept going back for more. Once you get laughing like that, it's hard to stop even if nothing particularly funny happens afterward.

Nothing particularly funny happened after that day for the four of them. Leanne and Molly finished their boring parochial school, where Leanne engaged in every activity and followed her mother's rules, while Molly engaged in zero activities and got high with the burnouts. Nora coasted through public school and took care of Gramp Shea the way he used to take care of her. Christina over-achieved in her private school, and Molly occasionally played a guest star role on the weekends when Christina's friends wanted to over-achieve at smoking pot.

They have grown to believe Molly is the only reason they are still in touch at all. But before she died, Molly wrote in her journal one last confession about her best girlfriends.

It was all my fault.

When they were twenty-two, they could have reunited and become adult friends. The high schools and colleges that had kept them apart were now just small pieces of the cool young women they had become. It would have been so smart for each of them to start out in the world alongside friends who knew the truest versions of themselves. Unfortunately, twenty-two is not the time any of them wanted to be reminded of that pureness. It was the time when they started trying on their new adult-person suits, and none of them were quite pulling it off.

The friends who know about the tears cried in the bathroom of a youth hostel may be the whistleblowers when wistful conversations about "time abroad" come up at dinner parties. It's pretty impos-sible to impress a boss or new coworkers during after-work drinks when an old friend keeps bringing up some sloppy college behavior or that NKOTB purse you carried around in elementary school and still refuse to throw out.

"Could you *please*?" Christina exclaimed at Leanne at a wine bar one night right around the time they were just old enough to legally be in such a place. When said with the right emphasis, the word *please* among longtime girlfriends can easily imply an unspoken "shut the hell up."

Christina had been talking to a handsome mature TA from law school, when Leanne made a casual reference to Christina's fondness for Meatloaf. (The singer, not the food. Though neither is anything to brag about in a fancy wine bar.) This Meatloaf exchange is one of many pieces of evidence Leanne presents when discussing the case of Leanne vs. Christina-Thinks-She's-Better-Than-Me. It's a pretty open-and-shut case. Christina would even testify against herself because, indeed, she *does* think she's better than Leanne.

"What's wrong with thinking I'm better, anyway?" Christina asked Molly once after a few drinks. "Of course I'd rather be me. I work hard to be me. I deserve it."

Molly agreed with Christina.

Leanne presented her argument that Christina was self-absorbed, cared too much about designer labels, and wasted too much money on expensive shoes.

Molly agreed with Leanne.

Nora had a separate case against both of them.

"Can't I just stay home, dye my roots, and read instead?" Nora would say when Molly proposed that they all get together as a group.

Molly agreed with Nora.

In her final days, Molly often wrote in her journal in an indecipherable scribble. Sometimes she even ran her pen across the page with her eyes closed, while her mind formed the words she wanted to write, but couldn't. One of her final scribbles could be translated this way:

I killed the friendship that could have existed for my three best ladies. I played all sides and kept them each all to myself. They think I am the link they share as friends, but I was actually the person who kept them from speaking directly to each other.

Molly opened her eyes and looked at the page of wiggly lines and added with great clarity and impeccable penmanship:

And that's why they have to have brunch on Sundays.

17

Many people appreciate the charm of colonial houses, but owning a historical home is a big drafty pain in the ass. All around Massachusetts are masterfully restored houses that date back to the 1680s just around the corner from whole subdivisions full of colonial-style knockoffs with gigantic back decks for barbecues. The latter is exactly Leanne's jam.

While sitting in her parked car in Leanne's neighborhood, Nora scribbles in her notebook.

If Leanne tries to claim her house is "a colonial," Christina is going to say something rude, I just know it. Is it rude to be honest? Yes, usually. I admit if someone's trying to pull off the colonial look, they should try harder. Why are the foundations so high above the ground in this "colonial" neighborhood? It does look insane. Never did a colonist walk up a front staircase to enter a home. Did they? I'm going to look into this.

Where is Christina?

Should I have offered her a ride? No. Then you'd be alone with Christina instead of Leanne. Why would that solve anything? It wouldn't. Never mind. Never suggest carpooling. Never never never.

Should I just go in? No. You won't have a menu to stare at.

It's so much more awkward to be alone with Leanne in her home. Why why why did we agree to this?

It's going to be harder to leave too. Can't eat and run when you're in someone's home. I'll have to linger. Holy crap, this is the worst idea ever. I wish Leanne never suggested this and I wish—

Nora sits back in the driver's seat. There are so many things she wishes. So many ways she could wish away the burden of being at Leanne's house for brunch on a Sunday.

The screeching voice of Axl Rose heralds Christina's arrival before her screeching tires turn hard onto the quiet suburban street. Christina's car slows in front of six identical neighboring houses. She checks the house numbers and speeds toward Nora.

"Mr. Brownstone" is Nora's cue to turn off her car and stroll toward Leanne's house.

Christina's car lurches into a crooked curbside parking space in front of Leanne's house just as Leanne opens her front door.

"You can park in the driveway! The driveway!" Leanne yells, gesturing wildly from the front steps. Nora pauses in the brick path to Leanne's red front door, unsure of whether or not she should re-park. "Oh, Nora. You could have parked in the driveway. We have plenty of space. It's okay, though. Whatever is easier."

Christina can't hear anything until she turns off her car along with the music that seems to propel the engine. She's already out of her car by the time she realizes she breached protocol by parking on the street.

"Never mind! You're good!" Leanne says, making an unsuccessful attempt to appear breezy.

"Hi," Nora says. "I brought you some honey from the farmers market."

Right away, Nora regrets sharing the origin of this honey and hopes Leanne doesn't ask for any more details about the farmers market, particularly with whom she attended said farmers market. Nora told her notebook that she didn't necessarily go to the farmers market *with* Sam. They just were there at the same time, walking and talking together. So, really, she attended the farmers market *adjacent to* Sam. Her notebook completely understood this, but Nora has a feeling Molly's other two best friends will not.

"Oh! How thoughtful! Come in! Come in!" Leanne says, ushering Nora up the cement front steps where no actual American colonists ever tread.

Nora passes through the doorway to Leanne's house and into a French cliché. The air smells like baking and lavender. The mauve walls are littered with black-and-white Eiffel Tower photos and faux-weathered signs that say stuff *en français*. The soundtrack is provided by Piaf. In short, fake Paris threw up in Leanne's house.

"Wow! Did you decorate like this just for the brunch theme?" Nora asks.

"No, no, I'm a *longtime* Francophile," Leanne says, laughing. "As you *well* know!"

Christina steps through the Franco portal before Nora has a chance to tell her to make a run for it. Now it's too late for both of them.

"Oh," Christina says, looking around and air-kissing Leanne at the same time. "Very well-themed."

"Thanks!" Leanne says. "I'll get started on the crepes. Café au lait for you?"

"Um. Sure. Thanks," Nora says.

Christina nods. They're both still taking in all the Frenchiness surrounding them. It's a lot.

Nora and Christina peruse the bric-a-brac on Leanne's mantel and discover their favorite piece of Leanne's decor—a familiar black-and-white photo taken through the window of a café, Le Sarah-Bernhardt.

It was Molly's crafty gift to each of them one Christmas when they were in college.

Molly had gone to visit Christina in her study-abroad stint at Oxford and planned to meet up with Leanne in Paris. Leanne didn't show up because she decided an internship at a museum would look better on her résumé. She sent Molly a letter (c/o Christina) saying she wasn't coming. A *letter*!

Christina opened the letter and called the hostel in Paris where Molly was staying, waiting for Leanne's arrival. Molly cried in her bathroom-less room because this was not the adventure she had expected. She didn't want to be in Paris alone. She had just gotten her heart broken by her (in hindsight) boring college boyfriend whom she was "supposed" to marry. He was a "supposed to" guy. They were supposed to get married and then they were supposed to go to Paris for a supposed-to honeymoon—an idea that was as corny as he was. His future wife was supposed to agree with everything he said and confirm that he was as important as his mother had raised him to believe he was. That fall, he had abruptly recast someone else who could play this future wife role without improvising. He had his script and Molly couldn't take direction, apparently. Still, he broke Molly's heart because she'd bought into his act—just as she was supposed to.

Leanne proposed this trip to Paris as her way of rescuing Molly from the heartbreak. Leanne later told her that it seemed as if she was "over" the heartbreak and that's why Leanne didn't feel Molly needed a rescue. Molly pretended to be "over" Leanne ditching her in Paris. Molly was very good at pretending to be over things—it's a skill she learned from almost every woman she met in her young life.

Molly left her hostel after crying for a few hours and watching *Friends* dubbed over in French. She decided Paris would be a great setting for a rebound romance. The problem was—the men in Paris were just entirely too manly. Men being masculine sounds like a wonderful predicament when you're older, but Molly couldn't get on board with this much manliness at nineteen. Ain't no way any of them could join a boy band. It took only one flirtation from a gravelly-voiced, wizened-faced Parisian and Molly was ready to race back to her room and into the boyish arms of Chandler Bing.

In every good rom-com, the leading lady ends up with a love she was not pursuing in the first place. Of course, the audience roots for her to fall for the one who has been standing quietly by—the one who was there all along. Molly's rom-com was no different.

Paris was the one who was there all along. The one Molly would fall in love with and the one who would embrace her, make her feel beautiful, teach her about passion, and whisper in her ear "*Toujours.*"

So, Molly spent the trip alone and Paris treated her just fine. Once you've been with Paris, you realize that if you ever do go to this city with a lover, you'll actually be engaging in a ménage à trois. Paris is the lover who won't let go.

On Molly's last day in Paris, she lingered at Le Sarah-Bernhardt in the fourth arrondissement. It's a touristy place that's good for coffee and people watching, but mostly she was drawn there because of the name.

"You're a regular Sarah Bernhardt!" was a Gramp Shea-ism for when the girls were being overly silly or dramatic. He explained that Bernhardt was a Belle Epoch–era stage actress known for her melodrama and exaggeration. Naturally, Molly, Nora, Leanne, and Christina began using this name as shorthand when they identified a drama queen in their midst.

In fifth grade, they cryptically diagnosed their shared nemesis Trish Walter as "S.B." when she hobbled around on crutches with a self-diagnosed sprained left ankle. Periodically, the injury leapt to her right ankle for a few limping paces until she remembered the specifics of her lie. Trish told the teacher that Christina had called her an "S.O.B.," for which Christina was subsequently punished. That is, she was shamed in front of the class and forced to stand facing the corner.

At the café, Molly snapped a photo of the street through the window, so the word *café* appeared backward in the photo. She had come to Paris looking for an escape, and when she thought of her friends and their shared shorthand, it made her remember that her reality was not one that needed escaping. And perhaps, she realized, she was being a bit of an S.B.

At Leanne's house on this Sunday morning, Christina and Nora stare at the café photo and each considers waxing nostalgic about Trish "S.B." Walter. But comical nostalgia feels too intimate for the kind of relationship they have now.

"Do you still have yours?" Leanne asks from the kitchen, when she sees them lingering near the photo.

"It's in my office," Christina says.

Nora has drifted into memories and forgotten she is supposed to speak.

"Nora?" Leanne says.

"In my kitchen," Nora says.

"I always wanted to go to France," Leanne says. "I should have gone before I—"

"Wait. You've never been to France at all?" Nora asks. There's really no need to ask a woman who's dressed in a black beret and a red neckerchief whether she's been to actual France, but Nora is just waking from a daze and has forgotten that she shouldn't state the obvious.

"No, you?" Leanne asks.

"No, but I just thought you . . ." Nora says. "Well, you're kind of into it, right?"

"You and James should go," Christina says.

"That's not our trajectory," Leanne says, flipping a crepe. "We're planning a baby."

"You're pregnant?" Christina says. There's no way she can ignore the bait this time. The word *baby* is more than bait.

"No, yeah, well, we're not telling people yet," Leanne says, offering the girls a platter of croissants, madeleines, and fruit. "So, yeah, no."

Nora doesn't know what that means, but this time it's not because she took Latin instead of French. It's because it makes no goddamn sense.

She and Christina dig into the croissants.

"I'll go when the kids are in college," Leanne says.

"The kids?" Christina baits her back.

"People always associate croissants with France," Nora says, mostly to herself. "But it's actually evolved from the Austrian *kipferl* which goes way back to—"

"*My* kids," Leanne says. "We're going to have a boy and a girl."

"I wanna say, the *thirteenth* century, even?" Nora continues. "Maybe earlier than that."

"Two years apart," Leanne adds. "So they'll be close."

"But croissants started up in the 1800s in *Vienna*, not Paris, so . . ." Nora has completely dissociated.

"Poor kids aren't even born yet and you're already blaming them for why you're not going to Paris," Christina says.

Nora failed to derail the train of conversation. Now they're all sitting in the Go Fuck Yourself Depot wishing they'd gotten off at Polite Small Talk Junction instead.

"Regardless, they're delicious. Buttery. I love butter," Nora says. "Did you make these madeleines too?"

"Yes," Leanne says, without taking her glaring eyes off of Christina.

Christina ignores the whole conversation and acts as if she's smug secret besties with her café au lait. She draws a slow bored sip from her cup.

Nora chews on the cookie and the tension.

"Airy," she says with her mouth full.

"Thank you," Leanne says. "Jacques Pépin's recipe."

"Bien sûr," Christina says.

Sure, Nora took Latin instead of French, but she understands snark when she hears it. Nora will later make a list of other brunch spots around town in case someone proposes "mixing it up" again.

She'll scribble next to the list:

Home-hosted brunches are too fucking dangerous.

Pardon my French.

18

There was only so much preparation Leanne could do during these few early weeks of pregnancy. She read all the reviews for each ob-gyn in the area, conducted interviews, and carefully selected Dr. Lola Cortez-Sheinemann. Then she waited weeks to get in.

Perfecting an outfit for her first prenatal doctor's appointment took hours. This is a day she will want to remember and possibly commemorate with a photo for the "Our Journey" pregnancy scrapbook she bought on Etsy.

She toyed with the idea of wearing leggings and leopard print flats for easy removal before the exam. She'd pair the leggings with a loose-fitting fuchsia button-down shirt. At the last minute, she switched her wardrobe, thinking she'd better save this outfit for later, when her jeans no longer fit. Instead, she chose her most formfitting sweater in emerald green, her skinny jeans, and yeah, those leopard flats still worked.

She asked James to change his clothes when he came into the kitchen in a thoughtlessly chosen T-shirt and jeans.

"Aren't we just going to the doctor?" James asks. A day off from work for James means a day off from dress shirts and suits.

"Maybe we'll want to go out for lunch after? Can you put on your Ralph shirt?" Leanne asks. "The blue, not the green. We don't want to match."

James complies, because let's face it, this is not really a request. Leanne has a plan, as usual.

This is the day Leanne will hear her baby girl's heartbeat for the first time. She'll remember what she wore, how she felt, what she ate. She'll remember the look on James's face and how his eyes matched his blue shirt. Leanne has so many plans for the future, she even plans what she'll remember.

The official story of James's marriage proposal includes Leanne wearing a navy-and-white striped sundress with a red sunhat and Jackie O sunglasses. They were on the Cape and had an early dinner at their favorite restaurant. Just as the sun was setting, they walked on the beach at low tide. The wet sand was packed beneath their feet. James slowed his pace and fell behind. Leanne turned to see him kneeling on the hard sand and she thought for a minute that he'd tripped on the ridges caused by the tide. Then she saw the shining, perfect solitaire gleaming in the twilight.

But that was the do-over.

Before the mulligan, the original proposal went like this: James had gotten the ring and couldn't wait another second to show her. James isn't one to postpone joyous occasions on the basis of optics. So, he didn't care that Leanne was slathered with bedtime moisturizers, wearing mismatched pj's, and reading *Twilight* in bed. He sat on the edge of the bed and kissed her once on the forehead, then once on each of her slippery lotioned hands and said, "I love you."

Leanne didn't realize this was the proposal, so she said she loved him too, said she loved the ring, but she didn't put it on her finger. Then she went back to reading. To be fair, James didn't officially ask the big question because he'd gotten stage fright and forgotten his lines. Leanne could have said yes to the unasked question, but she had already planned their engagement story out so clearly that she missed the spontaneous moment when it happened. Perhaps kisses on the forehead and nights reading YA sci-fi in bed are not social media worthy, but those tiny moments are true bliss, even if Leanne didn't realize it. That moment belonged only to them.

Leanne in her green sweater and James in his blue Ralph Lauren shirt arrive on time at Dr. Cortez-Sheinemann's office. Leanne researched what this appointment would be like and dutifully chugged water on the drive over so she'd have no trouble giving a urine sample before her ultrasound. At first, she is happy they have a few extra minutes in the waiting room for a selfie that they can show their daughter someday.

Several selfies later, the wait has become too long. James tries to add humor by taking a photo of himself checking his watch. The downside to seeing the best doctor in the city is that she's also the busiest.

"Can I just give a sample now, while I wait?" Leanne asks the nurse, who probably should have anticipated the situation.

"Sure thing," the nurse says. She scribbles with a Sharpie on a plastic container and hands it to Leanne.

Almost an hour later, Leanne tries to remain serene in the doctor's exam room. Annoyance is not the emotion she wants to collage into the baby scrapbook.

"Hi there. Sorry to keep you waiting," Dr. Cortez-Sheinemann says. "Good to see you two again. So, we're still trying to get pregnant?"

"Actually, no. We're here for our first prenatal appointment," Leanne says.

"Oh," Dr. Cortez-Sheinemann says. She checks her notes again. "Hold on."

She leaves the room.

"We almost had her attention!" James says. "Think she'll come back by lunchtime?"

"Oh, I'm sure she's just going to get my chart or something." Leanne laughs. "I don't think she had the right one."

"Hope she doesn't switch our baby at the hospital," James says. "Lifetime Original Movie style."

Leanne laughs. She'll remember laughing at this joke.

Dr. Cortez-Sheinemann returns and asks Leanne before the door fully closes, "So, you took a home pregnancy test?"

"Yes, I wanted to ask you about that," Leanne says, taking out her freshly purchased pink pregnancy notebook. "The pink line was pretty faded, but I haven't gotten my period and usually I'm like clockwork, so maybe that test was warped or something. Is that common? Or do you think we should check my hormone levels?"

"Oh!" Dr. Cortez-Sheinemann says. "Okay, so it was faded. That explains it. Our test says you're not pregnant."

"Well, I am," Leanne says.

Dr. Cortez-Sheinemann tries to read the confusion on James's face. Her usual recourse is to science her way out of confusion, but talking science can come off as heartless when discussing a mother and her baby. She's worked in obstetrics long enough to know that reproduction and childbirth often feel more like magic than science. And sometimes, this stuff defies magic and science. Sometimes, busy doctors' offices just make simple mistakes.

"Okay, let's take a look. Maybe your samples got switched. The nurses are a little overwhelmed today," she says.

Dr. Cortez-Sheinemann wheels her stool up to the examination table and wields the ultrasound wand. She turns the screen toward Leanne so she can watch a guided tour of her lady parts. The doctor points out Leanne's full bladder first, taking the scenic route to her healthy ovaries and, ultimately, her empty uterus.

"Well, then why haven't I gotten my period?" Leanne demands, as if she can outwit the blank ultrasound screen.

The doctor has no angle here. It's not as if there's some crazy con she can run that involves telling pregnant women they're not pregnant. If it ever happens, Christina will love watching it on *Dateline*.

"I don't know, have you been under any unusual stress?" Dr. Cortez-Sheinemann asks.

"I just got back from Bermuda," Leanne says, her voice shifting to a strident screech. "I've never been so relaxed in my life!"

She grits her teeth to keep from adding "God dammit!"

"I don't know then—it hasn't been long enough to cause concern," Dr. Cortez-Sheinemann says. "If it doesn't come back in a month—"

"I'm always exactly twenty-six days," Leanne insists. "There has to be something."

"All right, I'll run a few tests if you're really concerned," the doctor says. "But these things usually—"

"Okay, and will the tests tell us more about the baby?" Leanne asks.

James kisses Leanne's hand.

But the best busiest ob-gyn in Boston doesn't have time to be as gentle. "Leanne, there's no baby. I am so sorry."

"But I don't have my period and the test I took was positive," Leanne says.

The doctor looks at the blank ultrasound screen. Surely this test is definitive to a rational person. It's clear Leanne is no such person.

"We recently lost her best friend," James explains. "That's probably the stress."

"Yeah, but that's not *stressful*. That's just *sad*," Leanne says.

Leanne still thinks she can talk her way out of grief and into a pregnancy. Anyone who knows anything about either one of these processes will tell you that there are certain steps that can't be skipped. And none of those steps can be dashed away using semantics.

"How about *we* do another pregnancy test then?" Dr. Cortez-Sheinemann says. She does have time to be compassionate to someone who is clearly at wits' end.

"Yes. Let's do that," Leanne says, in such a tone that she might as well have said "challenge accepted!"

Leanne goes into the bathroom, takes the test out of the box, and reads the instructions. She has to get it right so the doctor will stop doubting her.

Her eyes fix on the number on the front of the box. "Results in three minutes."

Three.

Molly's magic number.

She sees the box fall onto the tile floor, not realizing it's still in her hand. She feels pain in her knees and the sensation that the floor has leapt up and slammed against them. The cold, hard floor smashes against her body and her mind assaults her with the reality she's been avoiding: She's not pregnant. She was never pregnant. And her best friend is dead.

Leanne crawls to the door and tries to call for James, but instead her guttural voice cries out, "Molly!"

James was already there at the door. He's been expecting this. He crouches down and holds her.

"Molly. Molly!" Leanne sobs. James rocks her.

It's here. The grief beast. She can't fight it off. With no baby to protect, Leanne surrenders to the beast and it devours her.

19

Silence and sleep until 9:00 a.m. on a Sunday may be sweet indulgence to most people, but Christina jolts awake with that startled feeling you get from seeing a flashing digital "12:00" on a failed alarm clock. For Christina, the flashing 12:00 is Lilly, who usually wakes up at 6:00 a.m.

"Mom!"

Christina runs to Lilly's room and finds Lilly in bed, snuggled right under the covers where Christina tucked her in last night. Christina stops and braces herself for the moment she's been fearing all her life.

When Christina was six, she saw a movie where someone died in their sleep. Until then, she didn't know people could just slip away while sleeping. Of course, this revelation gave Christina her first bout of insomnia and a painfully literal interpretation of her bedtime prayer, "Now I lay me down to sleep, I pray the Lord my soul to keep, and if I die before I wake, I pray the Lord my soul to take."

The little future lawyer modified the prayer with the addendum "but *only* if I die before I wake, can you take my soul, dear God." Then she began to think that "if I die before I wake" was too fate-tempting, much like that moment in horror movies when a character says "What's the worst that can happen?" or "I'll be right back!" She didn't want the hand of God to snatch her soul. God, after all, digs foreshadowing. Everyone knows that. Young Christina wanted to be clear, so she added the preamble "I am *unwilling* to die during my sleep at this time, however, now I lay me down to sleep . . ."

That's when Lilly rued the day she sent her to "that damn Catholic school," as she referred to it later when Christina was settled into the nondenominational private prep school. The stuff they teach in Catholic school was just way too intense for an already intense-minded (paranoid) child like Christina.

What kept Christina awake as a little girl (and throughout adolescence and into adulthood) was the added anxiety about death by slumber. Didn't her mother know that she could be risking her own life simply by falling asleep? Lilly hadn't seen that movie. Six-year-old Christina woke often around 2:30 a.m. to use the bathroom, and on her way back to bed, she always crept into her mother's room and held the backside of a spoon under her nose to see if it fogged up. She saw that trick in another movie. She'd go back to bed relieved that her mother was going to live through the night.

Now Christina waits at the door of her mother's room. She doesn't have a spoon and she fears she may get an answer that doesn't bring her any relief.

"Mom?"

Lilly moves and drowsily hugs her pillow. Christina sits down on the carpet to finish waking herself up. It occurs to her briefly that it might be a good time to meditate. Doomsday thoughts swirling, heart racing, short shallow breathing. Yup, this would be a prime meditation situation.

But meditation can be so annoying and Christina is cozy in her own chaos anyway. The doorbell saves her from processing her thoughts. She remembers that Maeve is due to take care of Lilly while she attends another terrible brunch.

"She's still asleep. We, uh, both overslept," Christina tells Maeve before she gets the door fully open.

"No, girlie. We hafta get her movin'," Maeve says, barreling past Christina. She takes over the house.

"Well, maybe she needs the sleep," Christina wonders out loud.

"You don't want her switchin' the days and nights. This is how it starts," Maeve says. She opens the curtains and makes a careless commotion in every move she makes. "Lilly! Rise and shine, lady!"

"Okay, we'll figure it out, it's just one morning. I gotta get ready and go," Christina says. "Can you—"

"I got her, girlie," Maeve says. "You go ahead, see those friends."

"They're not my . . ." Christina doesn't feel up to explaining the complicated dynamics of women who met as girls. "Okay, I'll get going."

Once she's driven a block away from her immediate neighbors, Christina blasts "Here I Go Again " by Whitesnake and screams the words until her throat hurts.

While singing along with the guitar solo (Christina sings all instrumentals), she feels better and figures she'll be over this harrowing episode in a day or two. One drum solo later, she ponders the point of going to caregiver counseling at all when she can get through a whole week without it. She must not need it. She makes a mental note to cancel. She's obviously fine.

She sails through a red light and turns the volume up even louder. Her head begins to throb a little from singing so loud. That's all normal, right?

Yeah, she's fine. She's totally fine.

"Fine" is the answer she gives Leanne when Leanne asks about Lilly's health today at brunch.

"And how are you coping?" Leanne asks, clearly forgetting the many subliminal layers of the word *fine*.

"With a counselor," Christina says.

"I wouldn't have thought you'd do something like that," Leanne says. "Don't you roll your eyes at therapy?"

Christina rolls her eyes about rolling her eyes.

"Well, it worked," Christina says, as if she's been cured for good and doesn't need to go back.

Nora takes her seat at the table, waves, and cracks open the menu without delay. The conversation continues around her, which is how she prefers it.

"And anyway, this wasn't therapy!" Christina insists, God forbid. "No. This is a *counselor*. She's part of my mom's program. When Mom was diagnosed, her doctor suggested I go to a support group. Said it was a necessary part of taking care of someone with—well, someone like Mom. But I said no fucking way do I have time to sit around in a circle and sing 'Kumbaya' with other caregivers. So the doctor said I could go to a counselor one-on-one instead. So I go every other week."

Christina has been in therapy and nobody told her.

After a long silence, Nora states the obvious as only Nora can. "Sounds like therapy."

"Anyway, it helped after Molly . . . you know, lately my *counselor* has been discussing grief with me for half of our session and talking about, you know, the other stuff for the other half," Christina says.

"That's efficient," Nora concludes.

"It is. So, how about you, Leanne?" Christina fires back. "How are *you* coping?"

"I grieved at the funeral," Leanne says, as if it were a task on her to-do list.

"No, you did not," Christina says. "You thanked people for coming and comforted her parents."

"I grieved in my own way," Leanne says.

"By not grieving," Nora says.

"I grieved while it was happening," Leanne says.

"Isn't it happening now?" Nora asks.

"No, I mean while she was dying," Leanne clarifies.

"So you *pre*-grieved?" Christina says.

"Wow. You're even more efficient," Nora says.

Leanne seems satisfied that she's won this efficient griever competition.

Nora wishes she hadn't said that.

"Did you do anything fun last night, Nora?" Christina asks, changing the subject.

"Yes, actually, I had a great time! Josh Groban was playing with the Pops at Symphony Hall. I got tickets through my friend who works at 'GBH," Nora says. Nora considers a public television hookup to be very valuable. She doesn't have the kind of extra cash to make a donation to WGBH, but she has been very tempted by the perks of becoming a member. She covets the Peter, Paul and Mary DVD boxed set during every telethon. Her contact gets her canvas tote bags, mugs, and occasionally, tickets to Symphony Hall.

"How are you ever going to meet a husband if your Saturday night out is at a Josh Groban concert?" Leanne says.

"Who says I want to meet a husband?" Nora says.

"Ohhhhhh," Leanne says. Aha! Leanne is relieved to finally figure Nora out. "Listen, I know this awesome lady at work. She's single . . ."

Christina takes a violent bite of her bagel.

"I'm not gay," Nora says.

Leanne is disappointed. Nora is a mystery freak again.

"Not everyone wants to get married, Leanne," Christina interjects, while chewing angrily. Thankfully her mouth is too full of carbs for her to go too far off course. They better tread lightly. Christina's dangerously close to using the word *patriarchy* in a rant. It's better to get out before that. Consider it a conversational safe word.

"I never said I didn't want to get married. Why are we talking about marriage?" Nora asks. "I just went to a Josh Groban concert. And it was really good by the way."

"*Most* people want to get married and have kids," Leanne says.

"Most people?" Christina challenges. "Do you know *most* people? How many people do you know?"

"Josh Groban doesn't just do Christmas music, you know," Nora says. "He does a cover of 'America' by Simon and Garfunkel. It's really good. Haunting, actually."

"I know a *lot* of people," Leanne says.

"But do they ever say that's what they want?" Christina asks.

"It's just what you do," Leanne says.

"It's not what *I* do," Christina says.

"I like a concert where you can sit the entire time," Nora says.

"You could get married," Leanne tells Christina.

"Thanks," Christina says, though she's not thankful at all for this strange compliment.

"I prefer it—there is absolutely no pressure to dance," Nora says. "I'm not a dancer."

"And I'm sure you'll make a great mother," Leanne tells Christina.

"I won't make a mother at all," Christina says. "I don't want children."

"Oh, you'll change your mind when you meet the right—"

"No, I will not," Christina says.

Patriarchy! Patriarchy! The safe word is coming.

Leanne takes her napkin off her lap and puts it on the table. They're done.

"Anyway, he has a good mix of original songs and covers, so there's really something for everyone," Nora says. "And no one has to dance."

"Sounds good, Nora. I'll check him out on Spotify," Christina says.

No, she won't.

Christina can turn up the volume all she wants, but Josh Groban's voice will never be shrill enough to compete with the part of Christina's brain she seeks to silence with music. The promise to check out Josh Groban on Spotify is one of the many little lies they all will have to tell one another to keep these monthly brunches pleasant.

As she picks up the bill, Christina tells one more lie. "Well, ladies," she says, "it's been great seeing you."

20

Nora has skipped every Content Monkey monthly mixer in the last six months, and she has run out of excuses now that her best friend is out of hospice. The only way out of the next obligatory Content Monkey bonding ritual is for her to be in hospice herself. No such luck.

Worse, this one is the holiday "extravaganza." Nora doesn't bother pondering what qualifies a social event as an extravaganza. The office party committee never shies away from cheeky holiday hyperbole—forever referring to their gatherings as galas. They love to pair normal holiday names with optimistic suffixes such as *-fest*, *-palooza*, and *-a-go-go*.

This year's Winter Holiday Extravaganza was so titled to emphasize inclusion, after two people complained to HR about Kwanzaapalooza last year. Assumptions swirled that the complainers were from the die-hard "Merry Christmas" crowd, but in fact, the complaints came from those who actually celebrate Kwanzaa. The moral of the story: don't "palooza" real holidays when they're not yours to palooza.

Nora has no delusions that this year's extravaganza will live up to its name. Despite the Evite's "dress to impress" caveat, Nora plans to wear only slightly fancier clothes than she normally wears to the office. Her coworkers will dial their wardrobe game up about ten notches for the night, while Nora will only dial it up by one tenth of a notch. Half of the staff left the office early today to get blowouts and spray tans. Spray tans. In New England. In December.

Nora consults her notebook once she's done putting on her tinted Chapstick.

I'll go late and leave early. If I take my time getting there, everyone will be plenty drunk. They'll have no concept of time and I can sneak out fast. I'll have the rest of my Saturday night to myself. When I get back: pj's, oatmeal, Mary Tyler Moore Show. Done.

Nora is wearing a nice going-to-a-party blouse with her pajama pants. There's no need to put on real pants until the minute she's about to walk out the door. Many people have shoe-free households, but homebodies like Nora go pants-free too.

The doorbell rings and Nora ignores it, as she always does. She continues to write.

Important: I have to be there during the period of largest attendance, so I'll get maximum exposure. If everyone sees me, I'll be able to skip next month and the next one too, maybe. Ugh, do I have to bring something? Yes, get wine. What kind of wine? I don't know. Ask the Trader Joe's guy. Oh, get the decaf Irish breakfast tea from Trader's Joe's for after the party. Almost out of honey. Get honey. Might as well get another bag of oats too.

Nora's phone lights up with a text.

You home?

She ignores it.

Sam texting me. In 20 minutes, I can text him and say I'm not home. Good opportunity to get credit for being out on a Saturday night.

Hey should I worry? Your lights are on and I hear your TV. You ok?

What is he doing here!?

Nora scrambles to put on pants before she texts back.

I'm doing well. Just getting ready to go out.

The doorbell rings again. It's obviously Sam. Nora has to answer, now that she has pants on.

"Hi," she says, opening the door. It's more of an accusation than a greeting. The crime: popping by someone's home when you're not a character in an '80s sitcom.

"Just coming back from an awesome new java spot called Grounded. Next street over. You been there?" Sam asks.

"No," Nora says. "I drink tea."

"Saw your lights on and thought I'd say 'what up,'" Sam says. "So. What up?"

"Just on my way out," Nora says. She never thought she'd be so relieved to say that. She feels compelled to deflect any possibility that Sam might invite himself. He did, after all, just knock on her door randomly. Who does that? "To a *work* party. The Content Monkey monthly mixer. It's going to be super boring."

Everything Sam needs to know about the Content Monkey monthly mixer is right there in the name itself. Nora doesn't get out much, but even she knows that no one cool has referred to a party as a "mixer" since the '90s.

"You want a wingman?" Sam asks.

Boom! There's the self-invite. Nora saw it coming. Sam's presence could lengthen the duration of her party-going, but he could also do all the talking for her. She weighs this.

"Not really?" Sam says.

"Not really," Nora confesses. "I want to get in and out of there as fast as possible."

"Yeah, but think of the time you *do* have to spend there," Sam says. "I could do the talking."

Nora wishes Sam could stop hearing her thoughts.

"Tempting," she says.

"Okay, let's go," Sam says. "Put on your shoes."

She'll have to start thinking more quietly around this guy.

℃

If Nora's coworkers entered a Boring Contest, they would come in second because the judges of the contest would fall asleep before getting a chance to give them a good score.

Husband-and-wife start-up duo John and Susan Miller make the rounds at the Content Monkey Monthly Mixer/Holiday Extravaganza and bore everyone in their path. But the vacuous victims of their witless stories seem oddly unfazed. Incredibly, John and Susan are actually quite a bit more interesting than the other people Nora works with. John and Susan, dressed like seat fillers at the Oscars, corner Sam and Nora for an unpleasant photo session with John's selfie stick. It takes John six attempts to make the thing work. Nora loses her fake smile by attempt number three. She blinks during attempt number six. Photo number six is immediately uploaded to every social media outlet John has ever heard of.

"Funny story about this girl," John says, starting what would seem to be an uproarious tale. Susan anticipates this hilarity with a misplaced cackle.

Nora knows the promise of "funny" will never pay off. Sam leans into the story—he's the newest guest at the party and a naïvely optimistic audience for John.

"The first time I met her, she came into my office. She sits down. She gives me her résumé. It's, I wanna say, four o'clock in the afternoon? Four thirty? I'm tired. End of the day. I look it over. She's quiet. I say 'How long did you work at Prodigm?' She says . . ." John builds suspense, if you can call it that. He delivers the punchline. "Sixteen months."

John dies laughing. Susan throws her head back and wails.

"Just like that! 'Sixteen months,'" John says again, shaking his head.

"That's when I knew. I just thought, *Yup. That girl. Hire that girl.*"

"Bam! Hire that girl! Right?" Sam plays along and bros it up with John, even though he's pretty sure he missed the point of the story. Unfortunately, the point of the story is that there isn't one.

"I did work there for sixteen months," Nora tells Sam.

"She kills me!" Susan laughs.

John and Susan carry on. Nora and Sam slip away while John and Susan select their next contestant in a no-win game called Find the Point of This Story.

"So, yeah . . . classic anecdote," Sam says to Nora.

"Don't worry, I don't get it either. He tells that story a lot," Nora says. "I really did work there for sixteen months. I don't see why it's funny."

"It's not," Sam says. "But neither are they."

"That's John and Susan for ya," Nora says.

"More like Yawn and Snoozin'," Sam says, stretching. "They make me want to nap, dude."

Nora smiles during an office party for the first time ever. Maybe bringing Sam was a good idea, after all.

"Caffeinated booze?" Sam says, offering Nora a rum and Coke.

Okay, maybe bringing Sam was the very best idea.

"Yes, please," Nora says, almost laughing.

Nora glides through the next hour and appreciates that enough time has passed and she can justifiably leave whenever she wants. She excuses herself from Sam for a bathroom break before heading for the door. Sweet freedom is so close.

As soon as Nora is away from Sam, Susan pops up out of nowhere and traps Nora into chitchat.

"Heyyyyy *you*. I have to catch up with you. It's been *forever* since you've been at one of these things!" Susan says. "I'm glad you're feeling better about your friend dying."

"Oh. Okay," Nora agrees, because what else is there to say to this? She isn't feeling better about it. People are so weird about grief when it's not their own.

Nora catches Sam on the other side of the room heaving an imaginary lever to deploy her trapdoor. She purses her lips and avoids looking at him while Susan talks about . . . well, who cares? Nora can't resist sneaking another look over Susan's shoulder.

Nora sees Sam acting confused that his lever doesn't work. He scratches his head. He lifts the lever again. Nothing. He tries one last time, but—oops!—the trapdoor was under him! He mimes his sudden fall with arms flailing and his face contorting in a silent scream. He disappears behind the couch.

Nora snorts out a laugh right in the middle of Susan's yammering snoozefest.

The gracelessness of this pure laugh gives Nora a way out. She can easily pass it off as a choke, a sneeze, or some other involuntary spontaneous outburst that needs immediate attention. She has to excuse herself.

Nora finds herself on the sidewalk where she's fled in hysteria. In a way, the trapdoor worked.

Sam follows close behind and tumbles onto the sidewalk as if he's just been launched from a curvy escape shoot. He stands, disoriented.

"What the? Where am I?" Sam looks around. He's so committed to the bit.

Nora sits down on the curb to laugh some more.

"Was it good?" Sam asks, beaming. "Did you buy it?"

"Yes, very convincing," Nora says, noticing for the first time that Sam's joyful expression seems to recruit every muscle and feature of his face. Nora wonders how he can smile with his whole face like this, when she can barely smile with just her mouth.

"Wait. Don't worry. I didn't *really* fall through a trapdoor," Sam says, starting another bit.

"Wow, really?" Nora says. Blinded by comedy, she plays along.

"Man, good thing it wasn't real. You didn't even call the cops or anything. Geez, lady." Sam laughs. "Remind me not to rely on you in a crisis."

The veil of reality filters Nora's laugh. She had forgotten about her crisis for about five minutes, but it has crept back in. The blithe light in her eyes flickers and then burns out.

"I didn't mean . . . okay, I'm sorry," Sam says.

"I know what you meant," Nora says. "You're just kidding around."

"Yeah, I know. I kid a lot," Sam says. "Seriously though . . ."

"Okay." Nora avoids the serious direction this is taking.

"No, Nora. I want to say this," Sam says.

The eye contact thing disarms Nora again. But she sticks with it for as long as she can.

Then Sam says it. "I'm glad I have you."

Nora searches the sidewalk to make eye contact with anyone or anything besides Sam. A bug perhaps? A piece of newspaper? That mailbox will have to do.

"And you've got me too," Sam says. "I think we're doing pretty okay in the crisis. Right?"

Nora stares into the eyes of the mailbox and can't think of a thing to say.

"Dude," Nora says. She hears herself say it, and wonders if she's been possessed. Is Sam rubbing off on her? She instantly wants to cancel the last thing that came out of her mouth. It's the kind of moment where she wonders why she didn't make a better effort in her twenties to invent time travel.

"Right on," Sam says. They land a clumsy high five and all's well. Sam knows a high five is a big step for Nora. He'll have to work his way up to extended eye contact.

21

Leanne feels her body wake up and she refuses to open her eyes. If she can keep her eyes closed, she can keep the day from starting. Her holiday deep dive into crafting and made-for-TV Christmas-themed rom-coms sustained her through December, but now it's all packed away. In January, Leanne is left with an undecorated house and too much time with her thoughts.

James comes out of the bathroom, toweling off his freshly shaven face. When the sting of man soap clears from his eyes, he makes assumptions about Leanne's mood based on her position in bed. If she were lying with her arms above her head, he could wake her up by just calling her name. But since she is curled and covered, he will have to approach her cautiously. It is going to be a dark day, indeed. Getting Leanne out of bed will take a careful choice of words. A cheerful "Time to get up!" might work on another day, but today, it could trigger hostility about being told what to do.

"Hi," James whispers. "It's seven fifteen."

Leanne's eyes open and focus on nothing.

On a day like today, the most James can hope for is that Leanne will snap, "I know!"

Instead, she's silent.

"Want me to drop you off?" James offers, though he can already tell she will refuse to go to work.

Leanne doesn't answer.

James finishes getting dressed and allows Leanne to stew in still-ness. He putters around the kitchen, hoping somehow the tide will shift and the happier version of Leanne might rally and get out of bed. After an hour, it's clear that the other side of Leanne has taken over Tuesday.

"I have a meeting at nine, so I can't stay home with you," James says, anticipating a desperate request.

Whenever Leanne hugs James goodbye before work, she assumes it will be for the last time. She sometimes goes out to the car and asks for one more kiss, just in case. Leanne grew up in a home where love had contingencies, so she expects that James will be only a fleeting part of her life. And if she forgets her fear for a minute, Joan will be there to remind Leanne in both direct and passive ways: "You got lucky. Be nice. Don't lose him." When a girl is raised to believe she is undeserving of love, she assumes the love she does receive is tempo-rary. The minute James vowed to love Leanne forever, she inwardly mourned his destined untimely demise.

"Leanne?" James tries one more time.

Leanne rolls over, trying to will herself out of existence. There will be no extra kisses goodbye today. There will be no kisses at all.

Leanne feels a childlike longing, as if she's away at a rainy summer camp and she's desperate to go home. But the home she needs doesn't exist—and it never has.

Leanne keeps a steady pace with the stillness of her empty house. The sound of the garage door breaks her trance. She bursts from her blanket cocoon and chases James for a proper goodbye. What if he's gone forever?

By the time Leanne finds herself standing in the driveway in her pajamas, he is gone. (Only until 6:30 p.m., though. Not forever.) Devastated by his taillights, she turns to see an even more devastat-ing sight: the back door, closed and locked.

Leanne begins the negotiation ritual familiar to anyone who has ever locked their keys in the car, dropped their phone in the toilet, or done anything else instantly stupid and day-ruining.

That did not just happen. NONONONONONO . . .

She seems to think she can change the event by sheer will or by tugging on a doorknob that she knows is locked. It's as if Leanne has never seen a door before. Pulling on it and saying "come on" a bunch of times? No. This is not how doors work.

She relaxes, remembering that James stashed a key in the garage when they first moved in.

"God bless him," she'll say when he inevitably dies later today. "He took care of me until the very end."

Even though she didn't give him a kiss goodbye before his final journey, he gave her one last gift: a hideaway key. The key will drip with meaning forever. It will be such a poignant story of their last exchange that she'll cling to the key and perhaps wear it around her neck as a totem.

But don't worry. James will come home at six thirty. He always does.

In the garage, Leanne finds the key right away—in a coffee can, which is absolutely the most obvious place to hide a hide-a-key. Such a coffee can comes standard with the garage when you buy a house in Massachusetts. Burglars who are interested in burgling without breaking glass (who needs the mess?) can easily find a key. They simply look for a rusty Chock full o'Nuts can, knowing it's chock full o'screws, nails, and a key to the back door of the house.

Leanne's mood has now reached the level of shittiness where she seeks new ways to bask in her shitty feelings. She remembers Googling *stupidity* when she thought she was pregnant. Locking her pregnant self out of the house would have been an adorable "baby brain" anecdote. But this was just non-cute dumb. Standing in a garage, barefoot, and wearing pajamas gives her more seasoning for this marinade of melancholy. Hey, why not throw in a dash of the dead best friend while you're at it?

Yup. Here we go . . .

Leanne takes the cover off her inherited Vespa and sits on it for the first time. Of course, she won't even go near such a vehicle without considering safety first, so she dons Molly's sparkly helmet and buckles it right up under her chin. You know. In case the Vespa spontaneously turns on by itself and speeds out of the garage, into traffic.

Leanne will never put herself in a position to test the effectiveness of a motorcycle helmet or risk the type of trauma the helmet is designed to withstand. Lucky for her, this particular helmet belonged to someone who loved her, and it is covered in silver glitter so it is capable of softening the blow in a different type of crash.

The tag still dangles from the handlebar.

Allons-y, chérie!

"Let's go *where*?" Leanne says out loud, because talking to oneself and sitting on a Vespa in pajamas are two things that go hand in hand. She half expects a ghostly whispered answer. In the absence of supernatural profundity, she assumes the answer is that she should go back to bed.

She retrieves the canvas cover she carelessly cast aside. When she drapes it over the Vespa, the fabric catches an easel and knocks a mason jar full of paintbrushes onto the floor.

For Leanne's birthday three years ago, James renovated part of their garage into an art studio. She used it once. Molly came up with this clever art studio idea after a conversation she forced upon James about what Leanne was like in high school. Molly assumed he'd want to know everything about Leanne because men in love will often ask for these kinds of origin stories with the same enthusiasm as a child asking their parents to tell the story about the day they were born. James didn't ask, but Molly told him anyway.

Molly told James that Leanne won an art award when they were juniors in high school. It was a big deal, but not part of Joan's plans for Leanne. It had quite a bit of prestige and the prize was a weekend trip to Paris with the Art Education Coalition.

Joan reminded Leanne that the three days in Paris conflicted with one day of her SAT prep course. So, instead of filling in her soul with Paris, Leanne filled in tiny ovals on an SAT practice test with a No. 2 pencil.

Leanne's brilliant painting was still displayed years later in the hospital's main lobby when Molly was getting chemo. The people waiting for the elevator got an earful about her artist friend Leanne.

James never thought this garage art studio was such a great idea, but he presented the gift to her along with an apology and a promise to get her something that fit into a small box. The apology made Leanne feel silly for loving the gift so much.

On this grumpy Tuesday morning, Leanne bends down and scoops up the handful of paintbrushes into a bouquet. She's tempted to smell them and there's really no reason not to. She plunks them back into the mason jar and nestles it against her chest as if it's a newborn.

When James returns home tonight, he will find Leanne in their bed with art supplies laid out around her. Fresh charcoal sketches will line the floor. She'll have a pad of drawing paper in her lap and colored chalk all over her fingers. Last night's pajamas will become tonight's pajamas. Her hair will be a mess, but it won't matter because she'll have a sparkly helmet on her head. On a day like today, this shiny protective gear is a very reasonable addition to her wardrobe, because after all these years, this type-A planner girl has been magnificently broken open.

22

At 10:00 p.m., Lilly has only recently gone to sleep for the night and Christina still has many online errands to run. Christina gets comfortable in Molly's meditation chair, flips on the television, and selects *The Long Island Medium* On Demand. Tonight was surely not going to be the night where this seat fulfilled its destiny as a place for meditation. She opens her laptop and lets her fingers fly across the keyboard.

The rattan chair has a low back that comes up just above Christina's lower back, and the seat is curved in a kidney shape that matched the shape of Molly's legs when she was sitting in a lotus position. Christina does not know to put her feet in lotus position. Her little cousin's kindergarten teacher referred to this manner of sitting as "crisscross applesauce," which annoyed the hell out of Christina because the arbitrary rhyme infantilized a little girl whom Christina considered to be the most advanced kindergartener on earth. Everyone thinks the kindergartener biologically nearest to them is a genius. And everyone is right. Kindergarteners live in a perfect moment between expressive human skill and intuitive nonhuman insight.

When Christina sits on this little seat, low to the floor, she feels the cool familiar comfort of a beanbag chair she used to sit in while doing homework in high school. But it's not long before her foot falls asleep from sitting in this position and reminds her that she's no longer a teenager. It also reminds her that adulthood means she can afford another pair of shoes.

Click. And another pair of shoes is on the way.

Christina pokes around Pinterest and makes a new board, "Brunch Places." It is going to be a long year of monthly Sundays if the only thing she has to look forward to with Nora and Leanne is conversation. They might as well try some new restaurants and maybe do a tour de Bloody Mary. She finds a list of the best Bloody Marys in Boston and pins each of these restaurants to her brunch board.

She sighs and slips into an unfamiliar state of relaxation. Lightning-fast Wi-Fi can bring on a state of nirvana for Christina. Finding answers is her meditation. She enters *float* into Google and finds five images of inflatable swimming pool floats and three of them have dogs on top of them. Adorable. Wikipedia's first entry mentions *float* as a bartending technique, which inspires Christina to go back to her Bloody Mary search.

After almost two hours of mindless internet deep diving, Christina stretches and closes her laptop. She can close her eyes and fall asleep with ease, having stayed online until it physically hurts to be awake any longer. She has won the nightly game of chicken she plays against her swirling thoughts. These monsters could cause insomnia if she doesn't outlast them by staying online with the TV blasting. Victory for Christina once again.

Her immediate deep sleep shatters when Lilly yells her name.

"Christina? Where are you?" Lilly's voice comes from her bedroom.

By the time Christina wakes up, her feet have already taken her sprinting down the short hallway to find Lilly.

"Mom? I'm here. What is it? What is it?" Christina asks, barely breathing and gasping for air.

Lilly has gotten herself dressed.

"I want to go for a walk," she says.

Despite Christina's best efforts, Lilly's night has become day.

23

"Girlie, I told you. Listen to Maeve." Maeve shakes her head. "*Always* listen to Maeve."

Christina holds her second cup of coffee and she may bite the hand of anyone who attempts to take it from her. Who would do such a cruel thing? This dark roast coffee appears to be all Christina has left of her soul.

Maeve insisted on driving Christina and Lilly to their appointment at Dr. Breyer's office. She said Christina was too sleepy to be behind the wheel. But really, Maeve wanted to go along with them to hear the doctor's advice firsthand.

"I let her sleep in that *one* day," Christina says. "Just *one* day."

"It's okay, we're gonna fix it," Maeve says. "Lilly, wake up, hon. We're almost at the doctor."

Lilly snoozes deeply in the back seat of Maeve's Toyota Camry. It was the first car Maeve ever bought brand-new, and it still looks and runs the way it did when she drove it off the lot in 1999. She paid cash. Maeve doesn't like to owe anyone anything.

"Can you wake her up?" Maeve says to Christina, who is barely awake herself at 10:45 a.m. It has already been a long day. Christina's morning started at 6:00 p.m. when Lilly woke up from her daylong nap—for the fourth day in a row.

"No," Christina says. The ability to be polite was not ground up and filtered into her coffee cup, so Christina has none of it. "I don't want to."

Once Maeve has parked the car, waking Lilly from her deep sleep in the cozy back seat takes a good amount of time. Dr. Breyer is patient about their tardiness when they stagger into his office. His office decor implies that he's not a man who has any sense of time anyway. He has a Garfield comic strip tacked up on a corkboard behind his desk. The black-and-white print has turned to yellow. It's from way back when people still read newspapers and called cartoons "the funnies."

"Lilly, it's pretty good that you're able to sleep so much during the day!" Dr. Breyer congratulates Lilly. She smiles.

"I have to work and I can't be up with her during the night," Christina says. "Do you have any advice on switching her back to night sleeping?"

"Circadian rhythms are tough for people like Lilly," Dr. Breyer says. "Right, Lilly?"

Lilly agrees because Dr. Breyer is easy to agree with.

"It's good that she's still sleeping so consistently even though it's not when you want her to be sleeping," he says. "Eventually, you might start to see a twenty-four-hour waking day for her with one-hour naps throughout the day and night."

"What? Wait . . . wait," Christina says, not sure if she heard that right. "*What?*"

"It's pretty common with the illness," Dr. Breyer explains. "It disrupts the sleep-wake patterns."

Maeve distracts Lilly with a *Real Simple* magazine as she braces for the coming explosion. And here it is:

"Holy fucking shit," Christina says. That coffee this morning didn't have a poker face ground into it either.

"Okay, Lilly, let's go for a stroll!" Maeve says, already halfway out the door with Lilly and the July issue of *Real Simple* from three years ago. There's no harm in accidentally stealing this magazine today—no one needs a watermelon-and-mint salad recipe when there's snow in the forecast anyway.

Dr. Breyer can speak more frankly without Lilly in the room. Still, he understands Christina's temperament by now, so he chooses his words carefully.

"I know you have everything under control, but there's no harm in exploring residential care options for later. That way, if the time comes—and maybe it won't—you'll know just what to do right away and you won't have to start from scratch during a crisis moment. Most people just look into it for peace of mind," Dr. Breyer says. "Getting information doesn't mean you are making a decision."

With more sleep and her usual swagger, Christina could have had a laugh about this. She could say "I'm not most people" or "peace of mind can suck it."

Instead, she says nothing for a really long time.

Dr. Breyer comes around his desk and sits beside her.

They both say nothing together for an even longer time.

"Okay," Christina says. "I'll look into it."

"Okay," Dr. Breyer says. He scribbles onto a Post-it note. "My mom went to this one. She liked it."

"Did you like it?" Christina says.

"Of course not," Dr. Breyer says.

Back in Maeve's car, Christina closes her eyes.

"I have to sleep when we get home," she says.

"No problem," Maeve says. "Lilly and I will go for a walk. A very long walk. If I keep her active during the day, that might help. We'll keep her moving."

"Good idea," Christina says. "I have to get to the office this afternoon after I nap. I have to just focus. Mom and work. That's it."

"And your brunch too," Maeve says. Christina slips into sleep in the passenger seat without Maeve noticing. "It's time to lean on those friends of yours, girlie."

Listen to Maeve. Always listen to Maeve.

24

Leanne returns to work on a Monday without her helmet. Her protective gear today takes the form of a decidedly bright pink blouse popping underneath a new fresh green cardigan. She bought both items in vibrant colors at the J.Crew outlet online two weeks ago, before everything turned gray. Today, she dresses it up with a glittering statement necklace—the statement being, "Don't ask where I was last week. I'm fine. Look at how colorful my clothes are. My mood is stable and I'm not on the brink of a meltdown at all. Isn't it obvious? Shut up and get back to work, you nosey bitch."

"Bonjour, mon amie!" Katherine says, saving Leanne right away from any potential nosey bitches.

"Hi!" Leanne presents a demeanor to match her bright and sunny attire. She rides the momentum of cheerfulness and attempts small talk. "How's Corfu?"

"I don't know," Katherine says. "I've never been there, have you?"

"I mean, your dog?" Leanne says, confused.

"Oh! Aha! Cor*bu*." Katherine laughs. "I should have understood, that actually happens a lot. Rhona and I named him after Charles-Édouard Jeanneret-Gris."

Katherine and Rhona clearly suck at naming dogs.

"Oh," Leanne says. "Sorry, I didn't get that."

"No one gets it!" Katherine says. "We thought it was so obvious, but I guess not many people know. He's the father of French modern architecture. He's better known as *Le Corbusier.*"

Worst dog name ever.

"Ah. Corbusier. Corbu. I see," Leanne says.

"A little obscure, but that's us," Katherine says. "That *was* us."

"When did you break up?" Leanne says, embarrassed that she's worked with Katherine for so long and never knew anything about her love life. That's the kind of talk that turns coworkers into friends. Leanne worries—maybe they hadn't been friends all this time?

"Never. She, uh, she's gone," Katherine says. "Elle a parti."

It's been seven years and Katherine still can't talk about Rhona in the past tense—at least not in English.

It would have been more appropriate for Katherine and Rhona to name their dog Corfu as Leanne had assumed—or after any island, actually. They lived in their own obscure world, using highly intelligent references that isolated them from others but insulated them together. An island can be paradise if you're sharing it with the perfect person but hell if you're left stranded there alone.

Katherine and Rhona did briefly consider naming their dog after the island where they have a summer home, Martha's Vineyard. But Rhona gagged at the thought that people might presume their dog Martha was named after Martha Stewart, to whom Rhona referred as "the biggest dyke ever." They ended up with a male dog, so the point was moot. It was all for the best. Even though Katherine continued to go to Martha's Vineyard every summer after Rhona was killed riding her bike on its narrow roads, Katherine still didn't want a little namesake running around. Corbu was the perfect name, and Katherine loved that she and Rhona still kept everyone guessing.

"I'm so, so sorry," Leanne says, quick to end intimacy. She's sorry all right. She's sorry she brought up a painful subject, as if mentioning it is what made Katherine think about Rhona. Everything makes her think about Rhona.

Katherine knows this grieving widow dance very well. The next piece of choreography in this sequence is to comfort her dance partner by shifting into an "I'm okay" vibe. She glides into it with grace. And in French.

"Allons-y, chérie," Katherine says breezily to Leanne.

"What?" Leanne says, startled.

"Walk with me to class?" Katherine says.

"Oh," Leanne says, regaining her composure. "Sure."

"Are you all right?" Katherine says.

"Of course!" Leanne says.

"I'm glad you took some extra time off last week," Katherine says.

"I wasn't feeling well," Leanne says. "I, uh . . ."

"Say no more. Everyone needs time for themselves," Katherine says. She accepts that Leanne is dancing too. "It's good to just push the reset button on your brain every once in a while."

"Yes. Reset button, that's a good way of putting it," Leanne says. "I worked on my art."

Leanne hears the words come from her mouth and she's immediately mortified by her own candor. *My art? Who says stuff like that? You're delusional! You don't have art!*

"Merveilleux!" Katherine shouts. "How lovely. That must have been restorative."

"You know what? It really was," Leanne says, realizing it for the first time. Katherine's enthusiasm quiets that voice in Leanne that scolded her for telling Katherine about her art.

"I didn't know you were an artiste!" Katherine says. "Quelle surprise!"

"Oui, je suis une artiste," Leanne says.

Katherine stops walking to behold Leanne Version 2.0. She's impressed that Leanne has finally uttered words out loud in French. And Leanne can't believe her first audible French words presented such a deep confession.

"Et en français? Lalalala! Mon amie!" Katherine says as she loops her elbow through the crook of Leanne's arm. "Bon retour parmi nous."

Welcome back, indeed.

25

"I'm not gonna take advice on how to drive from ya, girlie," Maeve says, stopped at a red light with Christina acting as an unsolicited copilot.

Maeve doesn't like turning right on red, and Christina has been known to turn left on red . . . and straight on red, and U-turn on red. They sit at the traffic light waiting—two drivers with one wheel.

"You drive like my husband—like you ain't afraid ta die," Maeve continues.

"I didn't know you were married," Christina says.

"I'm not. He's dead," Maeve says. The light turns green and Maeve turns right. "That's why he ain't afraid ta die."

They've gotten into an active routine in the last few weeks since Lilly's sleeping trouble began. Every morning, Maeve and Lilly wade in the shallow end at the YMCA pool while Christina swims her laps. Maeve finds their interactions to be more tolerable when Christina has done her swimming. The cool water keeps Lilly from surrendering to sleep in the late morning.

Christina can't defend her driving skills in her sleepless zombie state and her conversational filter is gone.

"Oh, so your *husband's* last name was Carney," she says. "That explains half of it."

"Half of what?" Maeve asks.

"Your Irish name," Christina says. "Uh, not that you can't have an Irish name because you're . . ."

"There are black people in Ireland you know," Maeve says.

"Oh, of course," Christina says quickly. "I hate that *some* people assume that . . ."

"I'm just kiddin' ya, girlie. There aren't," Maeve says. "Why you so touchy?"

"I'm not!"

She is.

Christina unconsciously fears, as many educated white people fear, that if she's not the first one to spot racism, then she might be racist herself. Christina never knows exactly when, why, or how she can be racist, but racism doesn't go with her well-informed-pro-everything-that-is-liberal-and-just outfit. And thus, educated people like Christina will never be fully educated. You can't learn what you think you already know.

It's a reasonable question though—why would a woman with an African accent have such a specifically Irish name? It's a long story and since Christina doesn't ask, Maeve spills out the short version.

"I always say, 'I'm African by birth, American by country, and Irish by marriage.'"

Christina still has questions about her first name, but lets it go. Ultimately, Maeve's name doesn't matter, but her story does.

Maeve was born in Burundi with her eyes wide alert from the moment she was born and she pretty much stayed that way for all of her infancy. At her naming ceremony when she was seven days old, her mother called her Mutarambirwa, meaning "the one who never gets tired." She lived up to her name as a kid, always working harder than the other girls and taking care of her younger siblings—all five of them. She was strong, quick, and clever.

One night when she was nine, she was awake late as usual and went outside to check on the family's goat, who had been making a lot of noise. She was far from the house, but she heard her mother whisper calmly, "*Kirukanga*." She turned to look for her mother, because it sounded like she was right beside her ear, telling her to run.

"*Kirukanga*."

She obeyed, running back home. When she saw her house in flames, she heard her mother's soft voice again, "*Kirukanga, kirukanga*."

Maeve saw six men, one carrying a bat, two others carrying machetes, the others in the shadows. This time, she heard her sisters' voices, *kirukanga*, and her father too, *kirukanga*. They were so loud and so clear. Their voices were coming from the trees and so she ran toward them.

She heard her grandfather join the chorus and then her auntie. All of them told her to run. Last, her grandmother's resonant voice boomed into her ear. Her grandmother's voice demanded something different, and seemed to harmonize with the others. "*Courage courage courage*," but this word, in English. Maeve didn't know this word.

When she found brief safety in the next village, her feet finally stopped and so did her family's voices. She was surprised to see they weren't with her.

She kept moving and made her way to a refugee camp in Tanzania. She still has no idea how her family died exactly, because she didn't look back during the attack. She worries they died in the fire—could she have pulled them to safety? Someday, she'll understand that they were already gone by the time she reached the safety of the forest and that's why she could hear their voices whispering as if they were right next to her ear, "*Kirukanga, kirukanga*," urging her to run as fast as she could.

Adults dismissed the details of her journey through the trees. They said it must have been the rhythm of her feet, the swishing of the brush, and the wind in her ears that made the sounds she heard.

Maeve accepted that she couldn't retell this story, but she didn't accept the adults' explanations. Because really, what's more fantastical, the leaves and the wind making that noise or the voices of her dead family? Come on. Talking leaves? Be real.

In the camp, there was a volunteer teacher named Maeve Laughlin, who taught English. The children were happy to learn greetings and common sayings, but this tireless girl from a village in Burundi had one question: "What is *courage*?"

This girl with no family was the first to get an educational grant for refugees, and she made her way to the United States as a teenager. Of course, there weren't enough letter squares on the American government paperwork for a name like Mutarambirwa Ntezahorigwa. Where she grew up, everyone's name told a story or announced a quality about them. And by her estimation, her newly shortened name, Mutarambi Ntezhori, was now merely a collection of random letters.

She so wished there were more boxes on that form so she could have a full name that had proper meaning. Later, she saw there were more boxes on her college application, but these boxes demanded she categorize herself by race.

Courage. She was sure going to need it in America too. She gave herself a new name that told a story, Maeve. And to her, this name meant "woman who understands the meaning of the word *courage*."

She later met and fell in love with Dennis Carney, a bus driver from Dorchester. He was a widower without children, and he loved the texture of Maeve's voice and the generosity of her smile. Maeve worked as a home nurse for Carney's mother, who had gone mostly blind and partially deaf. His mother had assumed that a woman with a name like Maeve would be a gal from the old neighborhood, so she encouraged Maeve to marry her son. Carney loved Maeve and everything about her and spent the rest of his life telling her so.

And that is how a girl from Burundi named Mutarambirwa Ntezahorigwa became a woman from Dorchester named Maeve Carney.

Christina should ask. Maeve wants to tell her.

26

Leanne puts even more effort into her brunch wardrobe today than she usually does. That's because it's Saturday and today's brunch is with Melanie and Fabiola—her friends from the Ladies' Volunteer League.

The LVL does not outwardly require its members to break ties with nonmembers the way that, say, Scientology does. In fact, it's usually the nonmembers like Molly who are likely to trail off a friendship with a member, the way one would trail off the sentence that begins "I cannot *even* . . ." Molly always became enraged by any antiquated organization that still referred to women as "ladies," while Leanne considered herself as a "lady" exclusively, first and foremost. It's possible, in this way, the LVL could have become the demise of their friendship. Molly had the good sense to die before this conflict became fully expressed.

"So it's a sorority?" Molly asked when Leanne dragged her to the introductory session after they graduated from college.

"No!" Leanne said. "It's a women's philanthropic organization."

"This kind of spin doctoring is also how beauty pageants still get to be a thing," Molly said. It should be noted, the application for the LVL requires a headshot as well as a full-length photo.

At the time, Leanne pretended she didn't hear the comment. She thinks about it a lot now.

When Molly was Leanne's maid of honor, Melanie and Fabiola

"took point" on her bridal shower because, as Leanne put it, "it's really just more their thing." Mel and Fab asked Molly to simply bring the champagne. Naturally, Molly loved this delegation of duties because she typically avoided showers of all varieties: bridal, baby, and for a time, she even avoided actual showers. Molly's patchouli phase was short-lived for obvious reasons. Her attempt at dreadlocks failed pretty quickly, and she decided to dye her hair purple instead. Her mom was so relieved that she had given up on dreadlocks that she happily helped apply the Manic Panic dye to Molly's freshly washed hair.

"I don't care what color it is," Mrs. Granger said at the time. "As long as it's clean."

At Leanne's bridal shower, Fabiola offered to lend Molly her cardigan right before the group photo was taken—because it was "chilly," Fab said. Molly declined and said she was comfortable (temperature wise). Fabiola ultimately became more direct and insisted that Molly wear long sleeves "to cover up—just for the photos at least."

For some, it was offensive that the entirety of Molly's failed love stories were spelled out in tattoos on her left arm. While Leanne had been falling in love with James, Molly had been falling in love too—and falling in love and falling in love and falling in love and . . . It was easy to lose count. Breakups always followed. Molly collected this artwork to depict each blissful time she was swept away by love and each subsequent time it knocked her down. Long after her first lotus flower tattoo, she was covered in ink and heartbreak—from her shoulder all the way down to her wrist. Some people might say they'd "give their right arm" for a chance at true love. As a leftie, Molly didn't see this as much of a sacrifice, so she gave her left one. Only her hand remained completely unmarked, with the hope that she would someday add one final tattoo—a band of ink on her left ring finger.

Evidently, such artwork didn't blend well with the contrived bridesmaid moment Melanie and Fabiola were trying to create. Molly went along with their request to cover up because she loved Leanne more than she disliked those lame bitches and cardigans on hot August days. Molly wore Fabiola's cardigan for the rest of the shower. Once someone comments on your body, it sure is "chilly" after that. Melanie was mostly appalled by Molly's tattoo of a woman's beautiful breasts on the inside of her wrist. Melanie and Fabiola concluded that these breasts must have belonged to a lover. Had they asked Molly, she would have told them—the breasts were actually her own. She had gotten this homage to self-love when she decided to be single for a while. ("A while" translates to about six weeks for a love-obsessed woman whose lifespan was only thirty-four years.) The corresponding breakup tattoo in that love story depicts the time Molly broke up with this fake version of self-love. It's easy to love the good parts, she realized during her affair with herself. Finally, it was time to break up with her best qualities and love the flaws instead. She got a tattoo that encircled a jagged scar on her shoulder. Melanie and Fabiola assumed this circle with arrows pointing to it was a tribal symbol conjured up during an ayahuasca ceremony. (Molly had one of those too.)

Melanie finally did ask Molly what the circle with arrows meant while they were killing time before Leanne's final wedding dress fitting.

"It means 'look at my scar, isn't it cute?'" Molly said.

Melanie didn't get it. That's Melanie.

When Leanne puts the final touches on her outfit for today's brunch, she reaches for a cardigan in case the restaurant is drafty. Molly never told Leanne about the chilly bridesmaid sweater incident, but Fabiola thought Leanne would want to know. Fabiola told the story as if she and Leanne would bond over a quirky acquaintance's antics.

"Classic Molly," Fabiola said, as if she knew.

The memory now causes Leanne's knuckles to lock. Her hands strangle the nubby blush-pink cardigan while her eyes assault a neatly folded stack of cardigans of every color.

In a swoop of righteous wrath, Leanne excavates the pile of sweaters as if she's a human backhoe. It's not a flattering thing for a woman to be compared to, but that's what Leanne is—a machine designed to trench the earth, tear up concrete, and make way for new things.

And she's angry. Yup. This backhoe is angry.

The cardigans land in the trash, where they belong.

She pins on the "feminist AF" button Molly gave her before the Women's March. She hopes these "ladies" ask her what *AF* means.

℘

The ladies who brunch meet up at a crisply decorated bakery café that makes Leanne feel as if she is living in a Nancy Meyers movie. It's a lovely escape from the no-frills diner where she usually brunches with Nora and Christina.

The conversation flows along the safe surface of reality TV and online shopping. It's light and easy to be with Melanie and Fabiola— which is everything that's right about their friendship, but also everything that's wrong about it.

Minutes into the brunch, Leanne's sinuses want to yawn with a weird urgent sleepiness. If she were in an at-home place with her best friend, she would simply sink into her seat and say "night night."

Unfortunately, she is in an environment where she can't sink into her seat. Instead, the Nancy Meyers bakery compels her to sit up straighter, lilt her laugh more, and elongate her vowels. She lifts her large latte cup and nods intently while Melanie talks about the "settee" she wants to get for her "foyer."

"Check my Pinterest page, I need opinions!" Melanie says.

"Oh, show us now! We're *dying* to see it," Fabiola says.

Melanie's arm is twisted enough by this. She taps away at her iPhone where photos of the settee are locked and loaded.

It gives Leanne a chance to order another giant and necessary coffee. While Fabiola gasps over the photos, Leanne's mind wanders. Is her grief so deep that she can't enjoy anyone's company anymore? Or has she outgrown these friends? Her mind wanders to her usual brunch companions. She doesn't like them either. Maybe it's depression. Maybe she doesn't like anyone. Maybe no one likes her. Maybe it's okay to have fake friends as long as you know they're fake? Christina keeps her fake friends in a corporate compartment, and Nora has the good sense not to have fake friends at all. Which one of them is right? Both? Neither?

"Hey. Have you talked to Steph?" Melanie says, leaning in. When a person leans in and asks this kind of question, they're not looking for an answer so much as an invitation to dish.

"No, I've been so busy," Leanne says.

"Okay, you didn't hear this from me," Melanie says.

Danger. Gossip ahead.

"She"—Melanie pauses for effect—"is becoming. . ."

Oh dear. More suspense-building pauses. What could it possibly be?

". . . a yoga teacher." Melanie sticks the landing on this strangely huge news.

"Not as her *job* though, right?" Fabiola is incredulous. "Wait. Tell me she didn't quit her *job*."

"Uh huh," Melanie says. "She did."

"I thought her husband wasn't working?" Fabiola says, very (fake) concerned about her (fake) friend whose husband is now a side item on this gossip menu. They're dishing so much, they're going to need extra plates.

"I don't know, maybe he's doing some consulting?" Melanie says.

"Yoga teachers get paid," Leanne says. "It *is* a job."

"I mean, I guess," Melanie concedes. "But . . ."

"Well, she does love yoga," Leanne says. "If I could make a living doing—"

"As a hobby though," Fabiola says. "I can't understand how some people just flit away their education and career and try to make their hobbies a full-time thing."

"Kind of irresponsible," Melanie agrees. "As if she's going to be able to make a living! And what about maternity leave? What about when she wants to have kids? Can she get maternity leave? Benefits?"

"Irresponsible," Fabiola concludes.

Suddenly, these two women are nothing more than talking cardigans to Leanne. And they have to go.

While Melanie and Fabiola squawk on about Steph's new career and potential bad choices, Leanne hatches a plan. When she gets home, her cardigans will land in a more poetic final resting place. Leanne imagines what she'll do with those cardigans. Will there be scissors involved? She thinks it all through—weighing out the best and most dramatic way to destroy them. She wants them out of the house. And today is the day. Planning her spontaneity gets Leanne through the rest of the boring brunch.

When Leanne returns home, she finds the overflowing heap of cardigans in the trashcan. She scoops them up, squatting like a sumo wrestler to ensnare every last one of them in her full-body grip. She marches out to the garage and dumps them into the town-issued curbside bin.

She dusts her hands against each other in a completed task clap— as if she were in a cliché commercial where she has just finished some pesky household chore. She's nearly reached her back door when Melanie and Fabiola's venomous words about "hobbies" toot-toot in her train of thought.

Not good enough.

Fueled by a wave of genuine spontaneity, Leanne marches back into the garage. She rescues the cardigans from the bin and flings them into the backyard fire pit. Exhilarated, she grabs the lighter from the grill that James forgot to cover up after last night's steak. *Why doesn't he ever cover up the grill?* God dammit, she's furious.

The cardigans burn.

Those motherhumping cardigans.

Leanne lets the fire blaze on while she goes back inside the house. She knows she's supposed to pay attention to safety. She knows she's supposed to be careful about the types of things she burns in a fire pit because of the noxious smoke it can cause. She knows she's supposed to monitor a backyard fire. She's decided, though, that "supposed tos" in life must finally burn away with every fiber of those sweaters.

Of course, somewhere inside, Leanne's act of defiance is tempered by an awareness of the fire pit's design for safety, especially when surrounded by cement and snow. This was hardly the most reckless act ever taken in a fit of passion. But for Leanne, this is a big one. She gets credit.

Leanne returns to her closet, satisfied to see the space on her shelf that her sweaters left behind. She fills the space with Molly's sparkly silver helmet.

It won't keep her warm during a drafty brunch or icy bridal shower the way a cardigan would, but it will perhaps help keep her head on straight.

27

"Where's your leash?" Nora asks Fred, while she rummages around her apartment.

Fred doesn't reply. He does, however, whimper the message that it's been too long since his last trip outside. Sam walked Fred while Nora was at work, and somewhere in between, the leash has gone missing. She'll have to text Sam.

Hi. Where did you leave the leash?

Fred dances beside the door, and Nora becomes desperate. She loops an extension cord through Fred's collar, and regards herself the MacGyver of dog walking.

Sam chimes in.

hi!!!!!!! How are you? the leash should be beside the door on the hook?

Nora has no time to respond. Fred pulls on the extension cord. It's time to go.

Extension cords are not designed for distance, so Nora and Fred are back indoors not long after Sam's follow-up text arrives.

Crap. leash in my bag. So sorry. I can drop it off. be there in 10.

Ten minutes. Oh dear, that will not do. Nora hasn't mentally prepared for a visitor and neither has her hair. She types a frantic reply.

No, that's okay. I fashioned a leash out of an extension cord. We'll be fine until tomorrow. Thank you, though.

An immediate reply from Sam.

The MacGyver of dog walking!!! Go you!

Nora scrolls back in their text thread to see if she typed it or merely thought it. It turns out, it's the latter. He may have some sort of special powers, she concludes.

Nora catches her reflection in the mirror. It's not as bad as she thought.

"I can work with this," she tells Fred and her reflection.

She types,

Actually, the leash is a short-distance solution. Any chance you're in the area? I can meet you?

She still has real pants on. Might as well.

Sam's reply is instant once again.

YAAAAAAAAAA.

e

Nora has had more beer tonight than she's had in an entire year, which is to say, she's had two beers. Sam suggested they meet at the brewery near Nora's house because that place makes the most outstanding French fries in the world. Nora took a when-in-Rome approach to brewery dining when the waiter took her drink order.

"A beer, please?" she said. The waiter simply brought her his favorite amber instead of making this brewery rookie feel unwelcome by demanding she order more specifically.

Sam took a when-in-a-brewery approach and ordered a whole flight so he could sample every variety.

Now, Nora has consumed two beers' worth of Sam's infectious laugh. She feels dizzy and brave. She's unclear about whether her head feels buzzy from beer or from Sam.

"I've been curious. Which tattoo were you?" Nora asks, hoping that he wasn't the dragon.

"I wasn't on there, actually," Sam says. "Not a Hall of Famer."

"I thought she got a tattoo for all of them," Nora says. She hears it out loud and cringes.

"*All of them.* Yeah, there were a lot," Sam says. "I knew the dagger and the pogo stick. Both of those guys were on my rugby team."

"The pogo stick," Nora says. "Yeah, I don't want to know."

"I asked her. It's not what it sounds like," Sam says. "She got the pogo stick tattoo because when she was with him, she felt like she was going to fall over if she stopped moving. She couldn't have stillness and be balanced at the same time with him."

"I shouldn't have said that. It was insensitive. 'All of them,'" Nora says. She's been so consumed with awkwardness that she wasn't even listening to the pogo stick explanation. Too bad. It's a good one. "I'm sorry."

"Don't be! I took it as a point of distinction, being the only one who didn't get a commemorative tattoo," Sam says.

"Maybe she just didn't get a chance, before she . . ." Nora says. "Since you were the last, I mean."

"I wasn't the last," Sam says.

"What?" Nora says. "You were there at the end. In the hospital and the funeral."

"Of course," Sam says. "She was my friend."

Sorrow eclipses the light spirit of Sam's face. Nora had no idea that such sadness was part of the emotional repertoire hidden in those bright eyes. He sniffs and chases away grief as quickly as he can.

"What about the peanut butter and jelly one?" Sam asks. "I didn't know that guy."

"Oh, that was a breakup tattoo. The guy was allergic to peanuts and she thought it would be a fun way to kill him," Nora says. "Death by PB&J."

"Good one," Sam says. His laugh is back. It never strays very far.

Nora soaks up his smile, shocked by how much she missed it during that brief moment when it flitted away. Nora has discovered Sam's capacity for sadness, but she is absolutely sure she never wants to see him fade into sorrow again.

Sam makes friends he never intends to lose. That's why he stayed on after his four-month romance with Molly ended.

When they broke up, he said, "Okay. Too bad you're stuck with me."

Only Sam could say such a thing without prompting a restraining order. His mouth smiled but his eyes cried and it was all too tempting for Molly to take him back. It was too late though. Molly had already broken his heart in a way that he didn't know about. Molly was not made from the same loyal flesh as Sam. Molly's flesh was covered with the marks of other men, and before she realized the friendship she had in Sam, she'd already designed her next tattoo.

Molly did a lot of things that Nora didn't understand, and when it came to her best friend, Nora found it easy to accept things she couldn't comprehend.

Until today.

Today, she cannot accept that any woman would choose to chase the joy off this man's beautiful, kind face, even if for a minute.

28

Faceless executioners, sent to secure the survival of the species, raise their weapons to destroy all women who are unwilling to procreate. Leanne begs for her life and for her child's life. She sees a little girl hiding nearby. The firing squad lower their guns, curious to know—was this woman pregnant? They seem relieved that they won't have to kill her. Leanne opens her mouth, but her voice is gone. She can't explain herself and the little girl has disappeared. No one seems to be listening anymore—they're killing more innocent women. She has to confess, no, she is not pregnant but she knows she has a child. Where was that little girl? Finally, Leanne's voice squeaks out three words: "I'm a mother!" It wasn't good enough. There had to be a baby. She feels bony hands lower a noose over her head and the rope waits around her neck . . .

Leanne wakes with the nagging feeling that she forgot something very important.

She transitions from the tumultuous world in her mind to the flat one where James lies beside her, still sleeping. Leanne's arms are raised up over her head when she wakes—her first indication that she might get through the day okay today. The second indication is that she actually wants to get out of bed for a change. She'd better get up fast, before James wants to launch the next mission in Operation Offspring.

She's not in the mood.

In the bathroom, she sticks a wired sensor in her mouth before brushing her teeth. She clicks a few buttons on an overpriced fertility monitor to determine her ovulation schedule for the month. While the wand measures the electrolytes in her saliva, Leanne catches her own reflection in the mirror and remembers that very important thing she'd forgotten: there had just been a noose around her neck.

The execution dream floods back to her.

Leanne becomes preoccupied with the specifics. Why did they switch murderous tactics mid-execution? What kind of sick mind did she have? How many ways can a person be killed in their own dreams? In dreams like these, there was always a little girl hiding somewhere nearby. Leanne optimistically uses the little girl's presence as psychic evidence and plans the mystical moment when someday, she'll get to tell her daughter, "I knew you'd come, I saw you in my dreams."

The monitor dings, registering today's electrolyte reading. It confirms that today Leanne is ovulating. Leanne stuffs the monitor back in the vanity drawer. If this thing works correctly, she will have a baby in about thirty-nine weeks, and she'll only have to have sex with James once or twice to accomplish it.

She's already running late this morning. They'll have to wait until tonight.

$$\mathcal{C}$$

"Bon anniversaire!" Katherine presents Leanne with a birthday card as soon as she arrives at work.

Leanne is genuinely surprised.

"I know it's not until next week, but the workshop starts Thursday so I wanted to get it to you in time," Katherine says. "The painting class was sold out, but I got us into a sculpting class instead. Les artistes!"

Leanne opens the card and sees she's been registered for a four-week series at the Cambridge Center for Adult Education. She didn't realize they were at the knowing-each-other's-birthdays stage of friendship just yet. Leanne feels an immediate burden from Katherine's generosity. Instead of enjoying the gift, she wonders right away whether she's worthy of it. Her gratitude turns to worry. How will she reciprocate?

"Thank you!" Leanne says, hoping her show of manners is big enough. She anxiously scrolls through the birthday calendar in her mind and decides it's official—she's a rotten friend and doesn't know when Katherine's birthday is.

"It was selfish of me. I have been wanting to take an art class, and if I signed up alone, I'd probably just blow it off and watch TCM or grade papers," Katherine explains. "Now you have to hold me to it."

Perfect. Leanne has a mission. She's not taking an art class; she's not receiving a gift. She's helping a friend.

That's how Leanne presents it to James and Joan later that night when they have dinner.

"It's sweet actually," Leanne says to them both, trying to head her mother off before the judgment begins. "She wants me to go with her to an art class at the CCAE. It could be fun."

"How long is the class?" Joan asks, exhaling as if this were a prison sentence.

There's a go-to adage for optimism versus pessimism: "Some see the glass as half-empty, and some see it as the glass half-full."

Well, Joan will see a glass with water in it, subconsciously conjecture that at any instant she might be shrunken down to less than half-glass size by someone who is out to get her, which by her estimation is everyone. She'll imagine that her tortured fate is to drown in the half glass of water because she never learned to swim. And then, looking at the half glass of water, she will reflect aloud (in a non sequitur to everyone around her) about how lucky her children are for having a mother like her who paid for their swimming lessons.

So, yeah. That's who Joan is.

"Four weeks?" Leanne says, looking again at the card. "But if we like it, we can continue—it's monthly, I think."

"Well, I wouldn't make any long-term commitments," Joan says, as if anyone asked. The last long-term commitment Joan made was to a smart bob haircut and a subscription to the Talbot's catalogue thirty-five years ago. They're still going strong. "You'll have plenty to do soon enough."

"That's probably why I should do this kind of thing now," Leanne says.

"Yeah, if it's only four weeks, why not?" James says.

"Again, if I like it, then who knows?" Leanne repeats.

Joan laughs.

"You're starting with this again?" Joan asks. "James, you're not into this artsy-fartsy stuff, are you?"

"No," James answers. Based on the shifting position of Leanne's jaw, he course corrects. "Well, I mean, I have no skill, so I'm not into it like Leanne is, but, it's cool."

"Once you're parents, you can't just be *cool*," Joan says. "You have to be responsible."

"It's not irresponsible to take an art class, Mom," Leanne says. "It could be therapeutic."

"What do you need therapy for?" Joan snaps. "What are you saying?"

"I'm saying," Leanne starts. She knows it's not worth it. "Never mind. I'm—"

"I did the best I could!" Joan says. "When you have a daughter of your own, you'll see. Everyone always blames the mother. You'll see."

And, here we go.

"Okay, Mom," Leanne says. It's still not worth it.

"Joan, I don't think Leanne was suggesting anything," James says. It's as if James is new here.

"It's fine. Forget it," Leanne tells James.

James doesn't forget it. "She just misses Molly," James says to Joan.

"Don't you think we *all* miss her, James?" Joan says, melting into a thousand forced tears.

Anyone with an even slightly well-calibrated bullshit meter can see through these histrionics. There's a part of Joan who's relieved she no longer has to battle with Leanne over her friendship with Molly. This friendship has been Leanne's only act of defiance in life so far. Joan wanted her daughter far away from what she perceived as Molly's wildness, mouthiness, and bad influence.

Thankfully, Leanne could see that Molly's wildness led to bold adventure, her mouthiness to outspoken advocacy, and that the goodness or badness of Molly's influence was just a matter of Joan's blind opinion. All along, it's Joan who's been putting dangerous ideas into Leanne's head—ideas that Leanne is not talented, not lovable and, worst of all, not free to make decisions for herself.

Leanne can't bear Joan's tears over Molly's death. She wants to run from the table, but it will only cause more drama. She ends it. "Forget it," Leanne says. "The classes were a gift, so I *have* to go. It's the polite thing to do. It's only four weeks. And then it's over."

Silence.

"Well. Just don't get carried away," Joan says, picking up her fork again. She forgets to dab away a final imaginary tear.

While chewing his steak, James hums a song that's been stuck in his head all day. It's the Giant Glass jingle.

"Who do you call when your windshield's busted . . ." James sings to himself, seemingly unaware that he's saying the words out loud. Breaking awkward silences have become his specialty ever since he started joining these two mismatched women for dinner on a regular basis. "1-800-54-Giant! One eight *hundred*!"

Leanne wants to slap his stupid face. Naturally, Joan finds his antics adorable. She incorrectly assumes he's mocking Leanne. And while most mothers would hate for their sons-in-law to be so cruel, Joan relishes it, as long as it means he might be in some way pledging his allegiance to Team Joan.

Leanne glares at James.

"Oh come on, Leanne. So now you're pouting?" Joan says, releasing an exhausted snort. "Really. You're making everyone uncomfortable."

James continues to hum. If he stops now, it might trigger another fight in which Joan blames Leanne for making him uncomfortable or stealing his joy. If only James had been this committed to keeping the peace at the beginning of this dinner. James just keeps on singing.

Leanne suddenly sympathizes with women who are driven to murder their husbands.

ɞ

While James brushes his teeth before bed, Leanne considers the beeping fertility monitor and her ticking ovarian clock. Neither are as loud as her blaring resentment for her husband at this moment. Operation Offspring will have to wait until next month.

And so, before James can finish flossing, Leanne rolls over and goes to sleep . . .

Leanne is trapped in a burning house and she can't find her prized scrapbooks. All her memories and lists will be destroyed. These photos and letters cannot be replaced. One book catches fire and she feels the memories tingle in her mind and disappear. If she doesn't rescue these books, she'll forget her whole life. She throws them out the window and they waft safely to the ground. Her past and her plans are safe and sound—but her life is still in danger. She climbs to the windowsill and hopes the dream's gentle lack of gravity will float her to the ground in the same manner. But there's something still missing. That little girl is hiding again. Leanne sees the girl's shoulder and long hair peeking out from behind a closet door. Leanne calls out to her, but the girl is too scared and she won't come out. Leanne can't leave her behind. She opens the closet door just before the flames consume them both. She finally looks at the little girl for the first time and sees her own face.

29

Tinkly bells typically plink gently when a student arrives at Golden Eye Yoga, but when Christina opens the door, the bells herald her arrival with a loud crash. She thrashes the door open just as a huge gust of cold wind sucks the door back. She overcompensated for the wind when she pulled the door with all her might. But the comedy gods stopped the wind just at the right moment, sending bells flying and Christina tumbling into a graceless heap on the floor. The tinkly bells land at the calloused feet of the Yoga Instructor. Full-time yoga ends the reflex to flinch when something like this happens. It also chases away any concern for pedicures.

"Hi! I'm here for the nine o'clock class!" Christina says at a volume that suggests she's never been in a yoga studio before.

Freshly dressed in designer athleisure, Christina carries a yoga mat that screams rookie—still packaged in its original plastic shrink wrap. The yoga mat arrived just yesterday from Amazon after a late-night online shopping session. Every night is a late night for Christina and Lilly now, and therefore Amazon gets many 4:00 a.m. visits from Christina, who uses cyber errands to stay awake. *Late* is an odd term for a caretaker, when the night is just another shift in a twenty-four-hour waking day. Christina has vowed to confront the next woman who claims Christina "doesn't know tired" simply because she doesn't have children. She knows tired. Christina's tired isn't balanced by hope for the future, joyful giggles, and messy snuggles. Christina's tired won't grow up and pass through this sleepless phase. Christina's tired will only get worse until it's replaced by complete loss. Christina *knows* tired. And she will sue anyone who dares to suggest otherwise.

"Of course," the Yoga Instructor whispers. She has the soul of an ancient, the face of a baby boomer, and the body of a millennial. Her impossible physique and serene presence make a strong case for yogic living. "The first class is free, so why don't you go in and set up your mat and we'll get started soon," she says. "We'll start in Savasana."

Christina, always preoccupied with punctuality, assumes that "we'll start in Savasana" is yoga speak for "we'll start in a jiffy."

Christina goes on to ponder whether anyone uses the phrase "in a jiffy" anymore. The answer is surprisingly yes. Sam said it last year, and of course, Molly made fun of him. In all fairness, it slipped out of his mouth and surprised Sam himself as much as everyone else who heard him say it. Without pause, Sam repeated the phrase as an immediate incredulous question.

"In a *jiffy*? Did I just *say* that?"

If there's ever an opportunity for a laugh at Sam's expense, Sam wants in on it and will be the first person to point out his own foolishness. The jiffy incident only made self-deprecating Sam use the phrase on a very regular basis from then on.

Christina rolls out her yoga mat and, because it's brand-new, it curls up at the corners. She flips it over to the side with the solid color so the curling will stop. From now on, she'll always have to make sure the patterned side is down because it has touched the always-sweaty yoga floor.

Christina takes a cue from the other yoga students who are lying flat on their backs with their eyes closed. Christina fits in, though she still doesn't know that this is their first pose—Savasana.

The other students' ujjayi breathing provides a sound similar to Christina's Brookstone ocean-sound white noise machine. The digital ocean sounds can sometimes lull Lilly to sleep if Christina is lucky. In a jiffy, the waves of breath hush Christina to sleep right there on her yoga mat.

Christina's snoring has a rhythmic drone that easily blends into the tonal sounds on the Yoga Instructor's class playlist. Her throat makes a buzz that sounds like a swarm of bees. Molly heard this type of beehive sound coming from a wat in Chiang Mai during an impromptu trip with a man she later commemorated with a tattoo of a honeycomb. While monks chanted in meditation, the beautiful tone resonated through the area and she felt it buzz through her sternum and ribs. The sound made her want to lie down on the grass and sleep, but within seconds of hearing the sound, she no longer needed to—she felt rested and restored. The sound filled her up. She told Christina all about it, but Christina only heard a third of it, becoming distracted when Molly used the words *fully nourishing.*

"Tell me more about the food," Christina said.

Christina feels a gentle tap on her left shoulder.

"Hey?" a gentle voice whispers. "How was that for you?"

Christina opens her eyes, in utter confusion. It's been quite a while since she's been whispered awake. The ambiguously aged Yoga Instructor perches on her tiptoes in a low crouch, balancing effortlessly beside Christina's yoga mat. Christina scrambles to sit up in the now-empty yoga studio.

"I'm sorry, I must have dozed off," Christina says. "When does class start?"

"The next one starts in fifteen minutes, if you want to stay."

Christina looks for a clock in this place, but since most people come here to escape that sort of thing, Christina's impulse to mark her experience with minutes and hours goes unfulfilled.

"Did I really fall asleep?" she says, beginning to remember where she is, but still not grasping *when* she is.

"It's what you needed," the Yoga Instructor says. "Stay as long as you want. I just wanted to make sure you don't have any other commitments because I don't think it was your intention to stay beyond the end of class. Is that right?"

"Oh fuck!" Christina ruins this moment by projecting herself into the next—one where she's late for brunch with Nora and Leanne. "I gotta go."

℮

"She says she's just parking and to go ahead and order," Nora says to Leanne, without looking up from her text. "And she wants coffee."

They almost got away with skipping last month's brunch when the first Sunday fell on New Year's Day. Leanne had politely offered to reschedule, but Christina countered that they should "just get it over with and grab a coffee." One of the few places open on a holiday was the Dunkin' drive-thru on the Pike. They shivered outside their parked cars, and toasted to the New Year before going their separate ways with to-go cups. If only it could always be that simple.

Now it's February and once again, they have to just get it over with.

Leanne waves to try to get Diane's attention. They've all become regulars at Sunnyside's, but they are certainly not Diane's favorites.

With coffee pot in hand, Diane chats away with the old cockers who will take full advantage of the bottomless cup of coffee policy at Sunnyside's. She's quick to warm up their coffees with fresher brew and even quicker to snub Ms. Cobb-Salad-No-Bleu-Cheese.

Christina misjudges another gust of wind and overcommits to opening the door of Sunnyside's. The door flies open. Christina blows in even more loudly than she did at Golden Eye Yoga. Luckily, the din of a busy diner makes her less conspicuous this time—though not by much.

Diane cuts off the chitchat and hustles to the table to pour

Christina a coffee. Christina lands in the chair and lifts the coffee mug in one motion.

"Thank you, Diane," Christina says. "Thanks for ordering for me, Nora."

"I didn't," Nora says. Diane is already headed back to the kitchen.

"Oh! Can I have a—"

"Tea with the bag out, yup," Diane calls over her shoulder.

"And a—" Leanne tries.

"Orange juice. Got it," Diane says.

"I don't know how you get people to do stuff without asking," Nora says. "It's as if you're a Jedi."

"I don't know what that means," Christina says, nerd-shaming Nora even though Jedis are obviously mainstream. "Hey, have you ever done yoga?"

"Absolutely not," Nora says, fitness-shaming Christina right back.

"I did it with some girls from"—Leanne thinks better of mentioning the Ladies Volunteer League—"from work. I thought it was a little boring. You?"

"It's too soon to tell," Christina says. "I will say it was relaxing."

"What kind of yoga was it?" Nora asks.

Christina is saved from having to confess that she slept through her entire yoga experience. Diane arrives with orange juice for Leanne, hot water for Nora, and a readiness to expedite food orders for Christina.

"What're ya havin' today, ladies?" Diane asks.

"Oatmeal, please," Nora says.

"Eggs," Christina says.

"Cobb salad," Leanne says.

"No bleu cheese," Diane adds.

"No. I'll have the bleu cheese. Thank you," Leanne says. "And may I have some coffee too, please?"

"Decaf?" Diane clarifies.

"Regular," Leanne says.

Nora and Christina each check the other's facial expression. They accidentally lock eyes for half a second, which is three seconds less than normal friends do. A half second was enough. Everyone at this table now understands that if there had been a pregnancy before, there is no pregnancy now. The social code in the case of potential lost pregnancy dictates that Nora and Christina wait until Leanne brings it up. She never will. And so they'll never talk about it.

As far as Leanne is concerned, ordering a caffeinated coffee that she doesn't want and bleu cheese that she doesn't even enjoy is her way of talking about it. She's just announced in the language of coffee and cheese that she will no longer be alluding to a pregnancy. And that's that.

"I'd like to try yoga again," Leanne says. This is a lie, but it's a way back into the conversation they were having before all the subtext happened. "Maybe I'd like it now. What about you, Nora? Any chance you'll ever try it?"

"Absolutely not," Nora says again.

"Diane!" Christina yells out to get Diane's attention.

"Yeah?" Diane yells back from the kitchen, continuing their loud exchange.

"Got any muffins?"

"I'll check!"

Leanne shrinks when the other regulars crane to get a look at this bossy muffin gal. Leanne slightly shifts her body to make it clear that she wasn't the one who had been yelling. When Nora finds herself in the crosshairs of a salty old dude's studying stare, her body language is less subtle. She freezes and points to Christina.

The Salty Old Dude nods once and resumes his game of keno. Now they have an understanding. When Nora surrendered Christina, she made an alliance with God-knows-who. Nora sips her tea as if she's trying to drown herself in it.

"They hate us here," she says.

"Yeah, they do," Christina says. "I don't know why. At least Diane likes us."

"She likes *you*," Leanne says. "I bet she spits in my food."

"Nah, she's too busy," Christina says. "She doesn't have time to do that."

"Thanks," Leanne says, feeling no comfort at all.

"Yeah, don't worry," Nora says, trying to make up for Christina's insensitivity. "There are much grosser things she could do to your food besides spitting in it anyway."

"And again, thanks," Leanne says, with newfound longing for Melanie and Fabiola, whose response to Leanne is always enthusiastic agreement, however disingenuous.

"Here's a bran one," Diane says, delivering the muffin to Christina. "We got blueberry, but it don't look so good, so I tossed it."

"Thank you," Christina says, rummaging around her purse. "This will do."

Christina produces a birthday candle and a lighter. She plunks the candle into the bran muffin, lights the wick, and musters a smile.

"Happy fucking birthday to yooouuu," Christina sings. Adding an expletive deflects intimacy very nicely in this situation. It's common knowledge that the only way to be kind and still authentic to someone you dislike is to throw in an f-bomb while smiling.

Melanie and Fabiola would have brought overpriced fluffy cupcakes to brunch and definitely would have steered clear of profanity, but Leanne appreciates Christina in a new way. At least Leanne knows exactly where she stands with Christina.

"Oh thank you!" Leanne says. "You remembered? This is so sweet."

"No, not sweet, but definitely packed with fiber," Nora says. "Which I hear you'll need as you age."

"I ordered you some monogrammed stationery, but it didn't get here in time," Christina says. "I figure you like that kind of thing, right?"

"I do," Leanne says, with an ache in a place she can't access in present company. She and Molly had been pen pals even though they spoke almost every day. It was a "lost art," Molly always said. Leanne has no idea how she'll use the stationery now.

"I'll give it to you next brunch," Christina says.

"Thank you, Christina," Leanne says. "That's so thoughtful."

"I made you something," Nora says, presenting an envelope.

Leanne opens a custom-made birthday crossword puzzle. Nora peppered the puzzle with artists, figuring Leanne would know every answer. She thought of making the Sunnyside Café the centerpiece of the puzzle, but accepts that Leanne can barely tolerate their regular brunch place when she's more of a mimosas-with-brunch type of person. Instead, Nora chooses a more aspirational center word. The clue: Melodramatic Eatery.

"This is . . ." Leanne shakes her head. She can't force any of her usual over-the-top gratitude, and she doesn't have to. "Thank you."

"Wow. Your gift is way better than mine," Christina says. "Good thing I'm not competitive."

Nora and Leanne make no effort to control their outburst of laughter.

"What?"

They laugh more.

"Okay, you two are hilarious, whatever," Christina says, grabbing the bran muffin. "I'm eating this. Yoga makes me starving."

"Hey!" Leanne says, laughing. "Gimme back my birthday fiber, damn you!"

Christina defiantly takes a bite. As a peace offering, she fishes a pen out of her purse to get Leanne started on her crossword. Leanne starts with the longest word in the puzzle.

"Thirty-two Across: Melodramatic Eatery," she reads out loud.

"Sarah-Bernhardt Café!" Christina says as fast as she can. "Boom!"

"Good thing you're not competitive," Nora says.

"Aha! Sarah Bern . . . that . . . *fits*!" Leanne says, looking over the other clues. She decides to keep the rest for herself. She'll finish it later. "This is perfect."

"Glad you like it," Nora says. "And I hope you get to go there someday."

"Paris?" Leanne says. "Me too."

"Me too," Christina says, but this time she's not one-upping. She really means it.

30

"Les artistes!" Katherine bellows from almost a block away. There she is, an elegant aging Francophile, carrying on like an MC's hype man. "ARTISTES!"

Katherine waits for a callback that she's just not going to get from a gal like Leanne. Leanne has barely been able to confess to herself that she is going to take an art class. The last thing she is going to do is yell about it in the streets of Cambridge, Massachusetts.

"Hi!" Leanne says, bracing herself for the fierce hug she's about to get from her new friend.

"Are you excited for sculpting class?" Katherine says. She doesn't wait for a reply. "I am!"

"Yes," Leanne says.

"Chérie, take off your rings," Katherine says. "I left mine at home. We're going to get messy."

Leanne hadn't planned to take off her rings. She'd packed her mid-class snack, filled her travel mug with herbal tea, and smoothed her hair into a fuss-free bun. She forgot she'd have to get her hands dirty. Her nails have just been freshly manicured. This whole situation is not ideal.

"Put them in your wallet," Katherine suggests. "You'll be careful with your wallet. You know they'll be safe in there."

"Good idea," Leanne says, impressed with this improvisation. She makes a mental note to improvise more. She makes good on this resolution right away. "Oh! I can just put them on my necklace."

"Voilà!" Katherine says.

Leanne arranges her rings on her necklace as she walks with Katherine to find the art studio. Leanne tucks her necklace safely inside her black turtleneck, which she's decided is what an artist, beat poet, or someone of that ilk would wear.

In the front row of class, Leanne readies her pen and paper to take notes, ever the good student. That's when she sees the art teacher for the first time and discovers that a black turtleneck is not what an actual sculptor wears—at all. For one thing, white clay and gray slime will mark a sculptor's well-worn clothing. For another, the physical act of sculpting works up such a stinky sweat, it renders winter garments of any kind completely absurd. This particular sculptor wears a tightly fitted tank to barely cover his chest, leaving his strong arms and filthy hands free to generate a heat of their own while he molds the clay of his latest creation. His head is shaven almost bald, and his black tattoos are smeared with remnants of his latest work in progress.

Though Leanne's wardrobe has proven to be a poor choice for this sculpting class, she's still glad she's wearing a turtleneck when she meets Reggie for the first time—if only to conceal the wedding ring dangling from her necklace.

31

"We're *just* looking," Christina says for at least the eleventh time since she and Lilly got in Maeve's car this morning. "It's good to—"

"It's good to have information," Maeve says along with her. She's heard this phrase looped in a constant conversation pattern for a week—a very long week.

Maeve and Christina recently took all the interior doors off their hinges after Lilly accidentally locked herself in the bathroom and couldn't figure out the lock to get back out. After that incident, doorknobs made Lilly panic and soon the doors did too. Even the doors had to go.

On Tuesday night, Christina was up late preparing for a deposition. Lilly watched a *Cheers* marathon on Nick at Nite in bed while Christina hunched over her laptop in her meditation seat. Christina has been sleeping in this seat. She thinks it's meditation, but in fact, it's emergency shutdown sleep. She always positions her seat to block the doorway of Lilly's room, so that if (when) Christina does fall asleep, Lilly can't get out of the room without Christina knowing about it.

It's often the case that if you don't take the time to indulge in dreams, then the dreams will indulge themselves in your waking consciousness. The dreams find a way.

Christina was typing on her laptop when she saw the letters fall into a senseless pattern. She began counting the letters on the screen, as if that's what you do with letters and words. She lost count of the words, and she felt her seat rise up. The floorboards beneath her had sprung open and Times New Roman letters poured out of the wood like a billion carpenter ants. She shrieked and gasped awake.

Her barely open eyes caught the next level of a nightmare: her mother leaning out her fourth-story window. Christina didn't react at first as she processed whether or not this was part of the dream too.

But this part was real.

Christina lunged to grab her mom and slammed the shutter-style window shut. It turned out Christina had been asleep for ten minutes, and during that time Lilly had gotten up to get some water. She was looking for a cup in the "cabinet."

"How did I not think of that?" Christina said to Maeve the next day. Every day, it seemed there was a new, unimaginable unforeseeable danger. "The window! The fucking *window!*"

"She sure keeps us on our toes, doesn't she?" Maeve said.

On Wednesday, Lilly took a nap during *The Price Is Right*, and at the office, Christina fought to stay awake during that deposition. That's the day when Maeve slid Dr. Breyer's assisted living pamphlet into Christina's pile of mail. Maeve arranged the envelopes and papers so Christina would think she had come across the pamphlet randomly on her own. That's how it had to be.

Today, they arrive at Covington Meadows Estates, and Lilly is the first to comment on this once-austere manor that has been turned into assisted living units.

"This is gorgeous!" Lilly says.

"A good start," Maeve says, mostly to herself.

"I went to a wedding here once," Lilly says.

"No, Mum," Christina says out of habit.

"Yes, Lilly," Maeve says. "I read in the materials—it used to be quite the venue. Before that, one family lived here. In this whole entire place. Can you imagine?"

Christina flips through the pamphlet to verify this. She realizes she has only merely skimmed these papers, unable to fully commit to reading the brochure, let alone the notion that she would drop her mother off to live somewhere other than her own home.

"It was the daughter of this woman my mother was friends with," Lilly says. "I didn't like her much. Mother said I should go because I wasn't meeting any men at school."

"No men at Harvard?" Maeve says. "I thought it was all men back then."

"It was mostly," Lilly says. "That's how I got Mother to let me go to school there."

Lilly laughs.

"Any nice ones at that wedding?" Maeve says.

Lilly is gone again.

"Mum?" Christina says, always hoping she can just beckon her back an instant after she's gone.

"Well, Lilly. This place is apartments now. Wanna go see it with Christina?" Maeve says, getting out of the car and out of the way.

Covington Meadows' marketing materials accurately represented the lifestyle at their facility, but the "active seniors" briskly walking in the photos were clearly just silver-haired models in their sixties. In real life, residents of Covington Meadows move a lot slower and are closer to a hundred than to sixty.

"I'm not sure she belongs here. My mother is only sixty-five," Christina says pretty loudly near a group of octogenarians. She does this kind of thing every once in a while when a rare moment of vulnerability makes her cagey. Thankfully, only a few of these octogenarians hear her and, even better, they don't give a shit.

"We have people closer to her age here too," an admissions representative named Nancy says in a pleasant voice. Nancy can handle Christina—she deals with hostile and terrified children of aging parents all day long. "And many people come here because we have such a great memory care staff, so when people need that, they can transition very easily."

Nancy's pleasantness deflates Christina's bravado.

"I think she'll need to start there, actually," Christina confesses.

Nancy already knows this. It's Nancy's job to know this. Her bigger job is to let Christina take the lead.

"Why don't I introduce you to some of the staff?" Nancy says. "I'll be right back. I'm gonna grab Shelly. You'll like her, Lilly."

Nancy could easily summon Shelly by phone, but she skillfully senses that Christina needs a minute alone with her mother.

As soon as Nancy leaves them, Christina sinks down in her seat and calls off the attack dogs that seem to be bursting out of her chest. She feels one of the octogenarians watching her. Christina can barely stand the shame, but she looks back at this nice lady anyway and receives a forgiving wink. She wishes she hadn't been so nasty about their age. But lucky for Christina, women who have lived more than eighty years already—yeah, they don't waste their time caring who's younger than they are. At some point, the game changed from youthfulness to longevity and now they're winning.

"I went to a wedding here once. A wonderful man asked me to dance," Lilly tells Christina again.

When she attended that wedding, Lilly was freshly annoyed by all the men she usually met at Harvard. They'd read Chaucer, they'd read Keats, they'd even read Proust. But none of them had ever read a room. They could study all day, forever, and still, none of them would ever learn from books what Lilly was looking for in a man. She was looking for intelligence over knowledge. "I told him no, but if he could recite the soliloquy from *Hamlet* backward to the tune of *Bonanza* while turning cartwheels, then I would let him take me out for coffee the next day."

"So, how did that go over?" Christina says, smirking. She perks up in anticipation—Lilly's punchlines always have a second punch.

"Oh, you remember," Lilly says.

Christina's shoulders drop in disappointment. It seems Lilly has mistaken Christina for someone who attended this wedding with her back in 1960-whatever. But then Lilly adds, "You remember how well your dad knew his Shakespeare, sweetheart."

Christina never knew exactly how her parents met and she never asked. Because George died so suddenly, Lilly coped with grief by staying in shock for the rest of her life. Her protective mind seemed to lock away the story of her husband and his death. Her mind did a great job of helping her forget the pain while she carried on raising her daughter and conquering her career. Then eventually, her mind began locking away all the rest too.

Christina's father died when she was young enough that if they were to meet again, she would only be able to identify him by sonnet and smell. Even though questions about him ate away at her, she sensed that Lilly wanted to keep quiet about it.

Christina's internal timer dings—it's almost time for Lilly to slip away again. Lilly can feel it too. Christina has a lot of questions she wants to ask first. Lilly intuits the most important question nagging her daughter and she answers it just in time.

"This is my favorite place," Lilly says. "Thank you for taking me here."

32

Nora hunches down at her desk to confide in her notebook after a meeting with John and Susan. She'd made a case for telecommuting, but it blew up in her face.

"So excited about our new office mascot!" John chirps at Nora as he passes her office on a Segway. The office isn't very large, yet John parades around this way, as if he's riding into the Colosseum. The first time he rode on one of these dorky things, he did a whole chariot bit and Susan started calling him "my gladiator." Apropos of nothing, they were vacationing in Colonial Williamsburg at the time. The trip was precipitated by a conversation with a millennial who extolled the coolness of a certain Brooklyn neighborhood where he'd spent the weekend visiting friends. John and Susan promptly planned a weekend getaway of their own. It's unclear whether they ever figured out they went to the wrong Williamsburg. The only thing the two Williamsburgs have in common is that they both sell hand-churned butter. (Though only one of them calls it "artisanal.") It probably doesn't matter. John and Susan felt young and alive the whole weekend. And ever since that trip, John rides around on a Segway because he thinks it turns Susan on. And it does.

How vile.

Nora smiles until John glides out of sight to find another victim to infect with his sickening enthusiasm. Then her notebook gets an earful.

Fred is not an office mascot!!! Epic fail. Should I call Sam?
No, you should text him. No, email him. TEXT. OK, I will
text him, but what should I write? Maybe we should hang
out tonight. Is that weird? I just saw him yesterday. I'm not
supposed to see him again until Friday. This can wait until
Friday. No it can't. I should call him. Text him. I'll text him.

Nora texts.

Hi. How do I get out of bringing Fred to work with me?

Her phone rings. It's Sam.

"Hi?" she answers, fumbling to stuff her Bluetooth earpiece into place.

"Hi there," Sam says. "Let me guess. Yawn and Snoozin' want to liven things up by having a dog around the office?"

"I guess so," Nora whispers. "It's my own fault. I tried to leverage Fred as a reason to work from home. They said to bring him in."

"Epic fail!"

"That's what I'm saying," Nora says.

John coasts by Nora's office again on his nerd chariot.

"A poochie in the office!" John says. "It's gonna be so lit!"

"Did he just say 'poochie'?" Sam asks.

"Yes," Nora confirms.

"And 'lit'?"

"Yes."

"Want me to come rescue you?"

"Yes."

"Okay, see you in ten. I got the poochie with me," Sam says.

"Lit," Nora says.

They hang up and Nora feels the closest thing to euphoria a person can feel in an office that's so full of happy horseshit. Case in point,

John now has Susan riding with him on the back of his Segway. She hangs on to his waist as if he's a young Marlon Brando on a motorcycle. Right. And they're both wearing bike helmets. Going one-half mile per hour. Indoors.

Nora's sex drive momentarily weighs the pros and cons of suicide—John, Susan, a Segway, and two bike helmets add up to five marks in the pro column. Too late though, Nora's sexual will to live is on his way over to the office to "rescue" her. Nora gags at the idea of calling Sam her gladiator. But is Sam her hero?

It looks that way.

Sam will no doubt gallop into her office on a noble steed called intelligence and wield a fierce sword called humor.

Her hero. Sam.

Nora bursts through ten minutes of work so she can leave the office and not come back. She exits without goodbyes and races down the stairs onto the sidewalk where Sam pretended to fall out of the trapdoor that time at the office mixer.

Sam said he would be here in ten minutes and Nora can rely on it.

Right on time, Sam hurries in her direction, waving with one hand and steering Fred with the other. When Nora walks toward him, her shoulders relax the way they do when she first gets home after work. Seeing Sam, she feels that lightness of being in perfect solitude after a day of navigating a world full of strangers. Typically, this sense of arriving home prompts Nora to remove her pants. (It should be noted as a great victory that Nora does *not* remove her pants right here on this sidewalk.) In such relished privacy, Nora greets Sam with a mindless kiss.

She startles herself, having lost her sense of place, and remembers that she's in public. (The good news can't be overstated: her pants are still on.)

Sam notices none of her hesitation. He pulls her back in and kisses her until she forgets where she is again.

Through closed eyes, Nora senses that Sam has raised his arm up near his head in a hallelujah. Nora opens her eyes and lands a perfect high five for the first time in her life.

"*Nailed* it!" Sam says, deflecting any awkwardness that lingers after a first kiss.

If not for the high five, one or both of them would have snort-laughed or blasted out some sort of adolescent giggle that would have ruined the whole moment anyway. At least now they can both pretend they're laughing because of the "nailed it" joke and not because they just shared a perfect first kiss together and they're both super giddy about it.

Nora snort-laughs anyway because she just can't help it. Sam scoops her up until he almost lifts her off her tiptoes. Then Sam kisses her again. Because he just can't help it either.

℮

On Saturday night, Sam is only seconds away from joining Fred in a chorus of snoring. Their Friday night turned into Saturday morning. And then Saturday brunch became afternoon drinks and then dinner.

"I'm so good at making pancakes," Sam says, facedown in the sheets of his bed.

Even when approaching sleep, he can tell when a woman is about to flee his bed. Nora has wrapped her sweaty body in a scalding blanket because she has had enough exposure today—both physical and emotional. She's got to hide at least a little bit. She overheats with thoughts of guilt and tortures herself wondering whether or not she just crossed a line. She hopes there's a death clause that nullifies Girl Code.

Even Nora understands that it's bizarre to journal while in bed with a man. Desperate, she scribbles in her mind instead. *At what point is it not weird to sleep with your best friend's on-again-off-again boyfriend? Surely I cannot mention this at brunch with Christina and Leanne. What if Christina is right about all her psychic medium bullshit and Molly is watching? Oh gross. Oh my God. What am I doing? This is a mistake this is a mistake this is a—*

Sam's pancake non sequitur jars her out of her thought spiral.

"Sounds like a pickup line, I know, but I think I already picked you up," Sam says, kissing her into the present. "So, I mean, really though, pancakes. I'm super good at pancakes."

"I can't stay," Nora says, bursting free from her blazing hot blanket cocoon. She finds her underwear and T-shirt, and throws them on. "I have a ton of stuff to do tomorrow."

"Ah, yes, the brunch," Sam says, fully waking up again. He sits up and pulls her onto his lap, soaking up all the Nora he can. "How's that going?"

"Oh, we're quite a trio," Nora says, allowing him to assume that "stuff" includes brunch. It's not worth explaining that the only thing she has to do tomorrow is wonderful *nothing*—she has a plan for no plans. "But it's just for a few more months and then our friendship can fade into oblivion again."

"Molly always said if you met as adults, none of you would have tolerated being around her," Sam says.

"Well, Molly and I met young and we turned out very different," Nora says, breaking free of Sam to find her shirt. "Then again, I met Leanne and Christina young too. We turned out even more different."

"Why did you stay friends with Molly and not Leanne and Christina?" Sam asks.

"I don't know that I was *ever* really friends with them, they just came with the Molly package," Nora says, stuffing her distracted head into the sleeve of her shirt before getting it right. "Molly was like a sister to me. To them, too. She never gave up on any of us, I guess."

"I get that. She didn't give up on me either," Sam says. "I mean, we always stayed friends."

"Stayed friends?" Nora asks, losing momentum on her departure. "Weren't you together?"

"Just like, you know, occasionally," Sam says. "But she kept saying we didn't belong to each other. She said it was a line from some movie. 'We don't belong to each other.' Something like that. And she was right. We didn't really."

"It's in *Breakfast at Tiffany's*," Nora says.

"I never saw that movie."

"It was our favorite."

"What's it about?" Sam asks.

Nora doesn't have the energy to discuss nuance at this hour, and she's distracted by the onslaught of another impending guilt spiral. She sits at the foot of the bed.

"Hookers," Nora says, feeling herself drift a little.

"Intriguing. I'll have to check it out," Sam says.

"Actually, that movie is why she named the dog Fred," Nora says, trying to change the subject.

"That's weird," Sam says, stretching out under the covers. "I thought she named the dog after me."

"What?" Nora sits up from her slouch.

"She called me Fred. She said you'd probably call me Fred too, once we got to know each other," Sam says. "Most of the time, I didn't know what Molly was talking about. She had a funny code."

"I have to go," Nora says. "Come on, dog."

Fred wakes up onto his feet and follows Nora around, while she grabs the last of her clothes. Pants are always last.

"What just happened?" Sam asks.

But Nora is already out the door.

33

Leanne began pondering her outfit for the next sculpting class as soon as last Thursday's class concluded. The identity she'd tried to project by way of beatnik black turtleneck was off the mark by about seventeen thousand miles. And it was embarrassing.

If she can buy shirts that are marked down enough, she won't feel guilty about buying brand-new ones only to destroy them with clay and plaster. She looks really good in jewel tones, particularly blue. She hits the jackpot at Target, where there are many to choose from—including an emerald green one with a bateau neckline. Leanne likes to show off her delicate clavicles the same way some women might reveal cleavage.

It sure is a lot of wardrobe fuss for an art class with a work friend. It would smack of common sense to wear one of James's old work shirts or a shapeless smock and just get over herself. After all, sloppy old sweatpants were the kind of thing she always wore to art classes in high school. But those classes weren't taught by Reggie and his gorgeous sweaty man stink. Sure, there's a certain manner of casualness in most art studios, but Reggie's shaven head, meaningful tattoos, and intoxicating pheromones have changed the game. She hasn't admitted it to herself, but Leanne plans to impress Reggie any way she can.

Granted, aiming to impress teachers has always been Leanne's modus operandi. When she was in seventh grade, she had heard that the teacher that year would be Mrs. MacDougal, who was from

Glasgow. Naturally, Leanne made a point to research how to say "good morning" in Scots Gaelic.

Bad news: it's "madainn mhath."

Any guesses on how that's pronounced? Right.

Worse news: Leanne was twelve. Twelve is that perfect age where some girls are still young enough to try unique things. Unfortunately, twelve is also when peers disallow such uniqueness.

Leanne's greeting was kindly received by Mrs. MacDougal but panned by the rest of the crowd. Those brats wouldn't let it go, and they left their mark. Now Leanne is an adult who refuses to speak a foreign language out loud, despite being fully fluent in French.

Mrs. MacDougal became Leanne's biggest champion that year, which made Leanne's desire to impress teachers almost pathological.

A side note about Molly and MacDougal. MacDougal was nice and all, but Molly could barely understand a damn word that woman said. For a while, Molly shamed herself for not being able to understand a dialect within her own language. It further strengthened her belief that she simply didn't have an ear for language. It later justified her poor grades in Spanish, which she studied for the minimum two-year requirement at their school. (The term *studied* is used loosely here.) As an adult, Molly felt vindicated when she saw a Scottish documentary on BBC in which all the locals were given subtitles.

Today, before class, Leanne picked out the perfect Caspian-blue T-shirt from Target, and she plans to pair it with a bohemian ikat scarf that she'll casually remove when she gets to the grubby task of molding clay. Bohemian is the way to go, she decides. Not Beatnik.

It will be difficult for Reggie not to notice her in this T-shirt because Leanne looks outstanding in this particular shade of blue. He has already noticed her though—because she's talented and her eyes light up when he talks about Paris, where Reggie lived for three years, just for the sake of it.

He likes Leanne because her raw talent is beyond that of the bored housewives who usually end up in his class. He likes her because she's radiant when she's lost in a project. He likes her because she's attentive when her friend Katherine asks her a hundred questions (*en français*). Most of all, he likes Leanne because she's so excited to learn and she wants to learn from him. This makes him feel smart.

But for good measure, there's the Caspian-blue T-shirt.

34

Nora wakes up in her bed on Sunday morning and Sam is there. He was there when she fell asleep and he was there yesterday when she woke up. Nora had initially lamented Molly's leaving her alone in the world. But, as it's turned out, since Molly has been gone, Nora hasn't been alone much at all. And it's a pain in Nora's ass.

Without precious solitude, Nora's mind has been constipated for weeks. When not expressed or examined, thoughts like the ones Nora typically purges onto the page will collect and conspire to create confusion.

Nora rolls over in bed and feels a charley horse in her mind. Things are getting too cramped up in that head of hers. She longs for a moment to make a list. If she gets out of bed to retrieve her journal from the desk, she might wake up Sam. Then this magnificent solo moment will be gone.

She moves only her right arm to fumble around her nightstand until her hand feels the familiar weight of her pen. Her hand grazes the book Sam got for her on his way over to her place on Friday. He'd had the forethought to tuck the receipt into the pages in case she'd already read this one. (Of course, she had.) She doesn't care about returning it. That receipt is made of paper. She craves paper.

Nora snatches the receipt and presses her pen into it, rationing the space by writing as small as she can.

what is the

When she exhales in relief, the sound of her breath stirs Fred. Fred's collar clinks against his dog tags—a jingle that usually serves as an alarm clock for dog people. Sam rolls over and Nora grabs Fred to snooze the alarm. It's a close call, but she manages to whisk Fred out of the bedroom before her other companion wakes up.

In her frantic state, Nora has left the paper and pen behind with sleeping Sam.

Nora slides her feet into Sam's shoes and throws on her trench coat. There's no reason to waste these rare minutes of solitude fumbling for appropriate footwear. She clomps out onto the sidewalk with Fred. Nora's getup clearly indicates to Fred that this trip outdoors is strictly business, so he gets right to it.

The rest of Nora's half-written sentence hovers in the air just above her head. She needs to land this word aircraft as soon as possible. *Mayday! Mayday! Mayday!*

Nora scoots Fred back into the house and trips over a three-week stack of unread newspapers—a pile of more unfulfilled promises of selfhood. She's tempted to mourn the neglected newspapers, but in this moment, she has tunnel vision.

Paper. There's tons of it.

She ignores all the printed words on the newspaper and scrawls her thoughts across it with a Sharpie from the junk drawer. This time, her handwriting is large and bold so it can eclipse the type and photographs.

what is the name of the place where Gramps got the coffee cake that time? I wonder if I should go to

"G'mornin', toots!"

Nora jumps as if she's been caught in an indecent, compromising position. In a way, she has.

"What's . . . uh . . . what's up, babe?" Sam asks.

There is no way Sam can pretend he doesn't notice that Nora was squatting on the floor over a pile of newspapers, wearing men's shoes, pajamas, and a trench coat. It's not the kind of thing a guy can unsee.

Nora makes it creepier with a clipped response. "Nothin'."

Nora's hasty and direct trajectory to her bedroom signals "playtime" in Fred's dog brain. He chases her with a wagging tail that just barely clears the closing door.

She grabs her journal and pen before diving onto her bed, as if she's a 1950s movie teen who's about to sing some sappy song about a surfer she just met—only this Gidget is brooding and fitful.

Nora yanks the pen cap with her back teeth and leaves it there to bite down on while she spits words from her pen.

Fred shuffles beside the bed, wondering when the fun will begin. So far, this playtime is kind of a nonstarter.

Nora scribbles her incoherent thoughts into illegible words. The letters spill out, tripping over each other to escape Nora's head and find their freedom on the page. Her headspace has no regard for penmanship—it's not a priority to untwist the letters racing out of her in ink.

Nora ignores the ringing doorbell.

Fred knows this game. At Molly's place, Fred used to dash to the door when a visitor or delivery arrived. But he has figured out that Nora's apartment is different. The way Nora plays it, the doorbell rings and the object is to stay super quiet until the visitor gives up and goes away.

Fred plays to win. He stops pacing and waits in silence.

Nora continues to write in erratic flourishes, but she stops short when she hears a voice respond to Sam's friendly greeting.

Nora's penmanship straightens to form an immediate and clear thought.

Goddamn Francine.

Why did he answer the door?????!!!!!!!!! Doesn't he understand
how things work around here?

Unfortunately, Nora is dressed (undressed) in a manner that
would provide more information than she's willing to share with
nosey Francine, whose vices are virtue and gossip. The combination
of these two only add up to one thing: judgment. Who needs more
judgment on a Sunday morning when you've just woken up with your
dead best friend's sort-of boyfriend and you have already done nothing but judge yourself for weeks?

Nora decides to continue to hide in her room. Sam can handle
Francine. Isn't that the point of having an extroverted other half? To
fend off neighbors? Nora plans to stay quiet and wait for Francine to
leave.

"Is Nora busy today, do you know?" Francine asks Sam.

"Sometimes she has a brunch on Sundays," Sam says. "But I don't
think it's today."

"Oh, perfect!" Francine squeals. "She *has* to come to my Sunday
soirée!"

"No!" Nora says out loud while her body flings itself into a standing position.

Fred responds to Nora's sudden motion. Finally playtime begins!

"Nice. I'll let her know," Sam says.

"No!" Nora says again, wrapping her clothes more closely around
her. She is no longer concerned about what her clothes might imply
to Francine. Nora doesn't care about protecting herself from judgment—she has to protect her Sunday.

When Nora lunges for the door, Fred lunges too.

"Oh, and hey, why don't you come too?" Francine flirts with Sam.

Fred snatches the journal from Nora's hand.

"No!" Nora yells. "No!"

Nora fights a tug-o-war with Fred over her precious journal, while in the next room her Sunday is being yanked away.

"Okay, cool," Sam agrees. "Thanks! We'll be there."

"No!" Nora wrestles with Fred.

She grabs the doorknob with one hand while her other hand clutches the notebook that's clenched in Fred's teeth. Now Fred and the doorknob play tug-o-war with Nora.

"Okay, byyyyyyye," Francine sings.

"No!" Nora frees herself from Fred and flings the bedroom door open just as the front door closes.

It's too late. Francine is gone and so is Nora's Sunday.

35

Molly met Sam at one of those massive wine-bar gatherings where Christina strategically networked her friends into jobs and dates.

Christina always kept the swirl of socialization spinning—pairing off her most fabulous friends into romantic relationships and merging business associates into lucrative (for them) unions. She has been asked many times to be a bridesmaid but always declines, knowing the gesture is merely a courtesy thank-you for the introduction. She doesn't like to wear matching dresses with other women anyway.

Sam was part of Christina's motley menagerie one night when she dared to invite her former college crush, Ted, to one of her get-togethers. Ted brought Sam, whom Christina had heard was a little "different." She figured this was the perfect opportunity to include Molly. Molly was the straw that stirred the drink at Christina's parties, but typically when Ted was around, Christina didn't want Molly stirring anything. That night, Christina thought Sam might keep Molly occupied. She was right.

Christina was confused by Sam because he was one of the few guys who found it embarrassing to mention his prestigious alma mater in casual conversation.

"I don't get it," she exclaimed. "Why wouldn't you be proud of going to Harvard?"

"Doesn't seem like a big deal," Sam said. "My parents went there, my grandfather went there, my sister . . ."

Turned out, Sam was from an erudite, wealthy aristocratic English family. He trained himself to drop his English accent when he was at boarding school by imitating American teen TV dramas. A roommate told Sam it was crazy. It seemed to be such a bonus from the standpoint of attracting women. But in the absence of an English accent, Brandon Walsh didn't have any trouble with the ladies and neither did Sam.

By the time Sam admitted his pedigree, Molly had already offered to get him high, which he'd declined. So that was a little awkward. Molly usually knew better than to offer drugs to Christina's crowd. Sam called Molly "The ABC Afterschool Special" for the rest of the night.

"You're that girl," he said. Then he affected a movie trailer announcer voice. "She makes it all seem so cool and then . . . you're hooked. On drugs. And on her."

That night, Molly went home with Sam and he put Curtis Mayfield's "Pusher Man" on repeat and no, they did not get high, but yes, of course Molly slept with him.

"He's your soul mate," Christina told Molly later. "If you're a person who believes in soul mates, I mean. Which you are. So, you should marry him."

Christina was very eager to close this deal and line up Molly and Sam with her other vicarious romantic achievements. Then Christina added a comment that was Molly's deal breaker. "He's the most normal guy you've ever dated."

Normal was not what Molly looked for in a soul mate. She had the misguided notion that soul mates were supposed to make you feel as if your soul was being torn from your body. They were supposed to conjure that feeling you get when part of you is hovering a few inches outside your skin. While she was sick, Molly looked around her bedside and saw her friends. It occurred to her that the out-of-body feeling she'd had with most guys was really just her soul trying to flee from major douchebaggery. She felt calm and sure with her best girlfriends. These were her soul mates—the ones who were there when everything else had fallen away and she'd been left with only her soul.

With Sam's friendship too, Molly could be quiet and still. She didn't feel the urge to pierce, dye, or tattoo anything when he was around. Sam always made her feel as if she were as normal as he was. But normal is just not who she wanted to be. She fancied herself a free spirit. Ultimately, she was unfair to him—only rotating him into her life when she needed a dose of normal—a dose of Sam, a dose of her undyed, unpierced, unaltered self.

C

Today, Christina took Lilly to a new doctor. Unfortunately, the only thing that impressed Christina about this particular medical errand was the valet parking. The new doctor didn't talk to Lilly at all. He barely examined her before writing a prescription based on which pharma rep had bought him the best lunch.

As Christina and Lilly wait for the valet to take their ticket, Christina feels a pang of regret for being disloyal to Dr. Breyer, even though he was the one who encouraged her to do more exploring.

"You might find more answers," he said. "It's always best to ask around. Nothing personal."

Dr. Breyer wins Christina's respect quite consistently. After all, the smartest people are the ones who know when they don't know.

The valet is nowhere to be found. Christina taps her foot because her body needs to make noise and she might get arrested if she screams and smashes windows the way she truly wants to.

Tap tap tap.

Harmless noise. It doesn't seem like enough. She wants to exclaim out loud about the weird double standard where protestors will rally against medical testing on animals but not bat an eye when the elderly endure experiments with wait-and-see trial-and-error medications.

Tap tap tap tap tap.

If anyone would listen, she would exclaim about doctors treating her mother as if she were a lab rat.

TAP TAP TAP TAP!

She might be able to exclaim about this kind of thing to Leanne and Nora if she had been more open about Lilly's condition. Instead Christina has just put her head down and powered through all the anguish—including her new forced friendships.

Christina's positive impression of a hospital with a valet service wanes—she and Lilly have been waiting way too long. Her angry foot taps louder as she considers her preference for the valet at her office. Louie has spoiled her with swift service. She'd rather just get her own keys and get the car herself at this point.

She hears someone walk up beside her, and when she glances to see if it's the valet, she's so blinded by her own furious impatience that she doesn't realize at first that she's staring right at Nora.

Nora freezes mid-step—as anyone would when encountering a predator in the wild. She wants to pretend she doesn't see Christina.

It's too late. They've seen each other.

Christina panics. She's not ready to be this version of herself in front of Nora. This is the version of herself who's afraid she's failing at taking care of her mom. This is the version of herself who is helpless, angry, and confused. This is the version of herself who doesn't know what she's doing. If Christina were open to sharing this version with acquaintances, then perhaps her circle of friends would still be intact and she wouldn't be floating friendless, watching sitcom reruns every night. Perhaps then she wouldn't, in her lowest moments, feel compelled to reach out to Monica, Rachel, and Phoebe instead of actual real-life human friends.

"Hey, w'sup?" Christina says. It's not a greeting she's ever used on this side of the 1990s, but when she accessed the file in her brain labeled "cool and casual," that's what spilled out.

"W'sup?" Nora repeats, if only to clarify what Christina has just said.

"W'sup!" Sam, just a few steps behind Nora, greets Christina with surprise. The turn of the millennium didn't change Sam's repertoire of slang. He will say "w'sup" until he's a hundred.

It's not possible for Nora to pretend she's running into Sam in the same unplanned way. She tries to work out an explanation where it might be pure coincidence. But it's too late. Nora is busted.

She launches into an explanation that no one has asked for.

"Sam said he makes the best crumb cake and I said that's impossible because the best crumb cake is at the coffee shop here, so we came here to get it," Nora blurts out. "But they don't make it anymore, it turns out."

"So, I win," Sam says.

"Only by default," Nora says. "Well, it was a long time ago, I don't know why I thought they'd still make it."

Nora will never be able to validate her rosy memory of the crumb cake from the coffee shop at the hospital. Nora and Gramps had it just before his diagnosis, and it was the last time food tasted good for the rest of the year. The fact is, the coffee cake was probably just okay. It was from an Entenmann's box.

Through a suspicious side-eye, Christina watches Nora and Sam banter.

"Where's Fred?" Christina asks.

"At home," Nora says.

"We're heading over to get him now and take him to the park," Sam adds.

Christina's left eyebrow shoots up at the sound of "we."

This surprises Nora because Leanne recently launched deep speculation about Christina's Botox use. Either Leanne was wrong about Christina's Botox or Christina's judgy face has just defied science and broken through medically induced facial paralysis.

"Oh," Christina says. "Interesting."

Nora would rather not be the subject of someone else's interest. Being "interesting" is an introvert's nightmare, for one thing. For another, Nora had given herself the day off from guilt over the Sam thing. Christina has put Nora's self-judgment back to work.

Nora turns to Lilly. "Dr. Ford, I haven't seen you since Christina and I were in college," she says, remembering that Lilly could always carry a conversation with easy grace. Nora hopes that perhaps Lilly can wash away this terrible awkwardness. Nora throws out the lifeline. "How are you?"

Lilly can't bring Nora ashore this time.

Having no reference for the former version of Lilly, Sam senses how to talk to this current version of her. "I like your shirt," he says. "Purple is my favorite color."

"Me too," Lilly says. "I'm Lilly."

Christina and Nora unwillingly make eye contact. They are so busted. They face the harsh unspoken truth they've both been keeping—they are not really friends. A friend would confide the details of a sick mother. A friend would share the news of a potentially complicated romance. But they're not friends at all. And now there's proof.

It would be an ideal time for either of them to acknowledge the need for a follow-up conversation. Perhaps Christina could say, "Let's catch up this week" or something breezy that conveys the need to talk about this weird moment. Instead, she deflects to mock Sam's unusual color preference.

"*Purple* is your favorite color?" Christina says. "Really?"

"Yes. I get that a lot. I realize it's not masculine. When I was little,

I couldn't decide whether to like red or blue, so I said 'Can't I like them both?' and my sister—she's a little aggressive—said 'No, that's purple.' So, I said 'I guess I like purple.' And you know what? I do. I like purple." Sam shrugs. "What can ya do?"

"I hate purple," Christina says, having lost her ability to banter about two years ago when she let her alumnae association membership lapse.

Sam takes this in and notices Lilly hasn't been involved in their banter for a long time and she's holding Christina's hand for safety.

"I bet. Breast cancer ruined pink for my mom," Sam says, acknowledging that somehow marketing people have assigned colors to particular illnesses. Maybe branding can save lives? It's worth a shot. "Four years ago. Weirdly, I still like pink even though my mom doesn't like it anymore."

"Pink? And purple?" Christina digs in deeper to insult his masculinity.

"Not *together*," Sam says to Lilly, as if they're the only two people in the world who make sense.

Lilly smiles and offers, "I like pink."

"Thank you," Sam says. "Please tell your daughter not to judge me!"

"I will. She's supposed to be picking me up," Lilly says.

It hangs in the air and the banter flits away.

Sam takes the valet tag from Christina's clenched hand and helps himself to the key cabinet. With Christina's key in hand, he runs to the far lot, pressing the key fob to make the trunk of Christina's car open so he can find it. He holds the fob to his chin, because he read online that this makes it work at a greater distance by using the human skull as an antenna and brain fluid as a conductor. It's troubling if you think about it too much, but it works.

Nora has been able to lie to herself that hanging around Sam is not a betrayal, but reflected in Christina's side-eye she sees her actions aren't totally innocent.

"You could have told me," Christina says when Sam is out of earshot.

Nora sits on the curb so she can be close to the gutter where the rest of her conscience splashes around in a sludge filled with broken loyalty. Nora's tiny stature and baby face make it easy for her to pull off something as childish as sitting on a curb.

"I'm sorry," Nora says. "I don't really know what I'm doing."

"Me neither," Christina says, relieved to dodge any knowing glances from Nora about Lilly. "Do you want to talk about this later?"

"No," Nora says. "Do you?"

"No," Christina says.

Sam returns mercifully fast with the car.

Christina thanks him and helps Lilly into the front seat. She wants to get on the road as quickly as possible. And she'd like to forget this encounter with Nora even more quickly.

"All good?" Sam checks in with Nora.

"Sure," Nora says and reaches for the nearest truth to cover her lie. "I really want crumb cake."

36

For two months, Leanne and James have been on a waitlist to see Dr. Gianetti-Wong—the top fertility specialist in Boston. In their case, however, a generally decent fertility doctor might be just as effective as the very best one. Every month, Leanne pinpoints her day of ovulation, and then during those fertile days, she promptly has a headache, is too tired, has too much on her mind, or is captivated by an episode of *Hangin' with Mr. Cooper* on Hulu.

On her best days, she lies in bed next to her sleeping husband and consults an online due date calculator for the pregnancy she might have if sex were to occur. She constructs the baby's first year of life and all subsequent birthdays. For example, she's sure she wants her child to be born a good distance from Christmas. People who have birthdays in late December often receive presents wrapped in leftover holiday wrapping paper. If they're even more unlucky, their birthdays are forgotten altogether. Leanne really wants her child to feel special. Well, as special as a child can feel when he's merely hypothetical.

She worries about having a child too close to any national holiday, if you get right down to it. Is it fair for a kid to always be obligated to attend Memorial Day cookouts on their birthday? Or Fourth of July parades? What about Labor Day? No one likes Labor Day. Who would want a birthday associated with something so boring? In the fall, she had decided that an August due date this year was also absolutely out of the question. Leanne has been asked to read a poem at her cousin's wedding and she can't risk going into labor. Reading a poem at the wedding of a blood relative she sees only once a year is such an important responsibility. There will always be weddings in August. Actually, people get married in the fall too. It's a lovely time of year to get married. Leanne decides to cross autumn off the list altogether. They'll have too many weddings to attend in the fall for sure.

These musings would imply that Leanne doesn't want a baby. But it's worse than that. Leanne doesn't know how to want anything at all. Wanting went right out the window when Joan told Leanne what color to wear, what songs to sing, what books to like best, which friends were her favorites. Leanne never got the chance to want.

She wonders, did she decide to marry James or did it just happen? James was easy to be around, and there was tons of data on his desirability because every other girl in her dorm wanted to go out with him. Anytime Leanne talked about "taking a break" from James to sow her wild oats, friends told her she was crazy. (Molly high-fived her.) Joan warned Leanne that James might not like her for much longer and that she shouldn't take advice from a person like Molly, whose love life was "a shambles." Leanne assumed most people had better authority on her shoulds and supposed-tos, so she stayed with James. She loved him. She just wondered. Then the wild oats just turned into oatmeal.

And now, there's a new wild oat and he smells of patchouli and danger. Reggie consumes Leanne's every thought. She smiles about things he said in class. She particularly loves the things he hasn't said but would (she assumes) if they were alone together. She once found herself wondering how Reggie takes his coffee. In the ongoing movie that plays in Leanne's mind, the scene couldn't go on until she knew. They were in their favorite imaginary coffee shop, which looked quite a bit like Central Perk. Reggie was running late because he was in the middle of restoring an old barn. Leanne had to daydream-order his daydream coffee. Leanne doesn't know much about her teacher crush, so she fills in the details: *He drinks his coffee with soy milk—no, he drinks it black—no, he drinks espresso. Espresso. Yes. He drinks espresso. He loves the bitterness and it keeps him up all night so he can create a masterpiece after hours. P.S. Fair trade coffee only, please.*

"Any luck with Dr. Gianetti-Wong?" James asks, snapping Leanne out of her before-work daydream on a Tuesday morning. She's somewhat disappointed to be back in her kitchen—far from Central Perk.

"No, they said they'd call when they had a cancellation," Leanne says, thinking that maybe Reggie likes chai tea. *That's so Reggie*, she assumes.

Leanne's untapped imagination is desperate for a chance to create. Her daydreams have taken a few liberties in the absence of actual interactions with this man. (He drinks Dunkin' Donuts coffee—extra cream, extra sugar, by the way.) More dangerous than unused talent is unused desire—creativity's sneaky sidekick. Desire can be such a defiant brat if you ignore it. It will throw your life into upheaval when you make it desperate enough to do so. Leanne has pushed desire so far, it's about to explode.

37

There is a baby at Sunnyside's who is doing nothing to support Leanne's recent ambivalence about fertility. This baby is so cute, she could be in a commercial where the product they're selling is *babies*. It's as if this particular baby has been sent out on a recruiting mission by a cult full of mothers. If there were such a thing as spontaneous conception, then Leanne would definitely be knocked up at this very moment.

"Is there a baby boom going on right now?" Leanne asks Nora. "Seems like there are babies everywhere."

"Huh?" Nora says, awakening from her crossword-induced trance.

"Never mind," Leanne says.

Without warning, the funnel cloud known as Christina whirls into the previously serene coffee shop. Christina, dressed head to toe in overpriced workout wear, looks well rested and refreshed, having just woken up from yoga. She's got a giant Starbucks coffee in hand.

"You can't bring in coffee from somewhere else," Leanne says.

"Oh, it's no big deal," Christina says.

Leanne searches for the words with the most zing. Aha! Here they are. "It's rude."

Those are fighting words. Leanne knows how to push Christina's buttons. They met as kids, so Leanne got in on the ground floor of this button factory.

"Fine," Christina says in that tone that indicates the opposite of fine. Her pronunciation of the word *fine* morphs its meaning into a totally new sentence (or even a soliloquy) altogether.

Christina huffs out the door and paces on the sidewalk slurping her Starbucks. Her glowing mortification can be seen from outer space because she's joined the ranks of other restaurant pariahs like smokers and dogs. Her folded arms telegraph that she is (1) tortured by the freezing cold weather and, (2) not speaking to Leanne ever *ever* again. It's some loud silence out there.

Immune to Christina's antics, Nora resumes her crossword puzzle.

"I don't know what she's so mad about," Leanne says.

"Who cares?" Nora says.

"Well, I think we should care if our friend is mad," Leanne says.

"I mean who cares if she brings in a Starbucks?" Nora says. "And, come on, you're not friends. None of us are."

"How can you say that?" Leanne says.

Christina finishes her coffee with a grand gesture. The last melodramatic sip might as well have been performed by a mime. She slams the coffee into the trashcan and flings the door open. She harrumphs into her chair.

"Okay, here's the deal. I don't know how we're going to keep this brunch thing going," she blurts out.

"What? We have to," Leanne says. "Molly wanted—"

"Yeah, Leanne. I know. But this is too hard. If I don't see you guys, I can just assume Molly is on vacation or whatever," Christina says. "This brunch is a giant reminder. Let's just admit it, we never got together without her before. She's gone and we're all sitting here together, so it's like this obvious gaping hole and I cannot keep staring into that void every month."

Nora continues her crossword puzzle.

"Are you even listening?" Christina addresses Nora.

"What?" Nora rouses from her trance again. "Yeah. You don't want to have brunch anymore. Fine."

Nora's "fine" presents no connotation. She takes care of other matters. "Hey, Leanne," she says, "you know, you can take Fred if you want."

"What?" Christina exclaims.

"I know you wanted him and you're probably better suited to take care of him," Nora says. "And I really don't have the time anyway, really."

"I thought Sam was supposed to help you?" Christina says.

"I'd rather not see Sam anymore," Nora lies. "He, uh, talks about Molly too much and it's just too hard."

"Okay, sure, I'll take him," Leanne agrees right away. Leanne's gratitude for the chance to nurture something overtakes her curiosity about the Sam situation.

Christina seethes.

"You can't give Fred away, Nora. Molly asked you to take care of him," Christina says, aware of her own hypocrisy. "I meant we shouldn't have brunch, I didn't mean for us to trash *all* of Molly's wishes."

"Here," Nora hands off the dog treats to Leanne and reassembles her newspaper. She gathers her coat and bag. Hallelujah, she can be alone again—where she's safe and calm. She'll be done with Sam and Fred and all their slobber—no one trying to kiss her and no one trying to lick her face (respectively). "I'll bring over the rest of his stuff later."

Once Nora is safely out of earshot, Christina explodes.

"CAN YOU BELIEVE HER?" Christina has gone almost full cartoon.

"You can't stare into a void during brunch," Leanne says. "What do you think it's like for Nora to see Fred every day? It's not like Nora ever hung out with Fred without Molly before. Give her a break."

Leanne stands up and bolts out the door, starving for some Fred time. She's excited to have a snuggly bed companion who won't demand offspring.

Christina finds herself alone at Sunnyside's. She wishes she hadn't finished her Starbucks so fast.

38

"C'est tragique," Katherine presents her left wrist, which has been freshly set in a full cast. "C'est des conneries!"

Leanne's week at the office has revolved around daydreaming and Pinterest. Leanne's thoughts are almost always occupied with Thursday night's sculpting class. Then she spends Friday in an internal postmortem, mentally reliving every moment of class, analyzing every nuance of every word and gesture from Reggie. Fred has been the perfect companion for this kind of internal pining. She tried bringing her new dog companion to work to make the days between art classes pass more quickly, but Corbu is not as easy to get along with as his owner. Fred happily agreed to attend doggy day care where there's less drama.

"Oh no! What happened?" Leanne says, awakening from her Pinterest coma.

"I had the audacity to walk on a sidewalk during the winter," Katherine says. "How dare a woman of my age do such a thing?"

"The ice!" Leanne says. "Are you okay?"

Though her reaction is genuine, a large part of her concern is that this injury might affect their class attendance. Can Leanne still go without Katherine? Is that allowed?

"My dignity hurts more than my bones this time," Katherine says. "Well, there goes my sculpting career!"

"Maybe you can still go and use the tools instead of bare hands?" Leanne says.

"Come on, you've seen the pathetic work I do with two capable hands," Katherine says. She holds up her plastered-up hand. "Can you imagine?"

It's true, Katherine's artwork does inspire pity. By comparison, if Leanne's art could be a source of artistic arousal for Reggie, then Katherine's flaccid attempt at art would cause all of Reggie's desirous feelings to hail a cab, ride clear across the country, and walk into the Pacific Ocean with rocks in their pockets. So, yeah. Maybe the icy sidewalk has done the art world a favor. The clay, in particular, may be most relieved that its destiny will now be in the hands of a more talented sculptor.

"There's only one class left anyway," Katherine says. "We had a good run."

Leanne panics. Can she justify enrolling in the next session without Katherine? Signing up for another month of classes will require that she admit to herself that she's felt more alive in these four weeks than she's ever felt in her life, which is to say that up until now, she's been walking dead in jewel-toned cardigans. Worse, it may imply that her life with James isn't enough.

"Let me know how the last class goes," Katherine says over her shoulder on her way out of Leanne's office. "And watch out for the goddamn black ice! Bâtard!"

č

Leanne walks into class and sits at the table in the back for a change. One class left, then it's over. Time to break up. Poor Reggie, he'll have no idea he's been dumped—as is usually the case with men who are unknowingly in imaginary relationships with dissatisfied married women.

"Where's Katherine?" Reggie asks.

"Injured," Leanne says, busying herself by laying out her tools. In the absence of her chaperone, any flirtation would be inappropriate and potentially less innocent than before.

"That sucks," Reggie says, saddling backward onto the folding chair next to Leanne.

Why do cool guys have to sit backward on chairs like this? Oh, it's so they look even cooler, that's why. Reggie's subconscious knows that Leanne's subconscious has seen various John Hughes movies nearly nine thousand times in her life. This convention of backward-chair-sitting on the part of the Cool Guy is deeply entrenched in the synapses of Leanne's brain. A backward folding chair makes Leanne's inner tween squeal. There's a similar phenomenon involving four or five moderately decent-looking guys singing a ballad on wooden stools, but boy bands are not Reggie's jam. Not even close.

She avoids looking at him. He's too close to her body. And she's very busy.

He rests his forearms on the back of the folding chair and then rests his chin on top of them. It looks as if he wants to really listen to her. A *listening* posture? Damn, he's good. Lucky thing Molly is dead, Leanne thinks for the first time. She absolutely would have made some bad choices with this guy.

"You can use her clay," Reggie says. "Start a bigger piece maybe?"

"Sounds good," Leanne says, popping up off of her stool to get the clay. There's no sense in starting a new project, especially one that's bigger than usual. But she agrees because she's only capable of clipped conversation with Reggie today. He's so dangerous, Leanne should be dressed in some sort of social hazmat suit. A Caspian-blue one, of course.

In the absence of Katherine's quips and questions, Leanne finds herself alone enough to concentrate on the pile of shapeless clay. Her preoccupation with Reggie's biceps and lips slip away. She has one responsibility today and that's to be an artist.

Leanne attacks the clay. There's so much of it and she guides her hands along the surface, warming the slab into a softer, more malleable pile. But there's too much of it to manage with her dainty hands. She loses track of where she is. She molds the clay using every bare surface of her body. The art has either granted her some form of privacy or it has stripped her of the need for it. She pulls the clay toward her and embraces the whole mound, the clay warming against her arms, chest, and neck. She's forgotten about Reggie, she's forgotten about her emerald shirt with the flattering neckline. She's covered in clay from the top of her jeans to her beautiful collarbones.

Though she has broken up with her imaginary boyfriend Reggie, art has swooped in for the rebound. Leanne refuses to resist this time.

James understood that this class was a good opportunity for Leanne to be social with Katherine. It was a way of expanding a friendship, which is healthy after so much loss this year. It sounds perfectly practical when it's framed in that way.

Leanne is tired of perfect practicality. The next three hours disappear along with all of Leanne's inhibitions and plans. For the first time, Leanne forgets about what has happened in her life until now and she forgets to plan the future. She doesn't even know what she'll do three minutes from now because it doesn't matter. Her body hovers above the clay and the rest of her—the part of her that has made decisions until now—hovers somewhere outside her body. She's free. And three hours pass in a blink.

Her classmates pack up and say their goodbyes and Leanne finally towels off her neck, having savored every last minute of her time in the studio.

"See you next week," Leanne hears herself say.

She's speaking mostly to the clay, but Reggie responds, "See ya," and blows past her like a hot breeze.

Leanne has tried a lot of new things this year. What's one more? So, it's been decided. Leanne is going to lie to James.

39

Last night, Christina did something before falling asleep that she hasn't done in a long time: she brushed her teeth, she got under the covers, and she closed her eyes. It was the night before Lilly's big move to Covington Meadows, so Christina let her guard down and surrendered her watch post in the doorway. It was the homestretch. Still, just in case, Christina slept in Lilly's bed and held her hand so Lilly wouldn't get up without Christina knowing about it. By the time Christina opened her eyes in the morning, she was clinging to Lilly's whole arm as if it were her life raft. Christina, still adrift in this big decision, anchored herself to her mother as if she could easily float away into infinity if it weren't for the ceiling above her.

Christina slept deeply despite her anguish over the upcoming move and despite Lilly blaring all-night TV. Christina wonders why she ever stayed up monitoring Lilly when she could have been sleeping this way all along. Her youngest memories were of mornings like this—waking up in her mother's bed as a child of a widow often does. She even wonders today why they ever stopped sleeping in the same bed. (Oh, because she's an adult and it's a slippery slope into *Grey Gardens*? Yes. That's why). That's the way it goes when there's an awareness that something is happening for the last time. It's the world as seen through graduation goggles.

"Should we give it a week?" Christina asks Maeve first thing that morning. "Maybe we're onto something here with this sleeping arrangement."

"No," Maeve says, without embellishment. Any softening language would only invite negotiation.

Christina waits for the second half of that answer. There's nothing. Maeve carries on preparing breakfast.

"Well, gee, I hadn't thought of it that way," Christina says, with as much snark as any human can. Christina's sarcasm is meant to bait Maeve into explaining her answer. And because Christina is gifted at poking holes in answers (it's her job, for crying out loud), it would be wise for Maeve to give no further answers.

And Maeve is wise.

"Your eggs are ready," she says.

"I don't want eggs," Christina says, retaliating in an egg battle that has not been mounted.

"Suit yourself," Maeve says, peacefully resisting Christina's campaign for the right to avoid eggs. "Lilly? Time for your breakfast. We gotta get to the pool on time today."

Maeve insists that they keep Lilly's schedule as normal as possible on moving day. Lilly has a better chance of sleeping tonight if she's been active in the pool, and so does Maeve.

The home aide agency that placed Maeve with Lilly has no idea that they're about to lose a client. Maeve can't bear the idea that Christina will be getting calls asking for Maeve's evaluations and recommendations. Maeve can't make the space for interviews for her next job when her dear friend is about to move to a memory care facility.

Maeve has kept professional perspective when caring for her clients. They've always been reasonably older and she sometimes sought their advice, missing the grandparents she revered when she was so young. Then time went on, and the clients became people who were around her parents' age, had her parents lived past their twenties. She wondered what her parents would be like at this age. She was honored to care for these people because she always wished for the privilege of seeing her parents grow to such maturity.

Lilly was the first client who could be Maeve's sister.

Maeve wishes they could have been friends for real and that they hadn't been brought together under such tragic circumstances as a Harvard law professor losing her mind. The sharp reality is that these are likely the only circumstances under which these two could have carved out a piece of life together, occasionally laughing at the same thing.

Their friendship was sealed at the very beginning when they both rolled their eyes at Dr. Breyer's stupid nurse, who stated the obvious "this is going to pinch" as she pinched Lilly's skin for a blood test. That's how friends are made—in that moment when you find validation with one look. It's when you observe the world in a certain way and then find a face looking back at you as if to say, "You're seeing this shit too, right? It's not just me?"

It's never just you. Never ever. There's always someone nearby, if you look for them, who will nod and say, "I see you. We're in this together." And that is your friend—whether it's a lady at the airport you never see again, a coworker you see every day, or a home health aide your daughter hired to care for you.

In Lilly's flashes of clarity, Maeve has always been there to catch her look—especially when it comes to Christina.

They both understand Christina. They have an unspoken agreement to let Christina run out her tornado of words when she feels frustrated and scared. Like all storms, they eventually dissipate if you wait them out.

"These are delicious, Maeve," Lilly says, momentarily clear. "You're quite a talent. I don't even like eggs, but the way you make eggs? I love them."

"I do have quite a talent for eggs. Thanks for noticing," Maeve says.

Christina slams the refrigerator door and cabinets as if she's a brooding teenager. How dare these two carry on as if this isn't the worst day ever?

"Fine! I'll have some eggs!" Christina exclaims. "Gawwwwwwwwd."

Maeve spoons some scrambled eggs onto a plate for Christina. Christina salts the eggs without tasting them first, knowing this is the very best way to insult a true chef. Maeve takes no offense. She knows her eggs are really just as average as eggs are in general. Lilly and Maeve exchange quiet satisfaction, like two parents who have just tricked their little girl into eating her breakfast.

They all finish their eggs in silence.

"I just think that we have to give everything a chance," Christina says, reopening the case for delaying Lilly's move.

"No," Maeve says again.

"No? Just *no*?" Christina exclaims.

"Just. No." Maeve says. "Get your swim stuff, girlie. Your mother and I will be in the car."

℮

Today, the pool is warmer than Christina would prefer it to be. She'd rather swim in a crisp water temperature so she can work harder without overheating. The Y recently expanded group classes to include mommy-and-me classes and water walking, which brings in droves of babies and old people respectively. Neither of these groups like cold water, so Christina and the scant number of other lap swimmers remaining at this pool are shit out of luck. The staff doesn't even bother to put up the lap lanes anymore.

They arrive at the pool just as it opens, and the water is so still and smooth Christina could skate across it if she were a full cartoon character. Unfortunately, she's only part cartoon—the part that's always dialogued with exclamation points and all caps.

Christina stomps along the tiled edge and sends small vibrations rippling across the empty pool. Without lap lanes to contain her, she sets her territory directly in the center of the pool, taking up as much space as she can.

Maeve enjoys the water temperature for the first time. She doesn't love daily pool-going at all, and cold water has been the worst part about the whole thing—worse than the dry skin, the terrible smell of chlorine, and just the general fact of putting on a bathing suit. After all this time, she's able to ease into the water today and exhale instead of holding her breath. She can hang her hands in a normal position at her sides instead of doing that shruggy dance that all humans do in waist-deep freezing cold pool water.

"Isn't this pleasant?" Maeve says to Lilly.

Lilly's face agrees, but her mind is somewhere else.

Christina splashes into the pool and registers her disgust with a loud *tsk* and an exaggerated huff. She puts on her swimming cap as if every bad thing in the world is its fault. It's hard to say how she didn't rip through the latex when she jerked it onto her fuming head.

Christina torpedoes herself away from the pool wall.

There's peace. Maeve squats into the warm water to submerge her shoulders.

"Pleasant," Maeve says.

Lilly faces Maeve and imitates her posture. Their chins skim the water. From outside the pool, they look like nothing more than two pretty lady heads. Their heads smile and Maeve soaks up Lilly's shameless prolonged eye contact.

Lilly's expressive eyes make Maeve wonder sometimes if Lilly is observing more than anyone realizes. Maeve behaves as if this is true and has cleaned up the few blue words in her vocabulary. Lilly is to Maeve what impressionable toddlers are to mothers.

Christina's rhythmic fluttered kicks break through the water at the opposite side of the pool while Maeve and Lilly wade in the shallow end. Maeve places the palms of her hands on the top of the water and gently pats the surface to make a tiny slapping sound. Lilly does it too. They alternate patterns of sound until Maeve escalates and claps her hands down into the water. The splash surprises and delights Lilly.

Their playtime is suddenly interrupted when Christina's swimming rhythm turns erratic.

Across the pool, Maeve sees Christina flailing far from the edge. Without a lap line to grab onto, she goes underwater.

Maeve stands up straight in the shallow end.

"Somebody help!" she yells to no one.

Float.

Christina reappears, gasps, and falls under the water again.

Float.

Maeve holds Lilly's hand and walks as fast as she can through the shallow end until the water climbs from her waist up to her chest.

"I can't get to you, girlie! I can't get you!" Maeve calls out to Christina, but Christina's own splashing eclipses all sound. Desperate, Maeve screams, "Float!"

As the floor slopes, Maeve feels water up to her neck and fears she may lose her balance. Only seconds ago, chin-deep water was serenity, now this non-swimmer is just a few inches from drowning. Instinct wins over heroism and she pulls at the water to get back to the shallow end of the pool.

That's when Lilly lets go of Maeve's hand.

Maeve grapples for her, but Lilly is already in deeper water—swimming swiftly toward her daughter.

Lilly grabs Christina by the wrist and tows her until the floor meets Lilly's feet again. Christina nestles into Lilly and cries as her mother cradles her weightless body.

Lilly rocks Christina in the water until she's almost done sobbing. Then Lilly passes her grown baby to the woman she trusts most in the world. Christina surrenders to Maeve's comfort.

Christina rests her head on Maeve's shoulder and Lilly's gaze slips away again. Maeve wraps her arms around both of them. "Courage, girlies."

And they float.

40

On a Friday morning, icy raindrops pitter pat on Nora's window. Her first half-waking observance of this sound tells her that this freezing rain has gone horizontal, which means there's wind too. A lot of it. A second later, it's confirmed—the whistling wind creaks the walls and rattles the windows. Her second half-waking thought is that this is no time to be a dog or a dog owner. Then Nora wakes up fully enough to remember that Fred is gone and therefore she's no longer the latter.

It's the first moment in weeks she's felt okay about her decision to give Fred to Leanne. In her journal, she's tried to sort through her lack of loyalty to Fred as an extension of her lack of loyalty to Molly. She's questioned herself as a friend and even as a human. But today, under the warm covers alone, Nora pities Leanne. Who, in their right mind, would choose to care for a being who can't pee indoors? Today, she doesn't even need to use her notebook to conclude that living dog-free is a very good decision.

In Nora's line of work, there's always the need for unusual words or phrases, but still, she's often annoyed by the seemingly endless litany of new buzzwords, especially the ones that are clearly created for hashtag purposes. As she burrows further under her down duvet, she totally gets it—*polar vortex* and *bomb cyclone* and other new viral meteorology terms make all the sense in the world. This kind of day deserves its own vocabulary.

Sam has been out of town for almost three weeks. With this weather, Nora suspects his flight will be delayed and she'll get a bonus day or two before she has to explain Fred's new living arrangement. Nora's journal has gotten an earful about disloyalty regarding Sam too. In the first place, her feelings for Sam (and all that went on because of those feelings) were clearly a direct betrayal of Molly. As Nora has begun a phase-out process during the past few weeks, the betrayal has shifted. This time her victim is Sam.

She has worked out the justification for breaking off their relationship. She doesn't even acknowledge that it's a real relationship per se, because she never intended to date him at all. It was an accident. And she's sorry.

"All by Myself" by Celine Dion has been stuck in her head for days and she hears the refrain like an anthem. (Celine comes up a lot on Nora's Josh Groban Pandora station.) She doesn't know the lyrics beyond the titular refrain "all by myself," and if she did, she'd realize it's about *not* wanting to be alone. Still, the title itself feels like a victory song this week, and she might as well enjoy it, since it's looping around in her mind anyway.

The day after she gave Fred to Leanne, Nora wrote:

I'm just better off all by myself. All by myself. I Googled "how to get a song out of my head" and it says to do some brain-stimulating activity like a crossword puzzle. Of all things.

Sam is in London. He extended a work trip to visit family. The time difference makes it easy to be out of touch. When he gets back, I'll have a conversation with him about everything. I'll figure out what I'm going to say. Then he'll leave and we won't even have to see each other anymore because Leanne has Fred. It's a clean break. I'm glad I have this sorted out. My life can go back to normal.

I have to do a crossword puzzle now.

In another part of her notebook, where she keeps to-do lists, she wrote: *Script out what to say to Sam.* But she hasn't gotten around to doing this yet. Maybe later today.

She opens her laptop to dash off a hastily worded email explaining that she's not coming in to work today. John and Susan would rather Nora call in for this kind of thing, but Nora can't waste the opportunity to enjoy a full day without speaking at all.

Subject: Inclement Weather
I won't be coming in today because I can't face the elements. I have not heard a weather report saying when this freezing rain and wind will let up, but I looked out my window and determined that I should stay home. Have a good weekend.
Nora Shea

She always punctuates exclusively with periods even though it makes her emails seem less breezy and more chilly. Nora is just as unlikely to use an exclamation point in an email as she is to shout during a conversation. She is sure this email will become part of her boss's comedy repertoire because it's always her directness that he finds so hilarious. She doesn't care. Commitment canceled. She wishes she had written the email task on her to-do list so she could put a check mark next to it. Later, she'll write it down and check it off retroactively. It still counts.

Last month, her life and home were filled with dog and man— one as gangly, consuming, and energetic as the other. She longed for space. Her building pitches in the wind and she feels the cozy walls around her. This eight-hundred-square-foot home feels expansive, even indulgent. Trapped indoors, Nora feels free.

If she were the dancing-in-her-underwear type, that would happen. If she were prone to squeals of joy, there would be plenty of that. Defying another rom-com trope, Nora won't participate in a quirky montage to express her contentment. She doesn't need it. She's home and she performs for no one. Her appearance doesn't matter. Her grooming doesn't matter. She probably won't even look in the mirror. Does she need a hairbrush? Nope, not today. Pants? Boots? Eye contact? No, no, and hallelujah no.

She makes her way to the kitchen. Chocolate chips? Yes, she will use those. She pops one into her mouth for breakfast. What a rebel. She'd like to write a thank-you note to the person she was two weeks ago when she bought a bag of flour just as due diligence for the kitchen. It would have been a terrible loss to be stuck in the house on this cozy day and not enjoy the pleasure of smelling cookies baking or—worse—not getting to eat the cookies.

She's glad she put on her favorite pj's last night—the flannel ones with the typewriter keys on them. She tosses her cozy slipper socks into the dryer for a five-minute cycle while she waits for the kettle to heat up. Slowly steeped tea, warm socks, and nowhere to go? This is going to be the best day ever.

She takes a sip of her tea and takes in the view inside her little apartment. The Hang-in-There Kitty Cat artwork catches her eye. She almost says it out loud:

Not today, Kitty Cat. I'm livin' my best life right now.

Around 2:00 p.m., freshly baked cookies (and the cookie dough she tested before baking them) have hit Nora's bloodstream. It's been a magnificent morning of baking, lounging, and reading. If she wakes up tomorrow with a sugar hangover, wearing the same pajamas from two days ago, then she's going to have a bad Saturday. She decides to take a shower and get dressed—into other pajamas. It's all about intention.

In the shower, Molly, Fred, and Sam intrude on Nora's thoughts again. No one invited Celine, but she's here too.

All by myyyyy self.

Hey, why not? Singing in the shower is a thing. It's one of the luxuries of living alone. And this day is all about making that point.

"All byyyyyyy myyyyyy self," Nora belts louder than Celine

herself. It's pretty fun—why has she never tried this before? But what are the other lyrics? It doesn't matter! She can make them up—no one can hear her anyway. That's the point. She improvises her own refrain, "All byyyy myyy self, *I'm better off*, ALLLL BYYY MYYYY SELF."

It goes on and on. It's loud, it's shameless, it's the sweet freedom of a snow day, shower acoustics, and made-up lyrics. Singing this song with great conviction means her solitude has been self-selected and therefore this whole day (and maybe her life?) of being alone is empowering, not pathetic. This solo life will be the subject of envy, not pity! Wrapped in a towel, she emerges from her bathroom in a victorious cloud of steam, like Celine appearing on stage in pyrotechnic glory.

That's when she realizes that she is not, in fact, all by herself.

"Nice pipes," Sam says. "That's a solid power ballad choice."

Nora gasps and reaches for a crocheted blanket on the couch and scrambles to drape it around her bare shoulders.

"Sorry, I thought I was—"

"All by yourself?"

"Whatever," Nora says, hating his cute humor and regretting the "sorry." Why was she apologizing? He's the one who busted in unannounced!

"I'm sorry I busted in on you unannounced," Sam says, doing that mind-melding thing that Nora finds so unnerving. "I thought you'd be at work, so I thought I'd stop by and check on Fred."

"Fred is with Leanne," Nora says. "She said she was going to call you."

"She didn't," Sam says. "What's going on with you? Why haven't you called me back?"

"Time zones."

"Okay, but I've been back for two days."

"You have?"

"Yes."

"I didn't mean for us to get involved like we did," Nora blurts out.

"Okay?" Sam says, anticipating the next thing. But there's no next thing. There's no "but I'm glad it happened!" which is what he hopes for. There's not even a "but this relationship has run its course." There's only silence.

"Sorry," Nora says again. But this time, she means it. She's sorry she ever let herself have feelings for him. She's sorry she didn't check her voicemail yesterday. She's sorry she's hurting Sam's feelings. And she's very sorry she hadn't gotten around to scripting her breakup speech yet.

"Okay," Sam says, definitively. There's nothing else to say to being dumped. Not without losing dignity and the potential for salvaging a friendship. He's learned this before.

Sam fumbles with his keychain and places Nora's key on the table by the door. He yanks his snow boots on and doesn't bother to zip his coat closed.

"I'll, uh, see ya," he says, before he opens the door to leave. The door shuts behind him and when he's gone, an icy breeze blows into Nora's space, shifting the frames on Nora's gallery wall.

Nora wonders why she never noticed the Hang-in-There Kitty Cat's smugness before.

"No. *You* hang in there!" Nora replies out loud this time, as if the Kitty Cat had thrown down a gauntlet of positive self-talk. Nora recoils. How did she stoop so low—standing alone, clothed only in a towel and a blanket, having some kind of imaginary tête-à-tête reserved only for total losers and their cat posters? This is not the best day ever after all.

The rain falls horizontally again, rapping on Nora's window with sinister urgency. Her unshared apartment feels small and over-crowded again—filled with ghosts of what used to be. She wraps the blanket more closely around her tiny still-naked body, cocooning her wet head in a hood of crochet. She sits down in the middle of the living room floor and waits for the storm to pass—all by herself.

41

Leanne orders a second drink, even though the first one has already taken up residence in her eyelids and unpacked a suitcase full of the word *really*.

"I really really LOVE your class, I mean, really really really love this class," she tells Reggie. The first drink also absconded with her ability to judge the volume of her voice. "*Really.*"

Reggie nods and clinks her empty first drink with his third.

Tonight when Bald Guy with the Wire-Rimmed Glasses suggested they all get a drink after class, it seemed like the right thing to do. The class was small, so even one dissenter would have made the excursion awkward for the few remaining takers. Still, Leanne considered declining and lingered until she knew whether or not Reggie was going too.

Reggie was definitely game for after-class drinks. Such is Reggie.

Leanne was careful to position herself near Reggie at the bar. Even though she didn't talk to him directly, she was acutely aware that he might overhear the conversation she was having with the Woman in the Wolf Sweatshirt. When the organic part of the conversation occurred where Leanne could mention James, she didn't take the opportunity to do so. The word *husband* has been banished from her vocabulary for the night.

Despite masterminding this whole get-together, Bald Guy with the Wire-Rimmed Glasses was first to leave. Soon after, the Girl with

the Constant Sniff bowed out too. Next to leave was Guy Who Looks
Like the Guy Who Lived Next Door Before That New Snobby Couple
Moved In. Weirdly, he really connected with the Girl Who Looks
Like a Weather Girl. They left, it seems, together. After what seemed
like forever, Wolf Sweatshirt said it was getting late and she'd better
head home to feed her alpacas. Leanne missed the obvious cue to
start a new conversation about alpacas. (After all, isn't that a large
perk of keeping alpacas—the fodder?) Leanne was too distracted by
her own joy that Wolf Sweatshirt's departure would leave her alone
with Reggie.

"I'm going to finish this drink," Leanne told Wolf Sweatshirt,
making sure that Reggie heard her.

She's been waiting for this. But now she has no idea what to say to
Reggie. She *really really really* doesn't.

Once they're alone, Reggie scoots in closer to Leanne and clinks
her glass again. Reggie waits for her to talk. Leanne can feel his
attention and it fills her up. He doesn't have one hand on his phone.
He doesn't have one eye on SportsCenter. He doesn't have one other
thought apart from wondering what Leanne is about to say.

Leanne's smile is always so brilliant and her eyes so lively, but it
has seldom been this genuine. She mastered the charade that girls
with difficult mothers are forced to carry on. Joan has always cast a
wet blanket onto Leanne's fire, yet she still demanded that Leanne
glow. Leanne has lived as a china doll—beautiful, radiant, but lifeless.

Leanne talks on and on about her job and perceives Reggie's smoldering silence as intense listening. In this loud, age-inappropriate
bar, he can't hear a word she's saying, but he can't stop watching her
talk. After watching her lips for forty minutes, Reggie leans in and
gently bites one of them.

The numbness drains from Leanne's paralyzed body. She feels
every unmet need she's been denying for her entire adult life. Until
now, she has felt nothing close to the pure reckless joy Molly seemed

to soak up during her short life. Leanne's blurry barroom haze brings on some much-needed clarity—this numb life of hers is profoundly more tragic than the brevity of Molly's.

He kisses her again and talks to Leanne directly in her ear as the grid in her black-and-white mind breaks into kaleidoscopic fractals.

"We should go," Reggie says, as if to suggest that they're going to the same place.

Leanne picks up her purse without thinking, also to suggest that they're going to the same place. Then Reggie adds, "Sometimes my girlfriend's sister comes to this place and she's weird."

"Your *girlfriend*?" Leanne explodes, jilted by a lover she never got a chance to love. "You have a *girlfriend*?"

She's just been made aware of everything she's been missing—and the exhilaration gives way to a fury it was able to conceal for only seconds. Turns out, it was anger that had been awakened by this kiss— anger that was only briefly mislabeled as excitement.

"Yeah, but we're cool," Reggie says, moving his hand to the nape of Leanne's neck and brushing his lips up against hers. "She's cool."

Leanne is not cool. Not when *cool* is defined by ambivalence about monogamy. She can barely tolerate her own infidelity, let alone someone else's. In the months and days and minutes of her nonstop fantasies of an affair with Reggie, she agonized and ultimately made her peace with being an imaginary philanderer. But with real-life adultery looming imminently about one centimeter from her parted lips, she's jolted by guilt. The idea of being "the other woman" in a cheating scenario sends Leanne's moral compass spinning past north.

"I'm not cool," Leanne says, proving it right away by standing up and knocking over two chairs in the process. It was supposed to be a bold moment. In the movie of Leanne's life, "I'm not cool" would be the song cue for Aretha Franklin's "Respect." She'd throw a drink in his face and then storm out. A stranger would high-five her. The movie doesn't do well at the box office because the premise is impossible to believe. Leanne having an affair? No. No one is going to buy a ticket to that movie.

"Hey girl, d'you want me to drive you home?" Reggie says. "I mean, like, you can't even stand up."

"I am *fine!*" Leanne says. Thankfully, Reggie has a vague understanding of the variations of the word *fine*. He has known many women . . . Many. Many. Women.

"At least get an Uber?" Reggie says.

"Yes. Totally. I will *Uber*," Leanne confirms. Even in her altered state, Leanne has the presence of mind to know her limitations. No, she cannot cheat on her husband. No, she cannot drive drunk. And absolutely no, she cannot summon a car using an app on her phone. She lives in the suburbs and just does not know how to do that.

Still feeling righteous, she demands, "Please call me an Uber!"

She stomps toward the door, each of her furious footsteps registering indignation with Reggie and his entire gender. The bouncer gets out of her way and opens the door for her.

And because she's still Leanne, she interrupts her own feminist inner monologue to smile and chirp sweetly to the bouncer, "Thank youuuu! Have a nice niiiight!"

℘

The next day when Leanne wakes up, her eyeballs feel achy and dehydrated. She considers a time when waking up with this feeling was a badge of honor for being exceptionally badass the night before. It didn't happen often, but whenever she woke up with a hangover, she milked it all day, groaning in all her hangover glory and making sure she had brunch plans with Molly. She always relished a chance to get credit for badassery from the biggest badass she knew.

This time though, the ache is not a hangover. It is heartache. She wonders why she ever wished away numbness when pain sucks this bad. Her grainy eyelids can barely open. She navigates herself to the kitchen with nickel slots where her bright blue eyes usually beam. She scuffs her feet in a way that always annoys her when teen girls do it at the mall.

It's really hard to remember that she and Molly are not those kids at the mall. On any given workday, there's always a moment when grown adults like Leanne have a feeling that they could be arrested by a truancy officer. Leanne once told Molly that she sometimes feels as if she's on the longest summer break ever.

"I feel like any day now, we'll be back at school telling stories about what we did," Leanne said to Molly when they were on a summer weekend trip to the Cape.

On some days, it's impossible to understand how the world is trusting kids in adult bodies with grown-up problems like cancer, death, marriage, procreation, aging parents, and even jobs. Christina, for example, shouldn't even be driving a car.

"Yeah. How did this happen?" Molly said to Leanne. "I never agreed to any of this. *Adulting.*"

Her phone rings and it doesn't even occur to Leanne to answer it. Her mind has finally shaken the habit of thinking it might be Molly. There is no one she's willing to talk to and there's nothing worth talking about. She doesn't recognize the number anyway. It's probably the fertility clinic. That stupid fertility clinic.

"Any word from Dr. Gianetti-Wong?" James asks as he fills his stainless steel travel mug full of coffee.

"Can you ever say *other* words to me?" Leanne snaps before leaving for work. "If I hear from them, I will let you know!"

℃

When Leanne arrives home from work and the sky is still bright, it forces her to resume her usual optimism about the coming spring when the days stretch and the light lingers. The late sunset gives Leanne enough peace that when she sees James pulling into the driveway, she offers a truce. She knows he wants to ask again. He's dying to ask.

"I think the fertility clinic called this morning," Leanne says. "I had a missed call and I didn't answer. I'm not sure how your days look this week, so I didn't call them back."

"Okay, I'll call them," James says. "Do you have the number?"

"Here," Leanne says, handing him her phone. "Just call back the last missed number."

Leanne goes into the house—she can't wait to take off her painful shoes. They've been killing her all day, but she got a lot of compliments so she plans to wear them all the time. She slides on her old Birkenstock clogs that, over the last twenty years, have formed perfectly to her feet. She wears them around the house every day. It took her a while to wear them in front of James though. She waited until after they were married. It's that kind of thing.

She washes her pink travel coffee mug from this morning and looks out the window above the sink. James walks back and forth at a brisk pace while he talks on the phone in the driveway. It seems he's negotiating his way into an appointment. James can do this kind of thing. He always manages to talk his way into top-rated restaurants, sold-out shows, and now, highly ranked fertility clinics.

Leanne decides to prep tomorrow's coffee before starting to make dinner. She's hoping James feels like going out tonight instead. She dumps this morning's coffee grounds into the compost bucket just as James comes in the back door.

"Wow, that was a long call. That receptionist can be quite a talker," Leanne says. "Were you able to get the appointment?"

"No," James says. "But Reggie wants you to call him."

Leanne starts to speak, but James interrupts. "It's okay," he says. "We're cool."

Leanne is not cool. Not when *cool* means ambivalence about monogamy. And especially when *cool* means ambivalence about her. James doesn't have the decency to accuse her. He doesn't have the urge to confront her. He doesn't have the passion to beg her to deny it. He just goes into the living room to watch baseball. It is Opening Day, after all.

"Cool!" Leanne screams on her way out the door that she slams behind her. She says it again when she slams the car door too. "*Cool.*" She says the word *cool* about twenty-three more times as she screeches out of the driveway and speeds down their street.

There's a part of Leanne that longs for James to feel jealousy or any sort of heightened emotion somewhere in the neighborhood of passion. She might even hope that he kicks her out and never trusts her again. Instead, she sinks with hopeless nothing—tonight, the fight for her fidelity came in a distant second place to a televised baseball game.

Leanne hears her phone buzz and feels vindication as she waits to reply. She wants to make James sweat. Her commitment to vengeful emotional extortion lasts about four and a half minutes. Desperate to see words that make her feel valued by her own husband, she pulls over to read the text. But it's just a message from her phone provider saying her data plan can be upgraded this month.

She imagines herself throwing the phone out the window. Leanne often mentally rehearses bold acts of defiance, like throwing a plate against a wall and letting it shatter into pieces, flinging a drink in someone's face, or tossing her wedding ring into the ocean. She often thinks, *Doing stuff must be so awesome.*

Her phone buzzes again. This time, it's Reggie:

broke up w my gf. i wanna c u.

She resists the impulse to reply right away. She needs to live in a moment where someone in the world might be pacing the floors in her absence. Maybe Reggie will agonize over the wrong things she might be doing right now. The idea of it comforts her and she plans to drive around until she's tired. Then she'll go home and imagine what it might be like to drive to Reggie's apartment and it will occur to her again, *Doing stuff must be so awesome.*

Later, Leanne arrives home, still unsatisfied and fitful. She's already driven halfway to nowhere and then circled the neighborhood sixteen times. There's only one light left on in the house—her bedroom. James had the decency to stay awake, but it would have been nice for him to stay dressed, eat his feelings, and be afraid of the dark. It would be nice if he found Leanne's absence unbearable. Instead, he enjoyed the conflict-free silence and embraced the opportunity to watch ESPN instead of Bravo.

Leanne can't bring herself to go into her house. Not yet.

Target closed two hours ago. The last movie at the multiplex was at nine thirty. She ponders the twenty-four-hour Super Stop & Shop on Old Connecticut Path in Framingham. Is there anything she could buy there that would stick it to everyone? What rebellious items do they sell at Super Stop & Shop? Maybe she could buy scissors and then run with them? Maybe she could buy a scratch ticket at the gas station? Yes! Gambling! Joan is so against gambling that she won't even play bingo at her church's fund-raiser.

It's too late to escape though—James has already spied Leanne from their bedroom window. She's furious that she missed the opportunity to stay out late to make him worry. He never worries about her. No one does. She always does the right thing.

She wants to do a wrong thing. Without immediate access to wrong things, she opens her car door and slams it. In the language of door-slamming, this one translates to "Fuck you, world."

Leanne beelines for the garage because sitting in one's poorly lit garage after midnight is a moody and dark thing to do. Leanne never had permission to be a brooding teenager, so this is her chance. Of course, no one has permission to be an adolescent pain in the ass, but everyone usually does it anyway. Leanne was the only teenager who sought permission. And that's how she got here—a woman in her thirties, alone in her dark, cold garage, spiraling about babies, brunches, art teachers, mothers, and husbands.

Leanne takes the cover off Molly's Vespa. So far, she has only leaned on it, sidesaddle. This time, she straddles it and braces herself on the handlebars. She bats away the kickstand with the bottom of her Birkenstock. She positions herself as a driver of this vehicle and of her own life.

She turns the key and lets the motor idle underneath her.

Allons-y, chérie.

Leanne is fed up with her lack of choices and—worse—her inability to make them.

Allons-y, chérie.

She's tired of circling the same old neighborhoods.

Allons-y, chérie.

She's tired of living in a life she didn't choose. She's tired of opting out of passion. She's tired of watching women graduate from a school she didn't attend and pursue careers she'll never have.

Allons-y, chérie.

She's tired of cardigans and smart haircuts and brunch.

Leanne reads the note that still dangles from the handlebar where her beloved friend left it.

Allons-y, chérie.

She hears Molly's playful voice in her mind.

"Yes, Leanne. Let's go!"

She rips the note off the handlebar.

She's going.

42

On the first Sunday of May, Christina wakes up from a full night's sleep and therefore doesn't see the need for yoga. She does, however, feel a gaping hole in her social schedule.

Her condo's silence must be eradicated immediately by way of television programming that revolves around tiny houses.

Christina believes that she could live in a tiny house. She doesn't cook, and there's no use for her kitchen now that her mother and Maeve aren't around anymore. There's really no need for anything more than her bedroom and a bathroom. She could negotiate with the *Tiny House* builder to increase the size of the bathroom and do away with the kitchen altogether. What she envisions is pretty much a hotel suite. Christina loves the idea of a hotel suite. It would be a fresh place to sleep where there are no reminders of the way life used to be. In a hotel room, she could rest her mind from reality and pretend that she's the one who's gone away—not Lilly and not Molly.

It seems that *Tiny House* enthusiasts tend to be empty nesters or doomsday preppers. Lilly's departure and Christina's off-grid social life qualifies her for both these categories. It's been almost two years since she's been in touch with her usual fancy corporate crowd. Two years is an eternity when talking about friends who weren't true friends in the first place. Her squad of networkers have long ago migrated to the next swarm of activity.

Christina misses Maeve and invents a Lilly-related excuse to call her. Maeve answers without pleasantries.

"Why aren't you at your brunch, girlie?" she says.

"We're not doing it anymore," Christina says.

"I told you to keep going to the brunch," Maeve says. "It's good for you."

"I'm going over to see Mom this afternoon, are you?" Christina asks, ignoring Maeve's unsolicited advice.

"Not today, I have to meet my new client," Maeve says. "I'll go tomorrow morning."

Tomorrow won't do. Christina wants to see Maeve just as badly as she wants to see Lilly. A long pause on Christina's end tells Maeve to keep talking.

"I saw her on Friday," Maeve says. "She likes that one nurse—Kelly, I think her name is."

"Shelly, yes," Christina says. "She's nice."

"She's the same age as you," Maeve says.

"Yup."

"It's a nice day for a walk," Maeve says. "Take her outside when you go."

"Yup."

"I know you're not going to cook anything," Maeve says. "So, you might as well stop at that restaurant you usually go to on Sundays."

"I see what you're doing," Christina says, snapping out of her pout.

"I'm doing nothing, girlie," Maeve says. "Get out of your bed."

"Do you think I could live in a tiny house?" Christina says, changing the subject.

"Put your feet on the floor and start your day," Maeve says. "Go bug your girlfriends."

"We're not doing brunch any—"

"Goodbye now, girlie," Maeve says, and hangs up.

Christina is alone again. She can't remember what she used to do when she had Sundays to herself. She types a text to Leanne.

Hi. Knocked up yet?

She deletes the message before sending it.

"Why am I like this?" she asks the host of the infomercial that follows *Tiny House Nation*. Christina is not the only person in the world who talks to the TV, but by the way she asked the question, she might be the only one who earnestly expects the TV to answer her back.

She dials Nora.

"You're calling me?" Nora asks, already wishing she'd let the call go to voicemail.

"Yes, obviously," Christina says.

"Aren't you a texter?" Nora challenges.

"Aren't you *not* a texter?" Christina challenges her back.

"Can I call you back?" Nora says, already tired of the nonsense. "I'm walking Fred."

"Why do you have Fred again?" Christina asks.

"You don't know?" Nora says.

"No, obviously not." Christina is losing her patience with Nora's slow speech patterns.

"Leanne's missing," Nora says.

"*Missing*?" Christina exclaims.

"Yeah," Nora says, holding the phone farther away from her ear. She should have known Christina was going to exclaim a few times. She always does. "James called and said for me to come get the dog because Leanne left."

"*Left*?" Christina exclaims again. "Where is she?"

"I don't know."

"Did James say where she went?"

"No."

"Did you ask?"

"No."

"I'm calling her!" Christina says and hangs up on Nora.

Christina dials Leanne fast and the voicemail answers after one ring.

"Leanne? It's Christina . . ." Christina realizes she didn't plan what to say on this message. What if Leanne doesn't want her to know she left James? This was a mistake. "Uh, just checking in. Talk to you later. Goodbye."

Christina puts her feet on the floor and, as Maeve instructed, starts her day. Now she knows what to do with her Sunday.

Stalk Leanne.

℃

Only two hours later, Maeve checks in via text to see if Christina has gotten something to eat yet. It's brazen for Christina to scroll through her phone so openly because of where she is. She replies.

No, not yet. I might get something to eat after church.

Maeve's typing speed is typically glacial, but shock accelerates her response time.

Church? Oh no. What are you up to?

Funny how Christina's church etiquette wins out just in time to avoid answering this question. She turns off her phone and waits for the end of Mass. She has found her target: Joan singing conspicuously loud in the center row of the church—right on the aisle, so everyone can behold her piety. She's off-key in many ways—most notably her sense of righteousness.

Christina passes the time in Mass by playing a drinking game in her mind.

- Drink every time Joan nods her head in agreement with what the priest is saying.

- Drink if Joan talks louder during the Latin parts.

- Drink every time Joan anticipates a move from standing to kneeling before the rest of the congregation, to prove she's a better Catholic than everyone else in the church.

- Drink for each person Joan snubs during the sign of peace, which only further thwarts her efforts to be crowned Best Catholic Ever. (Note: Best Catholic Ever is not a thing. Joan just thinks it is.)

If Christina had an actual cocktail during her little imaginary game, then she would be even drunker than the priest is right now. (Which is to say, she'd be unconscious.)

When Mass ends, Joan stays in her row until the recessional hymn is over, giving Christina time to position herself optimally for a chance run-in.

During the Mass, Christina clenched her teeth remembering how Joan had once corrected Lilly when Lilly referred to herself as Ms. instead of Mrs.

"Aw, sweetheart, you're still a Mrs.!" Joan said, pitying Lilly, who preferred Ms. over Mrs. because she was a feminist, not because she was a widow.

Christina didn't know exactly how she was going to strike up a conversation with Joan, but she was sure she was going to use her mother's preferred salutation. Because she's in church, she justifies her act of revenge as an homage to her mom.

"Oh hello, *Ms. . . .*" Christina begins her greeting to Joan, completely forgetting Leanne's maiden name. She can't very well call her "Ms. Leanne's Mom," but she's tempted. Instead, Christina finishes her greeting in a manner that infuriates the respect-demanding Joan even more. "Oh what the hell, right? We're adults. I should call you *Joan*! Joan! Ms. Joan! How the hell are ya?"

"Hello, Christina," Joan says, extending her hand for a lady handshake. Christina wonders if this posturing is meant to suggest that she kiss Joan's ring or some shit. "How is your mother?"

"Terrible! Thank you for asking," Christina says, so eager to complete her mission, that she can't even finesse the usual softening of tragedy for the sake of polite conversation.

"I'm sorry to hear that," Joan says, as if she hasn't already heard about it through her parish minions, who feast on other people's bad news.

"Oh, and how's Leanne?" Christina asks, as if it only just occurred to her. "What's she up to? I haven't seen her in a while."

"I haven't seen her either," Joan says. Her gossip reflex is so tightly strung, it can be triggered by a breeze—even if the target is her own daughter. "I assume she went off with that lesbian art teacher."

"There's an art teacher?" Christina says, her wheels turning. "Wait . . . there's a lesbian?"

"Katherine something or other," Joan says.

"Riker. Right. Her friend from work," Christina says. "She teaches French history."

"Whatever, they took an art class together," Joan says. "I don't know what's gotten into her. I guess she's gay now."

"I don't think that's what's happening," Christina says, laughing.

"She must be a lesbian!" Joan says. "Why else would she leave James?"

"There are other reasons to leave a marriage," Christina says.

"No, there aren't," Joan says. Having been freshly absolved of her sins, Joan jumps right into a new week of judgment and backbiting. "Not a *good* marriage like theirs."

"Wow," Christina says. It's been a while since she's engaged in this kind of repartee, so she forgets it's rude to say certain things. For example, the following:

"You're nuts."

"Excuse me?" Joan demands.

"You're totally batshit," Christina continues. "I just gotta say it. Man, no wonder Leanne is all wound up."

"How can you talk to your friend's mother like this?" Joan says.

"So easily," Christina says. "Leanne and I aren't really friends."

Back in her car, Christina turns on the engine and opens her windows so the sound of Mötley Crüe can more sufficiently appall churchgoers.

She clicks through her phone, still ignoring Maeve's inquiries lest they inspire Christina's conscience to call off her sleuthing and go to a farmers market or take up golf the way normal bored people do on Sundays. Christina has new information and she wants to jump on it fast.

She logs on to her Wellesley alumnae website and finds contact information for Katherine Riker. She dials the phone and peels out of the church parking lot with a trail of explicit lyrics wafting behind her, but not before she sets Joan in her crosshairs and expresses a parting post-church sentiment using her middle finger.

The phone rings over the car speakers, which are now way too loud for a phone call. She turns down the volume as Katherine's voice answers.

"*Bonjour*?"

"Hi, this is Christina Ford," Christina says. "I'm Leanne Stubin's friend."

"Aha! Yes. Christina. Part of her brunch coterie!" Katherine says, brightening right up.

"Yes, that's right. I'm trying to reach Leanne," Christina says, no time for chitchat. "Is she with you?"

"No, I believe she went on vacation with James," Katherine guesses. "I actually haven't seen her since I stopped going to art class."

"Thank you! I'll check in with her when she gets back," Christina lies, quick to hang up so she can follow the next lead.

She pulls over at the next gas station to search for the art teacher Joan alluded to. She remembers Leanne talking about Cambridge, sculpting, and Thursday nights. She's pretty proud of herself for actually listening to Leanne's stories.

Within a few clicks, Christina finds a picture of Reggie, who gazes back at her with smoldering photographic eye contact.

"Oh . . . *shit.*"

43

Leanne's phone has been ringing straight to voicemail all week. By Thursday night, Christina has no choice but to take up sculpting.

It's obvious that Christina believes art is a spectator sport because she arrives to class straight from work, wearing an ecru ladysuit. She finds the cleanest seat in the room and decides to stand instead.

When Reggie fills the room with his gorgeous presence, Christina can easily answer her own questions about Leanne's whereabouts. Reggie obviously has Leanne stored somewhere in his pants.

Still, Christina has come all this way, so she might as well get to the point of her mission. After all, she's not about to touch clay or any surface in this room for that matter.

"Hi," Christina says to Reggie. "I'm a friend of Leanne's."

"Nice," Reggie says, seeming to congratulate Christina.

"Yeah," Christina says, happy he bought it. "Just wondering if you were expecting her in class tonight?"

"Dunno," Reggie says, with a finality that would suggest this was the end of the conversation.

"Any idea where she is?" Christina says, noticing the jawline on this specimen of a man. It makes her already forget the question she just asked.

"Naw, she stopped coming to class," he says.

"Any idea why?" Christina probes.

"I mean, it's like, I don't know, I guess I feel like," Reggie starts.

With this much buildup, one would assume there was some major profundity on its way. One would be wrong. "Like . . . you know?" Nope. Didn't get any of that, Reg. Verbs would be good here. "Sure," Christina says. There's no sense in trying to decode such nonsense.

Leanne has obviously lost her mind, Christina concludes. True, Christina can understand physically cheating on James with a guy like this. A woman has needs. But Christina feels that indulging this man in conversation would be cheating on one's own intelligence. Intellectual infidelity can't be tolerated.

Reggie has been thinking deeply for the last thirty seconds. Or is he having a seizure?

"I mean, I feel like, anyone who doesn't travel is, like, wasting their lives," Reggie says. "I mean, what's the point? Know what I mean?"

Though he begins every statement with "I mean," it's still fair to say that most people have no idea what Reggie means. He rarely attempts to convey any concept complex enough to confound even an average thinker, but still, he fails at the basics—such as having a point.

He's a man who swears by a struggling artist's code but then spends six dollars on kombucha twice a day because there's a lotus flower on the label and the word *kombucha* sounds vaguely yogic. He projects a deep vibe that he concocted while traveling the world on his parents' dime. There are beads on his wrist too. Leanne asked him about their meaning once and his vacuous answer sucked all the air out of the room.

"I mean, just like, you know, clarity, peace, and you know, like, stuff I'm about. Know what I mean?"

At the time, Leanne pretended to know what he meant.

Reggie continues to talk as Christina concludes that he is officially the worst.

"I mean, like, right now, I'm on a cleanse," Reggie says to Christina as she scans the room, hoping to see Leanne and/or the nearest exit. "I'm off, like, everything, that like, you know, distracts me? Social media, sugar, alcohol, sex . . ."

Once he said he was on a sex cleanse, it blared in Christina's ear and deafened her. This confirms that Leanne is not having an affair with this dude. Now, about that exit . . .

Then, Christina tunes back in to hear him end his list of things he's avoiding.

". . . leather, and also synthetic fabrics and man-made fibers."

Christina ponders the idea of shoes made of hemp. She shudders.

"I know," Reggie says, noticing Christina's reaction. "I mean, some people say I'm going too far. But, like, I have one really sweet student—your friend actually—she told me I was being a 'total SB' and, like, I really appreciated her support."

Christina doesn't bother with goodbyes. On her way to the exit, she dials her phone. When Nora answers, Christina doesn't bother with hellos. "I know where Leanne is."

44

Nora has been dodging communication all day. First, there were countless unanswered phone calls from Christina and now there's a text from Sam.

Any chance I can see you?

Nora deletes the text and feels a steely-eyed judgment coming from a certain dog.

"I know what you're going to say," she tells Fred.

Of course, Fred never says anything when he disagrees with Nora's choices. For example, he thinks she should go to the park instead of the library. But does he say anything? Nope. He thinks she should go to the park instead of work. Keeps it to himself. And he thinks she should go to the park instead of brunch. He never says a word about that either.

But Fred has reached a breaking point with regard to Nora's poor decision-making about Sam. Fred just might say something this time.

Ever since Fred returned to Nora's care, there's been a firm system in place. Sam sees Fred during the day while Nora is at work. Fred and Nora spend time together alone on the weekends and evenings. Sam promised to never bring Fred home late and Nora promised she'll never come home early. They can co-parent Fred and never cross paths.

"It's for the best," Nora tells Fred (and herself).

Nora opens a fresh new notebook. The pages of the old one are too loaded with grief, confusion, and Sam. She believed that the feelings she expressed in the pages of her last journal were a crime against friendship, and it was best to destroy any evidence that may incriminate her.

The doorbell rings and Nora considers avoiding a third mode of communication. She peers out the window as a deliveryman walks away from her door. Opening the door to a package will be harmless, she assumes. She's wrong. That deliveryman was a Trojan horse.

"Aha!" Christina exclaims. "You're home!"

"Yes," Nora says, defeated.

"Someone sent you flowers," Christina says, shoving flowers at Nora and pushing her way into Nora's apartment. Christina grabs Fred's leash and hooks him up.

"We're all going for a walk," Christina declares. She picks up Nora's shoes and searches for a jacket for Nora to wear. For once, Christina doesn't judge the shoes. They'll have to do for now.

Nora stands on her front step, in shock from this ambush. Nora doesn't want flowers today any more than she did the day after Molly's funeral. She'll put them in the trash because that thing with Francine was a fiasco not worth repeating. It's too late though. Francine's interest was already piqued by the departure of the deliveryman. She appears in her doorway.

"Aw, so pretty!" Francine says. "Did you take those off my doorstep?"

Nora studies the card and Christina appears next to her just in time to butt in.

"Why would she do that?" Christina challenges Francine.

"They're from Sam," Nora says.

"Those are for me then, yes?" Francine says.

"My name is on them," Nora says.

"Did he ask you to deliver them for him or something?" Francine asks.

"To *herself*?" Christina interrupts again.

"No. To *me*," Francine says, as if it were so obvious. "I mean, you two aren't . . . because he was your best friend's . . . aw. This is awkward."

"Bye!" Christina ends this shit right quick. She hands the end of Fred's leash to Nora and Fred yanks them away onto the sidewalk where they're free of Francine.

"What the *fuck* was that?" Christina exclaims.

"I don't know," Nora says. She's surprised to feel gratitude for Christina's presence, but still. "Why are you here?"

"Is that dipshit going after Sam?" Christina asks.

"I don't know," Nora says. "It's none of my business."

"It is *all* of your business," Christina says. "When's the last time you had a boyfriend?"

"I don't know. Probably around the same time you had one," Nora says.

"Hey! I am *very* busy," Christina says.

"So am I," Nora says.

"No, you're not. You're a recluse," Christina says. "And your neighbor is trying to move in on your man!"

"He's not my man," Nora says. "He was Molly's man and I made a mistake."

"Gimme a break. He's the most normal guy she ever dated," Christina says. "Don't let him go to waste on your lame neighbor. She can't be his type, right? That can't be a thing."

"Can we talk about something else?" Nora asks.

"Yes, let's talk about Leanne," Christina says. "That's why I'm here."

"Can we talk about nothing?" Nora tries.

"She's having a crisis," Christina begins her opening argument.

"Just quiet time now," Nora says.

"We only have a few more brunches to wrap up," Christina says.

"I thought we weren't doing the brunches anymore," Nora says.

"Aren't you the one who's ditching a perfectly normal guy out of respect for the dead? Don't you want to honor Molly's wishes?" Christina says. She fights dirty.

"Fine! We'll have brunch again," Nora says.

"In Paris," Christina adds this detail.

"What?" Nora says.

"Yes," Christina says. "That's where Leanne is."

"I have to work," Nora says.

"Molly would go," Christina says.

"There are lots of things that Molly would do that I wouldn't," Nora says. She feels the word *Sam* hovering over both of them in a cartoon thought bubble. She resents Christina for thinking it. "Oh, shut up."

"I didn't say it," Christina says. "But since we're talking about Molly, I do have to say something."

"No, thank you," Nora declines.

"I actually think Molly was being a know-it-all with those stupid notes," Christina confesses. "She is still bossing us around, actually, and I'm not that thrilled about it!"

The exclaiming continues. "I mean, *where* does she get off telling us how to live the rest of our lives? She can't tell me how to be! She's always—she was—I mean, what the *fuck*? Float? A meditation seat? Me? Meditate? Gimme a break! I don't need to *relax*, don't tell me to fucking relax! I will relax when I want to relax and no one can tell me *how* to fucking relax. I am *plenty* relaxed!"

"Yeah, you're totally chill," Nora says.

"Out of all of us, you should be the most pissed," Christina says. "You don't even like dogs and now you have one."

"I don't mind them," Nora says. This is the first Fred has heard of Nora's anti-dog reputation. Now he's invested in this argument.

He stands between them and follows their verbal volley, shifting his weight among his four feet.

Fred hopes that Christina's off-message rant was merely her clever way of lawyering Nora into a trip to Paris. Fred is a smart dog, but he's still a dog. He can't understand that Christina completely forgot her agenda when rogue grief launched a sneak attack. Surprise seems to be grief's most common tactic.

"But did you want one? Did you ever agree to this huge responsibility? You like to spend time by yourself. So what? That's who you are," Christina says. "Doesn't it bother you that she couldn't accept that about you?"

"She did accept it."

"She's forced you into brunch with us," Christina says. "You don't like brunch, you don't even like *us!*"

"Oh come on," Nora says. "Brunch isn't that bad."

"I guess I'm the asshole who's not keen on these last messages. Couldn't she have just died without having the last word? It's just selfish!" Christina exclaims. "And now Leanne has gone completely off her rocker and who's going to help her? Those terrible LVL bitches? No! Molly would be the one. She's Leanne's only real friend. She's my only real friend. And yours too. But she's not here!"

"Fine! I will go to Paris!" Nora says. "Will you please drop it?"

"I am angry. Hey wait . . ." Christina says. She seems excited to have raged herself into a revelation. A few months back she Googled *grief* and had wondered what the anger part would be like. Now she knows. "Oh! The anger phase! This must be the *anger* phase of grief."

"Is that on your grief spreadsheet?" Nora jabs.

"Shut up!" Christina snaps.

"*You* shut up!" Nora says, her own anger phase commencing.

"No *you*." Christina says.

This could go on and on until someone says "I'm rubber and you're glue."

Nora feels her eyes sting. This time, the tears are stronger than she is. She coughs to distract her eyes from producing more tears. The cough sputters and she inhales a staccato breath and ultimately surrenders. It's too late. She's crying. Finally.

Christina's leg muscles protest her anger phase by going on strike. She begins to buckle and grabs Nora to brace herself from collapsing. Their mutual unsteadiness balances them from falling all the way to the ground as they cling and cry like two dudes watching *The Notebook*.

Fred wags and dances his love jig. He loves to see people hug, even when the two people are hugging because of desperation.

"I really do hate you so much," Nora sobs.

She means it.

"I know. I know. It's been so awful spending time with you," Christina wails.

It feels so good to say it.

In some friendships, honesty is the same as love. And it will have to do for now.

45

Done packing toiletries, clothes, earbuds for the flight. Everything is almost all set for Fred. I feel like I'm forgetting something major.

Maybe what Nora has forgotten is that she is not the kind of person who spontaneously flies to Paris with a non-friend to track down another non-friend who has gone missing. It's good that she has forgotten this about her own nature because Christina already booked their red-eye flights for tonight.

John and Susan agreed that Nora should definitely work from home today so she can pack instead of commuting. They were so romanced by the idea of a last-minute trip to Paris, they practically offered Nora a ride to the airport. Nora is considering playing into their penchant for dinner-party fodder even more. When she gets back, Nora may make up a story about moving into a yurt, way outside the city. This is exactly the kind of Instagram lifestyle John and Susan would willingly foster. They'll grant Nora permission (and their blessing) to work remotely if it will make them cool by association. It's the best John and Susan can hope for—adventure adjacency.

Typically, people who work on a departure day get absolutely nothing done in the office anyway. Still, Nora is determined to use today as a chance to prove to John and Susan that she is more prolific at home.

At noon, the doorbell snaps Nora out of work mode. The only downside to a home office is Nora's work-from-home neighbor, Francine. One neighbor like her is definitely worse than a whole building full of coworkers. Getting a new apartment might be easier than getting a new job. Nora will simply have to move. Maybe to a yurt.

The doorbell rings a second time.

Nora remains still and expects Fred to do the same.

She hears the sound of the front door deadbolt click open. Keys jingle as they move to open the doorknob lock. Fred leaps to greet Sam.

Nora stays still for a second, wondering if she might blend into the furniture. Could she be that still?

"Oh!" Sam says, surprised to see Nora. "Hey."

"Hey," Nora replies, still motionless.

"I didn't know you were home, I'm sorry," Sam says.

Aha! That's what it was. Toiletries, clothes, earbuds for the flight, stuff for Fred, *tell the man you're in love with that you are trying to avoid him.*

"How have you been?" Sam asks. Sure, Sam can always read Nora just fine, but this time he ignores what she's putting out there. He doesn't care that Nora wants to run into the other room and pretend she's alone. "How have you been?" is not merely Sam's polite greeting. He's desperate to know the answer.

"Okay," Nora says. Her commitment to stillness is betrayed by the motion of tears.

Sam steps toward her to hug it all away.

"No!" Nora puts her hand up to halt the hug. "I'm fine. I'm a crier now. It's Christina's fault. She started it."

"Got it," Sam says, tearing up. Sam has always been a contagious crier. He's also one of those people who inadvertently starts speaking in the accent of the person he's talking to. It even happens around dogs—he clearly thinks Fred's accent is that of Scooby-Doo. Sam's unintentional mimicking is even more pronounced when it comes to crying. It could be really embarrassing for him—that is, if he were a person capable of embarrassment.

Sam notices Nora's suitcase and last-minute travel stuff lined up next to the door.

"Are you going somewhere?" he asks.

"Yes," Nora says, between hiccups of sobs. "I'm going to Paris."

She submits to hysterical crying.

"It's really lovely there. They write songs about it," Sam comforts her. "I think you'll be okay."

Nora laughs.

"I'm projecting," Nora says.

"Hmmm. Maybe," Sam says.

"I'm going with Christina," Nora confesses.

"That explains the tears," Sam says.

"Just for a few days," Nora says. "And I meant to let you know."

Sam perks up for a second, loving the idea that he was a person Nora would check in with before leaving town, the way that everyone checks in with their people before a trip. Sam would love to be her people.

"I arranged for Fred to go to a dog sitter while I'm gone," Nora says. "This girl Kayla who works at the vet. I know you're really good about taking Fred out during the day, but I didn't want Fred to be alone all night, so while I'm gone, he'll just be with Kayla."

"Oh," Sam says. "Okay, whatever you think is best."

He squats, looks Fred straight in the face, and addresses him in a distinctly human tone for the first time ever—without a Scooby-Doo accent. "I'm gonna miss you so much," he says, in his own man voice, with his own man tears. "You're the highlight of my day. Wish I could see you all the time."

Fred looks up at Nora to see if this registered with her. If she missed it, she's not human, Fred decides. He'll have to teach her some things.

As soon as Sam and Fred take off for their walk, Nora flips to the pre-Paris checklist.

I can't believe I forgot to tell Sam I'm going to Paris. I should have told him. What else am I forgetting for Fred? Kayla said she has everything he'll need.

Maybe Molly's last wishes were very selfish—Christina might be right about this. My life was sorted and now it's not. Should I tell Kayla to take the dog bed too? Is that too much? Should I leave dog food? No, she said she has that.

I can't be with Sam. It's not right.

Molly's instructions for dog care say that dogs aren't supposed to eat chocolate and certain plants like poinsettias. I found this surprising and helpful. I am sure Kayla knows that stuff about chocolate and poinsettias. Do people have poinsettias right now? The receptionist at work—hers last until July even though she stops watering them. She just can't kill them. Maybe Kayla has a green thumb for poinsettias too. I'll just leave her the folder with all of Molly's dog-care instructions just in case? Is that embarrassing?

Working from home today was a mistake. I can't believe I was here when Sam came over.

And just like that, air quotes appear around the words *working from home* because when Sam walked in the door, any potential for work-related productivity walked out. This encounter needs to be processed, but more journaling requires Nora to sit still, which she cannot.

Nora buzzes around the apartment, wishing she could pack her suitcase again. Her bed has been made, her apartment is clean. She curses her efficiency. She's ready to go, but can she get readier? Yes, she'll simply get readier.

Nora prepares another stack of just-in-case items for Kayla. She puts Fred's dog bed next to the door; she packs up his favorite toy, his blanket, a bag of treats, his dog bowl. Maybe these comforts will fulfill Nora's urgent need for Fred to know she loves him even if she can't be with him.

Each item in this pile creates a clumsier maze for her to navigate in her tidy apartment. Every time she manages to maintain her footing among the piles, she congratulates herself for having a low center of gravity. It's one of the many reasons she's never worn high heels.

In a final swoop of impulse, she grabs Molly's dog-care file to add to the top of the Fred pile. And that's when she tumbles over her suitcase, sending papers flying everywhere.

The papers have flung in such a scattered fashion that they'll need to be collected one page at a time. Nora is grateful for the project. It seems as if Sam and Fred have been gone for hours. Nora takes her time reassembling the papers, and she places them back in the folder.

She picks up one more small index card that landed facedown under her chair. As Sam opens the door, Nora reads the final instruction Molly left her.

Go ahead and love him.

46

Red-eye flights are a spectacular travel option for a person who can sleep anywhere. Christina is no such person. She resents the sleeping passengers around her who will blink awake at the gate and feel as if the trip was instantaneous. The passenger seated to Christina's left takes an Ambien and Christina checks her watch. She'll keep an eye on this dude to see how long it takes for the pill to kick in. Sleep aids fascinate her, but she'll never take one—especially not in public. She's read all about Ambien gone wrong in one of her many late-night Google rabbit holes. What if she tried to sleepwalk into the cockpit and an air marshal had to take her down? What if she sleep-masturbated? What if she had sleep sex with a stranger in the bathroom? What if she sleep-opened the exit door during the flight, got sucked out, and woke up mid-plummet to her death?

Though there's no way Christina will sleep on this flight to Paris, she still has a ritual on overnight flights that makes her look like a seasoned plane sleeper: earplugs, an eye mask, moisturizers, and some sort of Evian water face spray. Still, she's brought along one rather not-so-fabulous sleep accessory—her mouth guard. In the unlikely event that she falls asleep, she doesn't want to damage her enamel when she inevitably clenches and grinds her teeth from the stress of airline travel with Nora.

Nora takes out her notebook and shields the page from Christina's prying eyes.

"Still with those notebooks, huh?" Christina says.

"It works for me," Nora says, barely looking up.

Five rows back. Ten rows up. The nearest exit is behind us. In an emergency, there will be a lemming factor. I'll get Christina to yell for everyone to turn around and go back. She's loud.

"What do you write in there?" Christina asks while moisturizing.

"Just stuff I need to figure out. It's a sounding board," Nora says. "Doesn't everyone do this?"

"Nope," Christina says.

Nope, Nora writes in her notebook.

"What are you trying to figure out?" Christina asks.

"An itinerary?" Nora says. "This is a weird trip. You have to admit."

"I admit," Christina says. "Well, I say, we wing it."

Nora continues to write in her notebook.

I'll want to check out the Musée d'Orsay. And I think the Louvre is free this Sunday, which means it will be most crowded that day. I would rather pay admission and go on Monday. Hopefully, we can keep the togetherness to a minimum, I'm sure Leanne and Christina will want to shop. They'll understand I hate shopping.

"Why don't you just talk to me instead of your notebook?" Christina says.

She looks like she's all suited up to sleep, I wonder if she'll take a pill or something. Maybe some wine. No, I can feel her twitching around next to me. I have no hope that she's going to fall asleep anytime soon. I should put on my headphones, listen to a podcast, and pretend to sleep myself. Then maybe she'll stop talking to me.

"Are you writing about Sam?" Christina asks.

"When we land, I hope we see Leanne right away so you can start picking on her instead of me," Nora says.

"I'm not picking on you!"

"You're on me. You're all over me," Nora says.

"I'm just talking to you," Christina says.

"Where are we meeting Leanne anyway?" Nora asks.

Christina rummages through her carry-on bag, looking for nothing in particular. She can look in that bag all she wants, but she will not find the answer to the question that has been bugging her ever since she spoke to James. Where the hell is Leanne?

"Christina?" Nora says. Now Nora is the one being ignored. "Hey!"

"What?" Christina says.

"Where are we meeting Leanne?" Nora asks.

"Uh," Christina can't avoid this conversation any longer. "I'm not sure."

"*What?*" Nora exclaims in a pitch that she's never used before.

Ambien Man's eyes flutter open. Christina flinches away from him. She watches a lot of zombie-related entertainment and she knows what can happen.

"I don't know where she is *exactly*," Christina admits.

"I thought you spoke to her!"

"Not *really*," Christina whispers.

"Not REALLY?" Nora's voice wakes up Ambien Man. His vacant eyes open. Now he's awake and high as hell.

Christina remains perfectly still, as if she's trying to outsmart a swarm of bees. On one side, she faces a raging confrontational Nora and on the other a defendable potential murderer. She read all about it online—sleep-aid-induced amnesia killers. They can get away with murder.

"Dammit, Christina!" Nora's voice booms louder than it ever has.

Christina makes no sudden movements, hoping Ambien Man will go back to sleep. "Shhhhhhhh, shhhhhhhhhhh."

Ambien Man gets up to go to the bathroom or, as Christina presumes, to murder a flight attendant.

Nora scribbles in her notebook.

"What are you writing?" Christina asks.

Leave me alone.

"Can you please just speak to me instead of scribbling in that thing?" Christina says.

I can't talk to her. She's driving me crazy. How can I get some alone time when she's sitting right next to me? I thought she'd sleep. Why does she have that sleep mask? I wish she would put it on and be quiet.

"The guy next to us hasn't come back from the bathroom," Christina says. "He took an Ambien. He could be in a psychosis right now. You woke him up. You shouldn't have done that."

"You're spiraling," Nora says. "Just go to sleep."

"Well, you're ignoring me."

"I'm not ignoring you."

"Yes, you are."

"No," Nora says. "I'm *trying* to ignore you, but you make it impossible."

"Fine. If you're going to write in your notebook and not talk to me, then I'm going to put in my retainer and stop talking to you," Christina says.

Christina clicks in her mouth guard. Her threat to stop talking goes unfulfilled.

"I thould have jutht come on thith rethcue mithion alone," Christina lisps.

"What?" Nora says.

"I thaid—"

"Can you just take that thing out of your mouth?" Nora says.

Christina takes out her retainer and holds it between her fingers as if it's the stem of a martini glass.

"I said I should have just come on this rescue mission alone," Christina says.

"Why didn't you?" Nora says.

"Because Leanne doesn't like me," Christina says. "It's weird that I'm even going. It should be you."

"Me?" Nora protests. "She doesn't like me either."

"That's true," Christina says. "But you wouldn't have gone on this trip if I didn't lie to you."

"Can you put your retainer back in?" Nora demands.

"No, I'm—"

"Please!"

"Fine!"

Making a trip to Paris feel like a chore is a difficult task, but somehow these two have done it. Whoever has been in charge of maintaining Paris's solid reputation as a cultural and romantic mecca for artists and lovers will have to do some serious PR damage control after this pair of frenemies hits the streets. Nora and Christina will undoubtedly disturb centuries of good vibes.

And somewhere in Paris, Leanne thinks she has broken free.

47

At Le Sarah-Bernhardt in Paris, Nora and Christina sit side by side, scoping the crowd for any glimpse of Leanne. The chairs of the crowded café are already set up this way; people watching is perhaps one of Paris's finest forms of entertainment.

"Wouldn't it be a pain in the ass if I'm wrong about this?" Christina says.

Nora turns her whole body toward Christina so she can more pointedly glare at her. She stares at Christina for longer than she's ever stared at anyone in her life. Christina cuts the tension by pressing Nora's nose.

"Boop!" Christina says in a high-pitched tone. "You can't stay mad at me, Norie."

"I *can*," Nora says. "You're the worst."

"At least we're in Paris," Christina says. "I'm gonna eat so much fucking cheese."

"Tomorrow, I think I'll check out this Lost Generation Montparnasse walking tour," Nora says, looking through an old guidebook she brought with her. "It starts at the Rodin statue of Balzac. That reminds me, I want to go to the Musée d'Orsay too."

"And Hermès," Christina adds.

"No," Nora says. "Not '*and* Hermès.'"

"Well, *I'm* going to Hermès," Christina insists.

"Just go to the Eiffel Tower like a normal person," Nora says, getting her notebook out of her bag.

"I have already been to the Eiffel Tower," Christina says. "Maybe *you* should go to the Eiffel Tower like a normal person."

I am not a normal person, Nora writes in her notebook. She can't talk out loud anymore. She doesn't notice Christina reading over her shoulder.

"Agreed!" Christina concurs. "We should get the waiter over here. I need food. I can't have any more coffee—I'm so caffeinated, I can see through time. I'm switching to wine."

"No wine for me," Nora says, putting her forehead on the table.

". . . and cheese . . . and *wine* . . . and bread," Christina mindlessly carries on. ". . . and *wine*."

"I've passed the threshold where the coffee is actually making me sleepy," Nora tells the tabletop. "I think it's my organs shutting down. If the coma persists for more than three weeks, just let me go."

"I told you we should have started with wine!" Christina exclaims. "We're in goddamn *France* for Christ's sake!"

Wine arrives at the table, compliments of a class act gentleman in the corner who heard Christina exclaiming about wine. Nora lifts her head, worried she blacked out long enough for Christina to order wine.

"Merci!" Christina exclaims to the man, and raises her glass. "Enchanté!"

"Enchanté?" Nora says, wanting to bury her face in the table again.

"I know," Christina concedes. "I cannot pull that shit off."

And that's the end of the Parisian affair with the class act gentleman in the corner. C'est la vie. In hindsight, he may have just been trying to shut her up.

"Well, it's a good thing we *didn't* start with wine," Nora says. "We've been here forever. What if she's not coming? Can't we just go check in to the hotel and come back tomorrow?"

"No, what if we miss her?" Christina says, her leg bouncing from the caffeine coursing through her veins.

Nora rests one eye at a time, winking to stay awake. Through her one open eye, Nora sees a familiar shape enter the café.

The shape is wearing a black beret and a red neckerchief. Christina raises her wineglass and greets Leanne in the most loving way she can.

"Well. Bonjour, Motherfucker."

48

"It's over," Leanne tells Nora and Christina. Walking side by side always minimizes eye contact, but there's no need—a stroll through Paris offers its own intimacy. "I just couldn't live like that anymore. It was a bad fit."

For three city blocks, she's been Leanne-splaining why she's wearing clunky Birkenstocks instead of a sweet kitten heel with her well-considered cliché Paris costume. She says that her relationship with her former footwear cannot be salvaged. She tried to make it work, but ultimately they just couldn't get along anymore.

"I can see why," Christina says, limping over cobblestones in her Manolo Blahniks. "Sometimes it's just not worth the pain."

This is Nora's first conversation about shoes, but when it comes to conversations with Leanne, Nora is no rookie. Leanne will only ever talk about James in the form of transferred shoe angst.

"You should have seen what I did to my cardigans," Leanne digresses. "I just had too many. And I didn't truly love any one of them."

"If I'm being honest, I never really liked your cardigans," Christina says, picking up on Leanne's special code. Christina can't resist the chance to take a jab at those bridesmaid beasts, Melanie and Fabiola—even when they're dressed in a metaphor.

"They didn't like you either," Leanne says, smirking.

They all laugh. Because honesty is hilarious.

"I do think it's better to just invest in one or two really good quality sweaters," Nora adds, really proud that she stuck the landing on this loaded fashion repartee.

"I still can't believe you're wearing clunky Birkenstocks around Paris, of all places," Christina says. "I don't even wear those things when I pretend to go to yoga."

"What can I say?" Leanne says. "I've had enough."

That's all there really is to say about Leanne's life right now—she's had enough. There are no further questions Nora and Christina can ask because it's clear that Leanne has no answers. Not yet anyway.

"Well, Birkenstocks are back," Nora says. "I read about it."

Christina and Leanne don't for a minute believe that Nora has ever read any sort of periodical or blog that would tell a reader which fashion trends are "back."

"Actually," Nora says, caught in a lie, "Sam told me."

"*Sam*?" Leanne's eyes flicker while a flood of information downloads. "Oh."

Their light promenade stops cold as Leanne turns to face Nora. It's impossible to tell how Leanne feels about this new information. Nora has no choice but to deflect.

"Yup," Nora says. "I'm still not gay."

"Molly probably planned on you two getting together," Christina says, running interference for Nora as they both brace for Leanne's full disapproval.

"I don't think so. Molly couldn't have planned it," Leanne says, starting to walk again. "But she would have loved it. Classic Molly."

"Classic," Christina agrees as she turns to follow Leanne.

Nora looks out over the Seine just as a boat passes below the bridge she's crossing with Leanne and Christina. She doesn't look to see if the boat comes out on the other side. She doesn't have to. She knows it will. There's really no need to reassure herself of the completion of someone else's journey when her own is still in progress.

Leanne and Christina walk ahead, lingering at a slower pace so Nora can catch up.

Christina, Leanne, and Nora follow the sidewalk—walking alone together in a staggered line—one after the other. They don't talk anymore, and they don't have to—they're all thinking about the same thing. In this silent strolling formation, they can all easily trick themselves into thinking that there's one more of them walking just a few paces behind.

And there is. There always will be.

𝓔

Christina sure does love a luxury hotel. In no time at all, she disrobes and re-robes into the complimentary white cotton softness hanging in the closet. She uncaps and smells the hotel's assortment of lotions and soaps while Leanne rummages around a hastily packed suitcase. Impromptu travel thwarted Leanne's typical packing-pod strategy. Don't worry though—even at the last minute, Leanne still managed to use a laminated packing checklist she'd created for this kind of spontaneous occasion. Still, it's a small victory that her sensible travel items are so painstakingly disorganized.

Christina lands on the immaculate and fluffy king-sized bed when Leanne finds what she was looking for: her extra-large gift-with-purchase Bloomingdale's beach towel. She promptly uses it to cover the beautiful French linens on the bed.

"Interesting bedding," Nora remarks before gravitating to a fully stocked floor-to-ceiling bookcase. She's devastated to discover that the books are merely decorative.

"I just feel safer sleeping on my beach towel when I travel," Leanne explains, spreading the towel out on the bed. "You know. Bed bugs."

"How do the bed bugs know that your beach towel is off limits?" Nora asks. "Are French bed bugs allergic to pink terry cloth?"

"There are no bed bugs!" Christina exclaims.

"I don't know," Leanne says. "You can't be too careful."

"*You* can," Christina says, rumpling up the towel and throwing it across the room. "This is a goddamn five-star hotel, Leanne. Get in the bed."

Leanne does as she's told. It's killing her that she's not going to get a chance to slip the TV remote into a protective baggie. There are so many germs on that thing.

"I got you your own room, Nora," Christina says.

"Oh, you didn't have to," Nora says.

"I got it on points, so don't worry about it," Christina tells her. "It's free anyway."

Nora lingers.

"Of course . . . hang out here all you want," Christina says. "But I know you like your space . . ."

"Maybe we should all stay together?" Nora wonders out loud.

"Good idea," Leanne confirms. There's no way she wants to go back to her Airbnb alone. Independence has been liberating but torturous.

"Yup," Christina adds, pondering the tiny house she no longer wants. She needs guest rooms and a dining room and maybe a home office. She wants a real home and people to share it with . . . and an occasional hotel suite. She's just loving this hotel suite.

Originally, the idea of staying together belonged to none of them, and now it seems like one of those ideas that's so obvious, you'd kick yourself for not patenting it somehow. *Stay together.* What a great idea. Good thing Molly thought of it.

Christina moves over in bed closer to Leanne to make room for Nora. Nora climbs in, leaving her journal in her backpack, where it will go untouched until she gets home in a few days. She'll talk to her friends instead.

They sleep until they are profoundly rested. It's the kind of sleep

that brings them blissful momentary amnesia when they first open
their eyes. None of them can figure out how they got to this place.
Not Paris, specifically. But here—a group of grown women, minus
one. For that first moment awake, they can't remember anything that
happened since the last time they woke up in bed together on that
Fourth of July in high school.

At almost noon, they wake up hungry.

It's Sunday and so they go to brunch.

Acknowledgments

I first jotted down notes for this book at my favorite brunch place in San Francisco, when I was waiting for great friends to meet me for lattes served in cups as big as our heads. We often stayed until brunch turned into dinner. It was that type of place, we were those kinds of friends, and it was that time of our lives.

I want to express my gratitude for the lifelong friendships that began as girls in Massachusetts, as well as those formed over brunch in San Francisco and Los Angeles. I couldn't have written this book without the support of these inspiring women who talked with me about everything and nothing; who laughed at my weird humor and then topped it; who said "you should write a book" and then believed that I could; who are always recklessly enthusiastic and loving when I am emotionally cautious. Thank you to all my lifelong friends, for saying "what if?" with me years ago and always believing in the whats and ifs.

I suspect that all my best gals are reading this acknowledgment and are deeply horrified that I'm pouring my heart out about them.

I'm uncomfortable, Suzanne. Cut it out. You're making it weird!

Fine. I'll move on. Consider yourself thanked, ladies. I love you.

Thank you to the incredible friends and teachers who lovingly cared for my son while I was writing. My son is a dream come true and you gave me the space to pursue even more dreams.

And speaking of dreams, I'd like to thank everyone on the SWP Team, especially Brooke Warner, for your leadership. Thank you to

Mimi Bark, for your inspired cover design and to Samantha Strom, for keeping everything on track. Thank you to Lauren Wise, Barrett Briske, and the rest of the SWP community for welcoming me into the publishing world and helping me share this story.

Thank you, Crystal Patriarche, Keely Platte, Madison Ostrander, and the rest of the team at Booksparks, for shining a light on this novel. Thank you, Staci Griesbach and Melissa Currier Briggie, for your expertise, enthusiasm, and friendship.

A writer is only as good as her editors. Thank you to Lizette Clarke, for holding my hand through the early phases of writing this novel; and to Rena Copperman, Akela Adams, and Sarah Williams for pushing me over the finish line. A huge thanks to Lesley Dahl— your kindness and insight have made me a more confident writer. And a special thank you to Hilary Thorne Banda, who's been checking my spelling since first grade.

Thank you to Kirsten Wolf and Robin Finn, whose advice helped me take big steps toward publication.

I have been blessed with lifelong friends who have become my sisters, but an even bigger blessing is to have a sister who has become my friend. Thank you, Allison Pasternak, for being a witness to my best and worst life stories and loving me through all my rough drafts. I am so glad you were born as my sister and as a fellow artist. Thank you for your friendship and support.

This book is about women, but I want to thank my guys most of all.

To my husband, Bill: I can never write a book about you because I write fiction and you are everything that is true and real. Thank you for your unconditional support, for encouraging me to follow my dreams, and for giving me the loving foundation to make it all possible.

To my son: On a practical level, I want to thank you for being a good napper while I wrote parts of this book. But more importantly, thank you for reminding me of what matters most in life: listening to our hearts, telling the truth, and finding the funny. All these things inspired this book and you inspire me.

About the Author

© Ashley Burns Photography

Suzanne Nugent is a writer committed to exploring women's lives and relationships through poignant comedy (or funny drama, depending on your level of optimism). She was shortlisted for the prestigious Academy Nicholl Fellowship in Screenwriting and has received accolades from the Denver Film Festival and the San Francisco Writers Conference. She holds a dual degree in journalism and film from UMass Amherst and studied screenwriting at UCLA. She lives in Los Angeles with her husband and son. This is her first novel.

Visit the author at www.suzannenugent.com

SELECTED TITLES FROM SHE WRITES PRESS

She Writes Press is an independent publishing company founded to serve women writers everywhere. Visit us at www.shewritespress.com.

Stella Rose by Tammy Flanders Hetrick $16.95, 978-1-63152-921-4
When her dying best friend asks her to take care of her sixteen-year-old daughter, Abby says yes—but as she grapples with raising a grieving teenager, she realizes she didn't know her best friend as well as she thought she did.

To the Stars Through Difficulties by Romalyn Tilghman
$16.95, 978-163152-233-8
A contemporary story of three very different women who join forces in a small Kansas town to create a library and arts center—changing their world, and finding their own voices, powers, and self-esteem, in the process.

Center Ring by Nicole Waggoner $17.95, 978-1-63152-034-1
When a startling confession rattles a group of tightly knit women to its core, the friends are left analyzing their own roads not taken and the vastly different choices they've made in life and love.

A Cup of Redemption by Carole Bumpus $16.95, 978-1-938314-90-2
Three women, each with their own secrets and shames, seek to make peace with their pasts and carve out new identities for themselves.

Again and Again by Ellen Bravo $16.95, 978-1-63152-939-9
When the man who raped her roommate in college becomes a Senate candidate, women's rights leader Deborah Borenstein must make a choice—one that could determine control of the Senate, the course of a friendship, and the fate of a marriage.

What is Found, What is Lost by Anne Leigh Parrish
$16.95, 978-1-938314-95-7
After her husband passes away, a series of family crises forces Freddie, a woman raised on religion, to confront long-held questions about her faith.